The Persian Rug

By Chelsea Isadora Teich

NEW YORK

Ithaca Press
3 Kimberly Drive, Suite B
Dryden, New York 13053 USA
www.IthacaPress.com

Copyright © 2009 Chelsea Isadora Teich

*All rights reserved under International and
Pan American Copyright Law, including the
right of reproduction in whole or in part,
without the written permission of the publisher.
Requests for such permission should be addressed to
Ithaca Press, 3 Kimberly Drive, Suite B, Dryden,
New York 13053 USA*

Cover Design   Gary Hoffman
Book Design   Gary Hoffman
Original painting for cover *Blood Fountain* by Heather Fisher

Manufactured in the United States of America

9 8 7 6 5 4 3 2 1

Library of Congress Cataloging-in-Data Available
Printed in the United States of America

Teich/Chelsea Isadora
fiction/fantasy/science fiction/young adult fiction

ISBN 978-0-9798494-8-0

www.ChelseaIsadoraTeich.com

The Persian Rug

The Persian Rug

Chapter List

Prologue		1
I	Surrounding Aralevena II, Princess of Laaven	3
II	Contretemps	11
III	The Musings of a Healer and the Madness of the King of Laaven	25
IV	Maveree	39
V	Departure	49
VI	What Does the Seeress Desire?	57
VII	Father and Daughter	69
VIII	Lord, the Steward	81
IX	Iarnel Eremnad	91
X	Kerúx and Risúrat	107
XI	An Interlude in the Ariyekk Forest	117
XII	The Letter	125
XIII	Róethel	131
XIV	The Revenge of Lord Fén	139
XV	Oran Itae	145
XVI	Queen Eríé	157
XVII	Merend Faaj	163
XVIII	Sahena	171
XIX	Phallé-Nal	177
XX	The First Battle	183
XXI	Cold	191
XXII	The Golden Mountains	195
XXIII	Merend Zetth	199
XXIV	The Final Battle	215
XXV	The Empyrean Stairway	219
XXVI	A Seeress's Advice	223
XXVII	Evil Hour	233
XXVIII	The Beginning	245
About the Author		253

Chelsea Isadora Teich

The Persian Rug

Prologue

The monarchy had long since lost the respect and loyalty of its people. All trudged on grudgingly through a land of poverty and disease, ravaged by the machinations of shrewd upperclassmen. The rift between the bereft and the wealthy became an abyss beneath the feet of the forgotten majority. To live on was a struggle, whether you fought for bread or were consumed by the endless war for power. There was not one haven left. Misery ensued.

Diseased urchins fed off of the corpses of those they might have once professed to love in the streets, creeping upon their frozen bodies like scavengers of prey, taking whatever little they might have carried upon their person, and then, like macabre insects, scuttling away with whatever meat they could manage. These same streets were traveled by men and women feeding from not only the ruin of the peasants, but the ruin of their fellows. After stealing all that they could from the dregs and then the average men of northern society, they turned on one another. War raged amongst the pretentious men and painted women unendingly while the figurehead king watched with blatant apathy. The people of these coexisting worlds lived in ignorance of one another, gracelessly floundering in their depravity.

All who might have remembered the days when the kingdom of Phallé-Nal was in its glory had long since passed, leaving only bred enemies with knowledge of suffering and the cold to carry on. Generations of malevolent children poisoned by misfortune only served to further their destruction. The poor cowered beneath the oppressive government, although they were just as cruel to one another. The wealthy waged war and destroyed one another less obviously. Within the divisions of society existed divisions and then hateful divisions spawned from these. Millions of divided people lived in squalor and chaos.

And after draining the common man, the economy, the land, and one another beyond finality, only the most cunning and hellbent remained. Five Lords, realizing that they could not overcome one another, had reached an incredibly tentative agreement. It was not long after their intangible ceasefire that they began to contemplate a new conquest.

Chapter 1
Surrounding Aralevena II, Princess of Laaven

Noon was swiftly approaching and the sun was high above the Kingdom of Laaven. In the fields, farmers were hard at work and, in the streets, merchants peddled their wares to passers-by. The rich did their business in lavish offices in grandiose stone dwellings and beggars did whatever they could to get their fill. The Laaven castle, in the very center of the kingdom, was buzzing with excitement for the very next day it would be the turn of the year and the Enembír Festival would take place.

Every year the Enembír Festival was held in Laaven, a festival that had been famous and attracted royals, commoners, and everyone in between from all kingdoms for nearly six decades. It was famous for its music, wide selection of exotic food and wine, and the often long-winded speech given by the king. However, it was also infamous for the chaos, both in the weeks before and after, for the preparations were always rushed and came close to creating mass pandemonium among all involved, regardless of how early they started. The party itself would leave the gardens practically in ruins and putting them back in order often took months.

Being that there was less than a day left to prepare and royal guests from the Kingdom of Nallel had already arrived, the castle was bedlam. One could almost meet their death walking down the corridors that teemed with people rushing to finish their various tasks in time. In the midst of this chaos, a short, bulbous man dressed in blue rounded the corner and stood erect in the center of the hallway, putting himself blatantly in the way of countless others. "Your princess approaches! Look alive!" He bellowed and every man and woman in the hallway haphazardly flung themselves against either wall of the hallway, leaving it for the princess to pass undaunted.

Less than a minute later, a lithe young woman who was fair of face stood at the end of the corridor. Golden hair flowed down her back in rivulets and her amber eyes closed almost entirely as she feigned a yawn to show that her servant had not cleared the hallway as fast as she would have liked. A slender youth who stood only a hair taller than her shifted uneasily beside her. He appeared even paler for his hair was deep black and his raiment was of the same color. His icy blue eyes were fixed on the heavy box he carried in his arms. He looked embarrassed at having a hallway cleared for him.

"The way is cleared," she stated more than asked.

"Yes Highness," the short man replied.

"Good. Now who will take Nerin's box for him?" She asked and Nerin began to protest when the short man gratefully accepted it.

"Is this all really necessary, Princess?" He asked, moving to take the box from the little round man who took several steps away from Nerin so he was out of his reach.

"Yes, I want it to be necessary," she proclaimed and led him down the hallway. "Must you return to the other healers or do you have time to spare?" She asked and Nerin looked back to the servant, who trailed behind them at a respectful distance, carrying his box.

"For you I have nothing but time Aralé, you know this well," he whispered so that the man could not hear.

"I am glad to hear it," she whispered back. "Servant, Master Nerin will walk with me. Keep his box of herbs safe until he calls for them." The servant acquiesced immediately and made himself scarce. When his footsteps were no longer audible, the princess took a key out of one of the long sleeves of her dress and stuck it into the lock on the wooden door next to them. It swung open revealing a room filled with crates. She stepped inside, quickly pulling Nerin in with her. The door slammed shut behind them.

Outside, in the warm southern winter, the warriors practiced hand to hand combat. Sweat and sometimes even blood glistened on their bodies and on their hirsute cheeks as they fought seemingly to the death. At least two dozen groups of two or three were spread out against the lawn.

"Gentlemen," a proud voice announced and the warriors stopped, some in mid strike, kick, or hold. They all turned to face the prince and bowed in unison. The prince himself was a vision to behold. Next to the dirty, sweaty, and weatherworn soldiers, he appeared almost ethereal. He had near the same face as his sister, being that they were twins. His was only more masculine and slightly thinner, for his sister was a glutton and few had actually ever seen him eat anything. He stood clad in red velvet, gems gleaming on his fingers, and his shoulder-length golden hair blew about him in the light breeze.

"Do any of you know where I might find Captain Sern?" He asked with his usual debonair grin. The look writ in his countenance was condescending, as it had been since he was four years old.

"He is in his tree, Your Highness," one of the tallest warriors said quietly, his eyes respectfully cast down. The prince thanked him and gracefully strode away. As soon as he was out of sight, the warriors went back to sparring. Several of them muttered things to the degree of "If I didn't know better I'd say he was a wench," "A good gust of wind could knock him over," and "If I wouldn't be tried and tortured to death for it, I'd beat that smirk out of the whelp."

"Aralé…" Nerin tried to speak as she pushed up her sleeves

and kissed him again, tightening their embrace. "Aralé there is talk-"

"Talk is common," she said, making as if to kiss him again. Nerin stopped her.

"I have heard that it is arranged for you to marry the new King of Nallel and you will be meeting him at the festival on Saturday."

"We have been betrothed since we were three. It means nothing to us," the princess replied, swiftly losing patience.

"But what of when you are married? Then what am I to do?" He said almost sadly and the princess laughed and kissed the tip of his nose.

"Dear Nerin, sweet love, I am of the House of Vénatheln!" she replied in a lighthearted whisper. When Nerin did not quite seem to understand, she sighed. "We are infamously unfaithful spouses. All with the exception of my father, who became a raving mad lunatic upon the death of my mother and spends his days talking to a portrait of her, have had multiple affairs." And she returned to kissing him with renewed vigor.

Atop the tallest tree in all the palace grounds sat the strong figure of Captain Sern. He held an apple in one of his calloused hands, grey-green eyes contemplating it as his mind wandered. He had been there since early in the morning, before first light, sitting quietly amongst the leaves. His deep meditation was interrupted by the sound of footsteps.

Sern sighed, recognizing them as the prince's clumsy footsteps. He found it almost remarkable that so slight a young man could make such noise when warriors who weighed three and four times what he did and wore heavy armor could be almost silent. The captain sighed, wondering exactly what the young man wanted of him and knowing that he would make him get out of the tree.

"Captain Sern," the young man's voice called up and Sern grimaced. "Your prince asks that you come down."

"Very well, Highness," Sern said, disguising his annoyance

completely as he deftly leapt or swung from branch to branch until he reached one low enough that he could safely drop to the ground. He landed and swiftly rose so he could bow in one fluid motion. The prince seemed in awe of this feat of strength as Sern rose from his bowing position, standing erect.

"Have you seen my sister? It seems that she has disappeared," the prince asked. He assumed that if anyone would know it would be the captain, for he had practically raised her.

"I am sorry Your Highness, but I have been here since before sunrise," Sern said quietly. It was Thursday, the day Master Healer Nerin came to trade herbs and elixirs with the castle healer, Master Dorin. He knew very well where the princess was and with whom. While it made him sick to his stomach, he could not find it in his heart to betray her trust. He could not bring himself to tell her brother what she had told him in confidence.

"You look troubled," the prince said suspiciously, reading the conflict on the older man's face before dismissing it, bidding him farewell, and strolling away. Sern sighed, running his hands over his hirsute cheeks and through his dark hair before climbing back into the tree.

"That was the bell signaling the midday meal!" Nerin gasped as a high pitched bell sounded for the second time. He began to scramble away but Aralé pulled him back to her.

"Nerin, can you stop this!? You act as if you have committed a crime by loving your princess!"

"Your father would have me hanged from the tallest tree in the kingdom if he found out what we have been doing for the past year-and-a-half—" he began and Aralé silenced him with a kiss.

"And I would but follow," she said and he gently pushed her away.

"I refuse to hide my love out of fear for your father and future husband. In Nallel, if a queen is unfaithful, she is run through with a sword! I cannot do this anymore!" He cried and burst out of the storeroom.

"He will come crawling back tomorrow," Aralé thought aloud after several minutes of sitting on one of the many wooden boxes. She pulled a small mirror out from underneath another box and began to fix her hair and straighten her dress. "He always does." She finished with a grin, making sure that the mirror was hidden again, before leaving the storeroom and making her way toward the dining hall for the midday meal.

The hall was large and rectangular with three long wooden tables, suits of armor of various ages lining the walls, and ceilings made of colored glass that swirled in beautiful, intricate designs. Aralé walked to the head of the middle table where her father sat when he had strength enough to join his subjects for meals. Instead, she found only her brother sitting to the right of an empty chair, staring disgustedly at the piece of pork on his plate.

"Hello brother. Do you know where father is?" Aralé said to him as she carved herself a large piece of meat from the whole cooked pig that sat in the center of the table and poured herself a cup of mead from the large pitcher. They were very early and there were only some of the younger healers' apprentices sitting in a cluster at the far end of the third table.

"Master Risúrat tells me that he's ill," the prince said as he idly poked at his pork with a fork. Aralé looked up to see Risúrat, a tall, thin middle-aged man with grey hair and a grey beard standing by the entrance to the great hall, looking entirely too pleased with himself.

"When you are king, you will get rid of Risúrat, yes?" She whispered, taking the untouched pork off of her brother's plate and starting to eat it after quickly finishing hers. "There is something most unwholesome about him."

The prince mock sighed. "Women are such suspicious creatures. He is harmless. Since father is ill and cannot give the speech at the festival tomorrow, he personally helped me write one." Aralé snorted before returning to her ham. After finishing, she gazed about the crowded room as if looking for someone and turned back to her brother who was idly pushing peas around on his plate. He still had not eaten even a bite of food.

The Persian Rug

"And what of Captain Sern, is he sick as well?" Aralé spat as she poured a double helping of pudding on her plate.

"No, he is in his tree. The man seemed troubled when I spoke with him this morning to find out where you were. Oh and speaking of which, where were you this morning? I wanted to make sure that our festival outfits are not too similar and it was as if you had disappeared!"

"I was..." she trailed off, an idea suddenly striking her. "Have someone fetch Sern and tell him that I called for him. Have them tell Sern that I was crying when I ran off," Aralé said before taking another bite from her brother's plate.

"What are you planning now?" Amíen replied with an exasperated sigh, but did not get an answer for his sister had already disappeared.

"Captain!" A short young man called from the base of the tree. He was clad in dark blue and his fair hair was long. "Princess Aralevena has called for you."

There was then a light rustling of leaves as Sern jumped from a tree branch and landed deliberately on the ground. "Is she well?" He asked casually and the servant shook his head.

"She was upset. She did not even say where she was going before she ran off," he said and there was a knowing look in the older man's eyes.

"Tell me. Were there tears in her eyes?" He asked and the servant nodded. Sern thanked and dismissed the servant before briskly making his way toward the castle. He quickly tore through the gardens and two castle floors before making his way down the almost forgotten corridor that led to an old library. He could always find the princess there when she was distraught. He came to the door and opened it to find a sobbing princess sitting on the floor with her back against one of the bookshelves that lined the walls. Light seeped through the moth-eaten curtains on the large windows and illuminated the silver tears on her alabaster cheeks.

"Sern!" She sobbed and he crumpled to the ground beside her, embracing her. "Nerin does not love me anymore!" She whispered through her tears and he began to stroke her hair softly.

"Shhh," he said gently. "He is a fool then." And he kissed her crown.

"I share everything with him and he abandons me!"

"Then he does not deserve you and when he comes crawling back to you…"

"He will not come back this time," Aralé insisted.

"Over the past year, he has done this four times. He has never lasted more than three days for he is enamored by your beauty. He cannot stay away." He wiped tears from her face gently with his calloused fingers, his voice almost catching in his throat.

"And I have been nothing but a burden to him! Does he think that his princess likes to hide from the world as if she has committed a crime? Does he believe that he is the only one who suffers?"

"Mayhap he is doing this because he thinks it best. Perhaps he is tired of all of this suffering," Sern said and the princess pulled away slightly and looked deeply into Sern's eyes.

"My suffering is tenfold when he forces me to doubt his love," she said and watched sadness cloud the older man's eyes. "You will not ever abandon me will you, my captain?"

Sern swallowed and cradled her against him so that she could not see his pained expression. "You would have to kill me first."

The Persian Rug

Chapter II
Contretemps

Nerin had returned to the House of Anív, where he did his healing work. He dutifully worked straight through the evening meal and until the head healer, Anív, forced him to retire. Near midnight, Nerin unwillingly returned to his bedroom that, due to his position as second in command, was private. He could not believe what he had just done. His heart ached for the princess and it had been not a day. There he paced until nearly sunrise when he collapsed on his bed, exhausted and distraught. They did not wake him when it came time to break the fast or even for the midday meal so he slept. It was not a peaceful sleep for he could be heard screaming late into the morning. It was five in the evening and all but the three unfortunate healers, who had drawn the shortest straws, had left for the celebration at the Laaven castle when he was finally awoken.

"Nerin, my healer." The young man's icy eyes slowly opened as a soft, lilting voice interrupted his dreams and a gentle hand nudged his shoulder. "You are back among the living I see," Anív said with a small chuckle after he saw the younger man had fully regained consciousness. Nerin looked up at the older man who sat before him, dark eyes regarding him kindly and the lines etched in his face accentuated in the light.

"You looked most troubled in your sleep," Anív finally said after a prolonged silence. His weathered hands were wrapped around one of the many crystals he wore about his neck. Silver rings embedded with stones of all colors covered his slender fingers and he wore gemstone bracelets. He held a small opaque stone of yellow hues in his hand.

"Only dreams," Nerin replied stiffly. He was clearly done talking.

"Dreams or memories, child?" The elder healer replied, ever patient with Nerin, whom in all of the years he had been there refused to speak of his past or anything even remotely personal. Men he had known for years could not have even truthfully told his favorite color or where he hailed from.

"Dreams," Nerin replied, trying to stand but being halted by Anív.

"I hold in my hand a stone called citrine. They will soothe your troubled rest. Would you like to tell me of them? You were screaming in your sleep last night."

"As I have done before and will do again. In any case, my foolish nightmares are nothing to burden you with. Keep your stones, they will not avail me," Nerin said and Anív sighed.

"I suppose you do not wish to tell me why you returned from the palace so distraught yesterday."

"I know not what you mean."

"Of course not," Anív replied sadly. "Several times over the past year you returned from your weekly errand at the palace in a similar state, once even near tears, and yet every time you deny it with vehemence. I care deeply for any healer who works beneath me and you are no exception. You cannot truly wish to keep all of your secrets," Anív said as he looked to Nerin's forearm, which had been unintentionally exposed in his sleep. White flesh marred with gruesome scars seemed to glow in the setting sun against his black clothes and bedspread. After noticing the elder healer's eyes on it, he swiftly buttoned the sleeve of his shirt and pulled a black glove over his slender hand.

"I have no secrets."

"Very well." The elder healer rose. "Are you going to the turning of the year festivities?"

Nerin thought on it. Perhaps if he went, there would be the

smallest chance that he could corner the princess and quickly apologize. He smiled almost imperceptibly at this, hoping that his princess would suffer him. He wished more than anything that she would for he was a man hopelessly lovelorn.

"Yes. After all, how often does one get to watch the year one-thousand-nine hundred-seventy-seven dawn?" Nerin said almost lightheartedly and Anív watched him with slight suspicion.

"Only once an age," the healer replied. "And before you know the second age will pass and the third will begin."

"I doubt that thirty-some-odd years will fly so quickly," Nerin said. "Now, I hate to be rude but I very well cannot dress with you here."

The older healer nodded and left, leaving Nerin alone to dress and ready himself. Nerin quickly went to the small dresser that occupied a corner of his bedchamber. He pulled out a rich velvet outfit of dark blue and laid it on his bed. He quickly began to dress.

As the festival was about to begin, Prince Amíen the Third sat by his father who lay wrapped up in his bed as he shivered. As a man of only thirty-nine years, he appeared to be at least seventy. His sickly and cadaverous body quaked beneath the thick coverlet, thin dark hair was plastered to his wan face, and his sunken eyes stared blankly into the distance at things unseen. The prince watched in pity and fear as his father muttered something unintelligible.

"I wish that you could be at the festival father," Amíen said sadly, wondering if his father could even hear him. "Sister will be meeting the King of Nallel, as you arranged…and Risúrat helped me write a speech to give tonight at the…" He trailed off, hearing his father croak loudly. Amíen was immediately struck with fear. He had seen servants die in similar states. "Father!" He exclaimed, reaching for one of the king's skeletal hands and becoming confused when his father callously shoved him away.

"Get…Risúrat," his father said through his wheezing and

convulsing. Amíen looked hurt for only a second before skillfully masking it.

"As you command," Amíen bowed and quickly exited the room. He found Risúrat waiting just down the hall, talking to a servant. He strode over to him and told him that the king had called for him. Risúrat bowed respectfully before heading nonchalantly toward the king's bedchamber. The prince made his way to the festivities.

Risúrat sighed as he turned the doorknob and gently slid the door open, admitting himself without his majesty's permission. He then slammed the door behind him and watched the writhing shape on the bed blanch and grimace before starting to convulse. It was only for a brief moment. However, it left the king hoarsely moaning in agony and dripping with cold sweat.

"Risúrat!" The king called as loudly as his hoarse voice and bleeding throat would allow.

"Yes, milord," the man said, bending by the king's bed. The king reached out with one almost transparent hand and gripped the older man's collar with a strength he did not look to possess. Sallow eyes bulged out of his head as he let out a moan of agony for his bones and muscles ached but hurt tenfold whenever he moved.

"Four days!" The king cried before letting go, as it hurt too much. He started to shiver again. "So cold."

"Milord—" Risúrat began but was interrupted.

"So cold!" The king bellowed, tears running down his cheeks. "Cannot take…" He trailed off, his face suddenly blanching and contorting as he leaned over and retched all over the floor.

"What are you asking of me, milord?" Risúrat asked, though he already knew and he did not bother to hide it.

"Knife," the king said as he rolled himself back up in the blankets, cringing as he did so for even the smallest movement caused him great agony. "There is a knife in the top drawer!" And he started to sweat. No longer feeling cold, he threw the coverlets that had been piled atop him away and the king cried as his muscles and bones protested.

"You want me to end it sire?" Risúrat asked mockingly.

The Persian Rug

"Yess," the king hissed. "Four days! No more!"

Risúrat took his time going through the drawer even though there was nothing but a long silver knife, a few letters, pens, and scattered papers stacked neatly within. Then he slowly drew the knife and looked at it, watching the room reflect in its lustrous surface.

"Risúrat!" The king whined and the older man smiled maliciously.

"If you try my patience I will have you wait another day," he threatened even though he had no intention of doing so.

The king croaked unhappily. "Sorry! Sorry! S-so…" he trailed off, his body started to shake violently. When the convulsions ceased and the king lay limp on the bed, Risúrat took out a small red satin pouch. He stuck the very tip of the knife gently into the pouch, cutting its contents into smaller pieces. He then propped the king up on several pillows and placed the pouch in his hand. The king cradled it and pressed it to his nose, there he inhaled its contents. His eyes rolled back into his head and his body quaked as he inhaled with all of the strength that remained in him. Tears streamed down his face as the sharper shards of the crystalline substance cut his nose and throat. The worse it burned and the more he bled, the more he wanted and the harder it was to stop.

He knew that one day he would simply take so much that it would kill him. Or perhaps one day Risúrat would decide to torture him and simply stop supplying him and wait for the seizures that came with withdrawal to finish him. However, at that moment, all of those macabre thoughts were far from whatever of his mind was left after a decade of torturing his body in such a way. He laughed as blood dripped from a nose he could no longer smell through. He laughed through a face contorted with pain as the jagged shards tore at him. He laughed until he had finally drawn in more than he could take and fell limp against his pillows, eyes open and blankly rolling about in his head.

Risúrat removed the pouch from the king's hand and tucked it back into a hidden pocket in his robes. He looked down in disdain at the king before taking his wrist and putting it to his ear, listening for a pulse. He scowled upon finding one.

"Perhaps next time then?" He said with a sigh. Then he wiped the blood and excess powder from the king's face and pushed his eyelids over his eyes before exiting the room and making his way to the festivities.

The prince and princess sat on their thrones before the fourth of the seven long tables that spanned the garden. Each was piled high with food and wine. The princess was feasting greedily on these while her brother only eyed the food nervously and sipped at a cup of wine. She was a vision in a light purple and silver gown with sleeves so long that they almost trailed the ground. Her long golden hair was wound in intricate designs with silver clasps. Amíen, who sat at the head of the table, was dressed in a glorious outfit of crimson velvet. Small rubies hung from his ears and his hair was pulled out of his face in a crimson clasp adorned with gems.

"Come now brother, eat. One could count the bones in your hands," Aralé said as she took a bite out of a leg of pheasant and got food on her cheek

"And risk bollixing this outfit! Hardly! Do you know how long I had to stand there as they made alterations?" He asked, wincing as his sister smiled, showing the food stuck in her teeth.

"Five-and-a-half days," she said in between gluttonous bites. Amíen found the sight repulsive. "And it would have taken less than three hours if his royal highness was not so fussy," she said taking a bite and her brother huffed.

"It is not my fault that they do not understand that you cannot mix different shades of red and that large buttons are not the fashion anymore," he said and took a sip of wine.

"You should hear yourself. You are such a woman," the princess said through a bite of food and the prince winced visibly at the sight.

"And you are such a slob," he said and grimaced as his sister stuck out her tongue, revealing a repulsive stew of half chewed food and vegetables. Amíen's eyes suddenly grew wide. "The King of Nallel is here! Oh my! Oh my!" He said as he looked at the group of people entering the gardens clad in grey. He immediately took Aralé's plate of food away from her and silenced her as she began to protest. "Clean off your face and get the food out of your teeth!" He said frantically and did it for her. "Now, King Seraavran will ask you to call him Seraav if he likes you. If he does, just do it and tell him to call you Aralé, but have him call you by your full name and call him by his until he asks you to call him Seraav. His left thigh is wounded from battle and never healed properly so do not brush up against it by accident when you dance or ever. Do not touch it ever. He has a weakness for blondes so if he tries to touch your hair, do not stop him. Oh, and when he makes jokes, which he will for he is a pretty wit and loves a person who can keep up, laugh and touch his arm lightly—"

"You know a lot about King Seraavran, Amíen. Maybe you should become his queen in my stead," Aralé said with a laugh.

"Hardly," Amíen rolled his eyes. "I am just trying to be helpful. You forget that I have known him since he was Prince Seraavran. He has told me all that he looks for in a wife."

"I personally think it a wonderful idea. You already have more jewelry than any queen I have ever heard of," Aralé said and her brother sighed before a genuine smile overtook his handsome face.

"King Seraavran!" He exclaimed and was enveloped into a warm hug by a man nearly a head taller than him. King Seraavran was a well-built man of twenty-two years with a thick head of tawny hair and deep brown eyes. He was dressed far more modestly than Prince Amíen in a simple yet elegant outfit of twilight grey. A silver circlet engraved with serpents and diamonds sat on his head.

"Why so formal Amí?" He asked and let go of the young prince. Aralé laughed inwardly at the pet name. "You have grown so tall! I suppose you are beating women off with a stick!" He exclaimed and Amíen blushed slightly. "But you are so very thin! Is your father not feeding you?" He asked only half jokingly and Amíen was about to respond when he was interrupted.

"He is too worried about getting food on his outfits to eat

much I'm afraid," Aralé said before she could stop herself and looked to the tall man before her. He was not exactly a man to her liking, but she found him tolerable and he appeared to be good-natured enough. He seemed surprised that she said anything at all, but there was definite mirth in his eyes. Her brother on the other hand looked mortified.

"Pardon me for being so rude, your highness," she said, seeming slightly embarrassed. She curtseyed gracefully. "I am Aralevena the Second, Princess of Laaven."

Amíen still looked utterly horrified. King Seraavran began to laugh. "With a tongue half as sharp as that, I would say that your sister and I are well-suited."

The princess smiled. She had always feared being married off to a man who believed that women should be seen and not heard or who would hit her and cover it with powder should she ever displease him. Prince Seraavran did not seem to be such a man.

"And with a mien half as pleasant as yours, King Seraavran, I would say that you and I are very well-suited indeed," she answered quickly and the older man smiled. Soon after, the pair was dancing and caught deep in conversation. Amíen, who was surrounded by his usual assortment of admirers, sat in a nook made of hedgerow where he flirted with at least a dozen maidens at once.

Sern stood at the other end of the garden by the musicians, casually glancing at everything but Princess Aralevena and King Seraavran. He was dressed in black and looked almost elegant even though his hair was not pulled back and his face was not clean-shaven. He wore no rings on his fingers or gems in his ears. A silver chain showed above his open collar. However, whatever hung at the bottom of the chain was hidden beneath his tunic.

"Captain." He looked beside him to see a young man only a hair shorter dressed in white and brown. Full red hair hung slightly below his shoulders.

"Danen," Sern said in greeting and smiled genuinely. "I heard that you lead the hunters who caught all of the food for the feast. I commend you, friend. There will probably be food enough to last well into the summer even after tonight!"

The Persian Rug

"Thank you captain. They tell me that I would be wasted as a warrior and should just be a huntsman," Danen said quietly. "Why are you not dancing?" He asked after a while.

"I am too old," Sern said almost sadly as he stole a quick glance at Aralé as she danced merrily with the King of Nallel.

"You are only twenty-nine. That is not too terribly old," Danen replied.

"Fine, then what is your excuse young master, for you are only sixteen?" Sern asked with a slight smile and Danen looked down at his feet abashedly.

"I am afraid that I do not know how to dance," he said and Sern chuckled before noticing one of the guests from The Isles of the Sun, a beautiful maiden with long dark hair, eyes, and skin, pretending not to watch them through her eyelashes. She was clad in a flowing wine-colored dress that hung off of her shoulders.

"I do not think that she would mind teaching you," Sern replied teasingly.

"She is clearly looking at you," Danen insisted and Sern rolled his eyes.

"Go ask her to dance or I will remind all of the other student warriors about the time you went swimming in the lake and forgot where you left your clothes."

"But captain, they were all just starting to forget about that!" Danen said indignantly and started to argue, but, upon seeing the incredibly serious look in his teacher's eyes, he went forward and asked the lovely maiden to dance.

Sern kept where he stood, simply observing. He tried to keep his eyes off of the princess, but he found it nearly impossible. His blood came as close to boiling as it ever had as he watched the visiting king snake his hands possessively about the princess' waist as the pair swayed together as if to say "mine." He watched as their hands touched and eyes met during the formal dances. He had been trying to avoid gazing at her all evening.

After the twentieth brief glance at Aralé and Seraavran, he turned his eyes back to Danen, who stiffly held the maiden as they danced. He looked as if he could name at least seventeen places he would rather have been at that moment. Since she barely spoke any Cancín, the common tongue of Laaven, and he barely spoke any Céremín, the common tongue of The Isles of the Sun, there was little conversation to fill the awkward silence. When they were positioned so that her back was to Sern and he was facing him, he caught the older man's eye before mouthing "She was looking at you, not me."

Sern sighed. Even as she and Danen danced, she still cast glances his way from time to time. He noticed only about a quarter of these for he spent almost all evening pretending he was not watching the princess and the king.

Nerin and Aniv had just arrived at the festival to find the party already in full swing. Nerin had every intention of finding Aralé and apologizing. However, after nearly a quarter of an hour of shoving his way through the crowd, he could scarce tell where he was let alone where the princess was. It was then that he accidentally came upon them. He saw her encircled in the arms of a man nearly a head taller than him as they swayed together. They laughed genially and the man suddenly held onto her a little tighter, as if by instinct alone he knew that another man was watching *his* princess.

"No, it is golden like the sun." He heard the man say as he touched one of the curls hanging loosely out of the princess' intricate hairdo. He watched as the princess near melted in a puddle at the older man's feet.

"It is for the best I suppose," Nerin said, before walking away. He suddenly did not feel like celebrating or joining in the merrymaking. He fought his way out of the crowd and then let his feet carry him away from the party. After approximately an hour of aimless strolling, he found a secluded spot in an unoccupied part of the gardens, far away from any of the lights, sounds, or smells of the party. Overcome with grief, he fell to the ground. He sat there awhile in the dirt, not caring that he was ruining the one nice outfit he owned. Perhaps in another year or so, he would be able to afford a new one if he saved his earnings.

The Persian Rug

After a while, he became uncomfortable and changed position. When he placed a hand on the ground, he noticed that it felt uneven. Upon turning his head to examine it, he found an ominous shoeprint with a large spike jutting from the front. He rose as if planning to leave and act as if he had never seen them, but he was curious by nature. Even though he knew that he would most likely rue the decision later, he began to follow them. He followed them as they wound through the garden, completely disappearing in some spots and then altogether as he neared the thorny hedgerow that appeared to lean against the outer castle wall. Nerin sighed, perplexed, before closing his eyes and sticking his hand into the bush to find that he felt no thorns and no castle wall. Berating himself every step of the way, he closed his eyes and warily stepped through.

There he found a narrow path between the outermost castle wall and the innermost thorns of the hedgerow. The ominous footprints continued on, nearly invisible in the dark. After several minutes of following silently in the dark, he caught a familiar scent. In his few years of healing he had encountered enough wounds to know the scent of blood. He froze as the sound of a sword slicing through flesh and being sheathed followed by the sound of heavy metal armor falling to the ground rang throughout the night. By the time Nerin had realized his mistake, it was too late. One dirty hand held him painfully by the hair and the point of a bloody sword was pressed dangerously against his back.

"Please...don't hurt me! I will do anything you want! I won't tell a soul that you are here if you just let me—" Nerin's words were muffled as the stranger roughly gagged him. Nerin closed his eyes and did not even dare to make a sound as the tip of the sword cut through the back of his tunic and made a shallow cut that ran along his spine. Red blood ran, dripping from the fresh wound down his horribly scarred and disfigured back.

"You will be silent. You will walk in front of me and if you so much as make a sound I will carve your innards out through your spineless back Nerin the Healer," he growled in a low dangerous voice, his rough hirsute chin digging into Nerin's cheek and foul spittle flying from his lips, which were almost pressed against the healer's ear. Nerin shook as he walked forward, barely even daring to breathe with the sword at his back. He felt himself start to become lightheaded as they stepped over the decapitated cadaver of one of the palace guards. When he so much as started to stumble, the cad carved a big enough piece out of the flesh on his back to hurt Nerin, but not enough to hinder him longer than necessary. Nerin still seemed unresponsive to the pain he surely must have felt. More blood ran briefly from this wound as the stranger pushed him forward.

Soon the stranger stopped and Nerin found himself pressed hard against the cold stone outer wall of the castle. The way the moon shone made Nerin seem almost ethereal, red running in rivulets down milky skin, which held unworldly phosphorescence beneath the gruesome scars. "Climb," the voice commanded and Nerin only looked up at the immensely tall castle wall and started to try and protest through the gag. He only felt another chunk taken out of his back and sighed in annoyance.

"Do you not feel pain?" The villain snarled, slightly surprised for he had never heard anyone sigh in annoyance as their skin was peeled away. He did not give Nerin time to respond before giving Nerin a choice. Either climb or have a sword driven through your stomach. "Climb," the masked man barked. Nerin gulped and put a foot on the first brick and started to climb, fearing for his life even though he was barely even an arm's length off of the ground.

He simply kept climbing. He did not dare to look down or to either side of him for he thought his fear of heights might overtake him before the wet and dry blood on his hands caused him to slip off of the wall. Since being a healer did not entail much physical strength, he could barely climb a tall tree, let alone scale a castle wall. While the masked man seemed to scale the wall as if he were a preternatural great black spider, Nerin had to be carried on his back and hauled over the edge before they had even climbed halfway. He was too exhausted to continue.

The man gave him little rest once they finally set foot on the angular castle roof. While the masked stranger skillfully made his way around the various parts of the roof, Nerin stumbled behind ungracefully. The more progress they made, the closer the sounds of the Enembír Festival became. There was an almost deafening roar before an eerie silence. Just as Nerin could see the garden, he was roughly pulled behind one of the towers that protruded from the roof. It was then that he noticed a quiver full of foul smelling arrows. He watched as the stranger began to adeptly assemble a bow. He gasped.

"You were sent to assassinate the king!"

The masked cad said nothing as he pulled two arrows out of the quiver. He readied one to shoot and, in that exact moment, Nerin heard someone begin to speak and looked to see Prince Amíen standing behind a large dais, calmly and genially delivering a speech. There was a swell in laughter from the crowd as the cad pulled back on the arrow, aiming it directly at the prince. Nerin closed his eyes and turned his head away from what he was sure would be a gruesome murder.

"Coward, how dare you call yourself a man!" The assassin spat and Nerin winced before he felt a heavy blow to the back of the head. The assassin had struck him with the back of his bow. Then, after regaining his footing and his aim, he shot the arrow. Without waiting to see if it hit its target, he disappeared.

The crowd screamed as an arrow pierced the chest of the young prince. Many fled. His face contorted in shock as blood poured from his mouth and out of the wound in his chest. He fell, first clinging to the dais as he desperately clung to life. The shock that had dulled him to the agony finally dissipated and then he fell to the ground as he let out his final breath. He did not suffer long, for the arrow was poisoned. He could see his sister leaning over him and talking to him as tears poured down her face. As the last of his life left him in a final breath, his head fell to the side. Through the pandemonium he saw Risúrat waving discreetly to him, a sadistic smile on his withered face. The prince let out a moan, realization in his eyes before he succumbed to the darkness.

"Amíen!" Aralé cried before she fainted. From his appointed seat at the table of the warriors and their leaders, Sern saw this and ran forward despite all those who tried to stop him. He flung himself at the raised platform behind the dais and looked at the hideous scene before him. It was apparent that the prince was dead. The steward and others who should have taken the role of controlling the crowd and seeing to it that certain things were done had already run away or were in too flustered a state to do their duties.

"SILENCE!" He bellowed and the crowd, which was quickly becoming a frantic mob, stopped, many looking at him in utter shock for he had always been so soft-spoken. Even though he was most imposing, unshed tears glistened in his eyes.

"There must be some semblance of order! Master Dorin see the prince and princess to the healing wing!" He said and he looked to the head guard as healers gathered with long pieces of wood used to carry the incapacitated wounded or ill. "Agír! See to it that the palace is surrounded. Take all of the able-bodied men that you can! Send a small party to search the roof for evidence. Women, children, and the elderly enter the castle in an orderly fashion."

There was silence aside from the head guard, Agír, assigning tasks and directing the warriors and volunteers as all of Sern's orders were carried out. Just as the head healer Dorin, a man with long greying brown hair, was about to leave with his healers, Sern grabbed him by the arm and stopped him for the briefest second.

"I meant no disrespect by ordering you about old friend," he said and the healer shook his head.

"You take control beautifully when the circumstance calls for it. I will send someone to report to you the conditions of both the prince and princess. Knowing you, you will not remain idle and it will be quite a task for them," he said and before Sern had a chance to wonder at how he could seem so nonchalant when something so tragic had just taken place, the man was gone. Sern immediately busied himself making sure that the women, the children, and the elderly entered the palace in an orderly and safe manner.

Chapter III
The Musings of a Healer and the Madness of the King of Laaven

"Time of death of Prince Amíen of Laaven, approximately ten fifteen at night, December thirty-first, year one-thousand-nine-hundred-seventy-six of the second age," Dorin said sadly as he looked down at the cadaver of the prince of Laaven. The arrow had been removed from his chest and the wound bandaged. He lay dead and stripped of all his clothing. A light blanket covered all of him but his bandaged chest, the tops of his arms, and his face, which was still contorted in agony.

"He was so young," Dorin remarked as he closed the young man's eyes. As he sat back in his chair beside the bed, he grabbed the arrow that had slain the prince. As he handled it, a poignant stench assaulted his senses and he realized that he recognized it. It was a rare and complex poison used to subdue rabid animals. He wondered at this. Perhaps the assassin found some kind of twisted irony to it.

Dorin also wondered if the king would weather the death of his son. He had always been weak in every sense of the word. He had only survived the death of his father, King Garthermor, through the steadfast strength and love of his wife, Queen

Aralevena I. After the death of his wife he had been left hanging by a thread and by that thread he had remained for near two decades. He survived with the knowledge that he had an heir to the throne of Laaven to rule in his stead once he was gone. The healer doubted he would survive knowing that his only heir was the child he had discounted and had in essence wanted nothing to do with.

Dorin sighed at this. A part of him cringed at the logical fact that the assassin had in all likelihood done their kingdom a favor. The monarchy was corrupt and the ailing king had lost all control of it years ago. The prince had been weak, vain, gullible, and impractical just like his father. King Amíen had even thought to name both of his children after himself even though one was female. He had also managed to drive their kingdom into the dust with more poverty, crime, and disease than any could remember. This was all aside from the fact that they were on the brink of war and neither Amíen would have been fit to lead or take any part in it. Out of cowardice they would have most likely ran as far away as fast as possible.

Then Dorin's thoughts turned even darker. The princess, he realized, was no better than the prince. While her brother was basically good and only clueless, she was manipulative, shiftless, ruthless, and cared for only herself. Then the only hope for Laaven would be her marriage to King Seraavran of Nallel. However, that small hope was easily crushed, for the young man was well-known for being able to deny a beautiful woman nothing and, if nothing else, Laaven's princess was the fairest-looking woman to be found. Some even said her beauty surpassed that of her belated mother, who was famous for looking like a goddess in the moonlight when she was alive. The only good thing that would come of her becoming queen would be that Risúrat would be dismissed and, in all probability, assassinated himself for the princess was not fond of him and would have no qualms about it. Then again, she had never had qualms about anything.

"Of course the princess would hate Risúrat. The two are so similar in nature," the healer sighed and looked out the window where he saw Sern helping hand weapons to the unarmed civilians who stood guard.

Even Sern, who was usually a succinct judge of the true nature of a person, was blinded by her charms. The healer put his head in his hands. He knew that she would find a way to destroy the captain as well. In all his life, he had met less truly decent people than he could count on one hand. Sern was one of them. In fact, he had never met anyone who did not like Sern apart from Risúrat. However, since Risúrat did not like Sern, it was more than likely that the king did not like him.

Every decision, every thought, and every move the king made had something to do with Risúrat. Dorin knew that Risúrat had something—if not everything—to do with the fact that whenever the king was ill, he would not allow any of the healers to even bring him a glass of water. He then looked again to the prince, remembering that he had become a healer because he did not like the backstabbing and underhanded nature of politics and that, to a healer, any time a young man of not even twenty years dies, it is a tragedy. Regardless of who he is, what his death will entail, what preceded it, politics, or whether it is deemed necessary or not, it is a tragedy. The healer called from his room and one of the apprentices entered.

"Master," the young boy said respectfully.

"Have Sern report the death of the prince to the king. Traditionally it would be the job of the healer to take on such an unhappy task, but it would seem that the king will not have any healer set foot in his chambers," Dorin said and looked at the novice, who stared with tear-filled eyes at the corpse of the prince.

"Lord Secretary Risúrat said that the king will not let anyone enter. Perhaps we should simply tell him and let him do it," the novice replied quietly.

"Risúrat already knows!" The healer cried, anger blazing in his eyes. "If it were up to me, he would tell the king nothing! In fact, he would never speak again! Captain Sern will not cower before him as we all do! I will get him myself!" With that, the master healer stormed from the room.

A party of six soldiers had been sent to investigate the roof. Two of the six were walking, exploring the roof. Four stood quietly hovering over a spot in the roof where they discovered that, if you looked down and a woman wearing the right kind of dress was standing up, you could see far more than she had intended.

"You four are ridiculous! How could you be thinking about *that* at a time like this?" The one of the two, who had not spoken before, Éumes, said as he glared at the four men. He then remembered the other various times he had been sent to carry out tasks with these men. Each time, they had done something of this nature or even worse.

"Do not blame us. Blame Íerles. He always walks with his head down!" One said and the others agreed quietly. Íerles grimaced angrily, his head still hanging low.

"I only walk with my head down because if I ever *dare* to look you in the eyes, you will have your father harm my wife and children," Íerles muttered under his breath. No one paid any attention to him.

"You four would not even be here if your fathers weren't rich," he said angrily and this time they did look at him.

"Yes, so unlike you who can be so easily let go for even the smallest mishap, we have nothing to worry about," one said smugly and the others agreed with smug chortles before returning to what they were doing before.

"Have you no honor or pride in yourselves?" Éumes groaned, very well knowing the answer.

"Who needs any of that when your father owns half of the country you live in?"

"Don't lecture us because your father mends shoes for a living."

The two who were actually doing their jobs moved forward, stepping carefully over the roof. After several minutes, one of them stopped.

The Persian Rug

"There is a body by the edge of the roof at the very spot the assassin would have shot his arrow," Éumes said and the other nodded and followed. Soon, a body came into view. One began to draw his sword and the other stopped him. They soon came to the body, which lay in a heap on the roof. Blood ran from his back through a tunic that had been shredded.

"In the name of all that has ever lived and died!" Éumes exclaimed, not even turning the body over. "From the looks of it he has been tortured!" He peeled bits of the torn tunic away from the wounded back to reveal old scars and new wounds marring silvery skin. He winced as he knelt over the prone body.

"Do you think that this man was the assassin?" The other, who stood as far away as he thought he could without being seen as a coward, asked as he looked out over the palace grounds and what he could see of Laaven. Hundreds of men worked tirelessly below them.

"If I had been tortured this badly, I would certainly want to kill someone. However, he seems to be more of a victim than anything. Though all of the gruesome scars are old, these wounds are fresh and there is a bump the size of a fist on the back of his head. If he is lucky, he will only awake to a severe concussion."

"I think I know who he is," the other replied suddenly sounding somber. "Gently turn him over."

The body was turned over and both men gasped.

"Nerin the Healer? How did he get those scars? How did he get up here—"

"I have a more pertinent question as of this minute," the other said. "How are we going to get him off of the roof without killing him?"

Sern walked down the corridor that led to the king's chambers. He had known that the prince was dead for hours. He had been shot through the chest with a poisoned arrow. If one were to survive such a thing, they would be deemed unnatural and most likely either exiled or killed anyway. Sern had always been one to give hope to others when there seemed to be none, but against a poisoned arrow in the chest, there was no hope. He had never thought that he would be the one to do this. It was a healer's duty to inform loved ones of death. He was surprised to learn that the king had banned all healers from his room through Risúrat. Sern found it more likely that Risúrat had banned healers from the king's chambers through the king.

He nodded in greeting to the two guards who stood in front of the short hallway before the king's chamber, walked to the door, and knocked. He was not at all surprised when Risúrat answered.

"Captain Sern, what a surprise," he said with cold and forced civility. He held the door open just enough so that he could fit but closed enough so that Sern could not see into the room.

"With all that has just happened, I would have expected you to be out offering your aid," Sern replied in the same manner. Risúrat looked as if he were about to make a reply before finding that he could not think of one and scowling.

"The king will allow none admittance. Good day to you," Risúrat said and quickly tried to slam the door in Sern's face. The warrior put his heavy boot in the door and Risúrat found that it would not shut.

"I will ask you nicely one last time," Sern said and the advisor only attempted to crush his foot with the door. Sern sighed and pulled him out of the room roughly by his collar, threw him on the floor, and stepped into the room in one swift motion.

"Did you see what he just did!?" Risúrat cried, struggling to get up off of the floor. He looked to the two guards who stood where the small corridor that led to the king's room met the main corridor. After several minutes, one sighed and turned around.

"As of three days ago, by *the king's* orders, we do not guard the door," the guard sneered.

"Then what in the name of all that has ever lived and died do you do?" Risúrat snapped back and the other guard turned around, smirking.

"Stand around and act like we are doing something so no one suspects you of anything."

"You will pay dearly for your insolence," Risúrat snarled and yet still the two guards did not seem intimidated.

"The king will be dead in a week and the prince is dead. That leaves Princess Aralevena and she despises you. The first thing she will take care of as queen is Master Risúrat, son of Néiro. We have no need to fear you anymore."

With that, Risúrat snarled and fled from the corridor.

Sern stood inside the king's chamber. He slowly moved toward the large bed in the center of the room. Candles burned low all about the room casting eerie shadows against dusty furniture. "I suppose *the king* banned the maids from his room as well," Sern thought as he continued forward, noticing a thick layer of dust covering a woman's shoe that lay on the floor. Sern recognized it as the belated Queen Aralevena's. He slowly moved toward the bed.

"In the name of all that has ever lived and died!" He gasped upon seeing the king's face. He looked cadaverous and breathed heavily through a nose deformed by scabs and scars. Thin, knotted, dark hair hung limply against his head. He was thinner than Sern had ever seen him and his skin was transparent.

"Highness," Sern said quietly and the king only continued to breathe shallow breaths. His eyes did not even flutter. Sern decided to stay until the king awoke to reveal the news. He shook his head as he looked at the pitiable state his lord was in.

"What has he done to you?" The warrior thought aloud as he pulled a chair by the king's bedside.

Three hours passed before the king awoke. Sern had almost fallen asleep when suddenly King Amíen awoke with a strangled cry. He sounded as if his throat was closing and he writhed in agony. There was blood in his yellowed rotten teeth and his bloodshot eyes bulged as he coughed.

"Highness!" Sern exclaimed as he began to pour water out of a pitcher and into the cup for a king, thinking that the man was coughing because he needed water. When the king had stopped coughing, Sern began to help him drink. The king's face contorted in agony as he drank the water.

"Sern, what are...wha..." The king swallowed and trailed off.

"Your majesty, there is something I must tell you," Sern said. However, the king did not seem to hear him. "Your majesty," Sern began quietly before remembering that the king was almost deaf. "Your majesty, last night at the Enembír Festival Prince..." Sern trailed off again upon seeing the recognition in the king's eyes for twice before he had heard a similar speech.

"My son!" He cried in a hoarse voice. His fists clenched and he bit so hard on his scarred bottom lip that his teeth went clear through it. "My son!" He cried through the tears and the blood that dripped down his chin. "He was not yet a man!" Suddenly the king stopped, growing even paler before leaning over to the side of the bed and retching on the floor. Sern held back his greasy strands of thin hair.

There was a knock at the door and, when the king had finished, Sern went to answer it. "Who comes to call?" He asked, once again the soft-spoken man with an unassuming and kind voice.

"Sodró," a voice came from behind the door and Sern opened it and kindly greeted the young man. "Captain, the supposed assassin has been detained and the guard dissolved. All of the citizens have been sent back to their homes. Both Lords Dorin and Agír want to meet with you. Agír says that you know the man who shot the prince."

At this, there was a wail from the king who clutched his head and started to sob. Sodró's eyes opened wide at this. Sern looked to the men who were standing at the door to the king's room. "You, guard," he said, pointing to the one on the left. "Go in and watch over the king. Take care of him." He then looked to the other guard. "See to it that no one goes in or out besides myself or the princess without my permission. It is for our lord's own protection," he said and turned to the young man beside him.

The Persian Rug

"Sodró, tell Master Dorin that I will meet with him when I am finish—"

Suddenly, they heard the king mutter something and all became silent.

"I order that you take me to the assassin!" The king cried in all that was left in his voice. "I do not care if I have to be carried there! I want to see the man who killed my son!" Then he ordered for someone to fetch him the royal robe and attempted to climb out of bed. He would have fallen and hurt himself had Sern not caught him. The messenger helped him get into his robes as Sern held him up. It turned out that the king was indeed too weak to walk, even with a person on each side of him helping him, so Sern had to carry him. The sun was rising as they made their way to the castle dungeons.

Upon entering they were met by the warden, Nevate. He led them to his office, where the king was given a chair and Sern was dismissed by the king. He then made his way to meet with Dorin. Once there, he and the older man spent hours reflecting and talking of the future regarding themselves and the kingdom and simply comforting one another as two friends would in the face of such a tragedy.

Nerin choked as he felt dirty cold water hitting his face. The ache in his head was almost unbearable and the dark room spun about him. In order for him to even begin to be bothered by the pain, it must have been bad enough to make any other wish for death. He suddenly heard someone yelling at him to get up. He tried and found that he could not, not only because he was dizzy but because something was hindering his arms and legs from moving beyond the length of a few fingers. He fought against them weakly, not able to register that it was shackles that were hindering his movement so and that he was lying half naked on a prison floor and the warden was standing over him, screaming at him to get up.

Nerin eventually fell gracelessly against the ground whimpering. Another bucket of the frigid and disgusting water stung his eyes and blinded him. This time, it was accompanied by a kick in the side. Nerin barely felt it. Before he knew it, he was being dragged down a dusty hallway and there were hands all around grabbing at him (and had been for quite some time before he realized it). These were the dirty and skeletal hands of the condemned prisoners in the cells that lined the thin strip of hallway between cells. His boots were even stolen, revealing feet that were scarred and bloodless. He mumbled incoherently and kicked weakly several times. The warden had to beat away several of the hands that refused to let go. Nerin closed his eyes, half out of agony and half in a attempt to help sort things out through a mind that seemed to have no memories, no information, no ideas regarding anything at all, and able to process next to nothing.

Next, he felt rough hands letting go and a cold floor beneath him. He looked up to see what appeared to be a feeble old man in a chair before his eyes lost focus. He thought that the man had said something to him, but he could not tell. Upon putting his head in his hands, he saw the scars that covered them. He looked at his arms, shoulders, torso, feet, and the parts of his legs that were either not covered by his short leggings or visible through tears in them. He screamed. He began to mumble incoherently and panicked inwardly before he felt a sharp pain in his side and saw another man standing over him.

"Why did you kill the prince? Why my son!?" The king shouted at Nerin, who only looked at him blankly after finding that he could not understand the words the man said.

"Why did you not just kill me!?" The king bellowed and Nerin barely even heard him for his head began to spin again. It was his intention to ask who he was when he fell to the ground shaking. Bile poured from his mouth and he moaned as the aftershock wracked his body.

"The boy has a concussion," the warden said, looking down worriedly at Nerin. He seriously doubted that the healer had killed anyone.

"The very second he is well, I want him hanged from the

tallest tree in my scepter!" The king tried to cry but only managed something between a whisper and a wheeze.

"But sire, there is serious doubt as to whether he actually—"

"He will hang! Are you trying to protect the man who murdered my son? Are you a traitor? Do you want to die with him?"

"Never!" The warden declared and bent to kiss the king's hand before dragging Nerin back to his cell and leaving him there. So it seemed that the fate of Nerin the Healer would be to die.

It was an hour before noon and Sern had fallen asleep by the princess' bed in the healing wing. It was there that she had slept peacefully through the immediate aftermath of her brother's assassination. The king had been too busy mourning Amíen and then planning his son's funeral to even spare his daughter a second thought so Sern took it upon himself to watch over her. Last Sern had heard, the man had ordered servants carry him to his study and there he had sequestered himself. Instead of thanking Sern for taking over and seeing that things had run smoothly when even his most loyal advisors did not, he bitterly kept his distance. That was fine with Sern. He had never liked the king, even when he was Prince Amíen.

Aralé opened her eyes and looked around in confusion for several seconds before the realization of all that had come to pass hit her harder than anything had ever hit her in her life. She refused to believe it.

"Sern," she said quietly and he awoke and looked at her worriedly, immediately leaning by her side. "Where is our brother?" She asked quietly and Sern looked at her sadly. "Sern…" she said again and he did not answer for long moments. The princess grew impatient and flew out of bed just as he began to answer. There was a book resting on the dresser by her bed. She quickly opened it and tore out three pages. When Sern began to ask her why, she ignored him and started a frantic run. Barefoot, she tore through the healing wing and then down the castle corridor. Sern followed closely behind her as she ran through several levels of the palace, stopping at the door that opened to the staircase that led to her father's secluded tower study. She clambered up the winding staircase in almost total dark before coming to the wooden door of her father's tower study. Sern still followed. He watched as she kicked at the locked door with all her strength.

"Leave me in peace!" was the muffled cry that came from within.

The princess was breathing heavily as she quickly placed the three pieces of parchment on top of one another and folded them in half. Sern watched as she forcefully slid the combined and folded pieces of parchment in the small space between the part of the door that swung out and the wall. The pieces slid right through, the lock clicked audibly, and the door swung open. The king bellowed indignantly as his daughter entered his tower study. Sern did not.

"What in the name of all that has ever lived and died do you want girl?" He spat. The princess had almost never seen a day when her father did not seem to be grieving silently. However, on this day, it appeared that he suffered tenfold. One look at him told her that what she had feared to be true was indeed true. She saw that the portrait he usually held close, a portrait of the late Queen Aralevena, had been replaced by a portrait of her brother, the late Prince Amíen.

"Amíen…" she gasped and fell to her knees. The king began to weep anew.

"Get out girl!" The king howled.

"Father?" The princess said through her tears.

"You have no right to cry! I told you to watch over your brother!" He spat.

"Blame me for whatever else you will, as you have always done, but you cannot be sound of mind and blame me for this!" The princess wailed.

"But it is your fault! You have been doing disgraceful things with the very man who slew my son for months! I know your mind, you wretched girl! What did you do to drive him to do it? Harlot!"

The Persian Rug

Aralé only stared at him before whispering, "Nerin?" She turned pale.

"So you admit it then! Was your plan to supplant your brother?" He then started to cough and, when his coughing fit subsided, he continued his cruel and, above all, untrue accusations. "Or perhaps it is just a matter of finishing what you started. You killed your mother! Am I to follow my son in short order?"

"It was your sickness that killed my brother!" She screamed angrily before the tears stopped falling and her face became rigid and cold. There was an almost unnoticeable grim satisfaction about her. "And it was your seed that killed my mother."

With that, the king snarled and began to throw books, paperweights, and anything else within reach at his daughter. Aralé ripped one of the daggers that was only for decoration off of the walls and pointed it at her father from across the room. He froze and immediately ceased his tantrum. He was so drained of energy from the exertion of his tantrum that his body collapsed against his desk chair. Aralé glared at him murderously before throwing the dagger so hard against the floor that it stood there upright as she stalked out of the room. She walked with her head held high, back to her chambers. Sern followed behind mutely.

Once they were in her chambers, she locked the doors and collapsed to the floor. Sern knelt beside her and she clung to him. After several seconds he carried her to the bed and laid her down gently before fetching her handkerchiefs for her to dry her tears. A short while later, when her tears were almost dry, she looked up at him and took his hand.

"Does everyone really think that Nerin…"

"The king has told Laaven that Nerin assassinated your brother," Sern said quietly.

"But do they believe it? Do they believe that Nerin, a healing prodigy, a man who helps everyone and often asks for nothing in return, would be reduced to murder? He has saved the lives of sons, mothers, fathers, wives, and often free of charge!" The princess cried and the older man shook his head.

"People will believe whatever they might be told," he said and Aralevena fell back into his arms.

Chapter IV
Maveree

He could make sense of none of it. All he knew was that he was cold and that he did not like it. He knew that the bread he had been given was not even marginally appetizing, and ominous looking black specs swam about in the cup of water he had been given. When he lay down on the cold floor for a while, unmoving, like a battered corpse, he would forget how weak his legs were and how much the rest of him ached and how much the room swam every time he attempted to rise. He would even fail to remember the heavy shackles. Then, when he would try to rise, he would be reminded as he came crashing back down to the ground.

It did not matter overmuch that the food and drink were so unappetizing, for he could keep only little sips of water and absolutely no solid food down. He tried to make sense of his situation, but found that he could not. After a while, he realized that he had no memory of his past, how he came to be so badly injured, or even his name. Being that his brains were as addled as they were, he came to this startling realization several times. Every time he looked at his scarred body, he would scream, not remembering even that.

When his dinner of stale bread and dirty water was brought to him, he did not even move until well past dark. The torches blazoned outside his cell, hurting his sensitized eyes, and the pain in his limbs made it impossible for him to sleep. Eventually, the thirst in him was so strong that he had to drink. He slowly dragged himself over to the cup and plate. Upon lifting the plate, he found a piece of yellow parchment underneath.

He clumsily unfolded it with shaking fingers to find that there was something scrawled in dark ink on the inside. It was wet and sticky against his fingers. He looked confusedly at it, not knowing exactly what to make of it. He stared at it before he became too dizzy and attempted to toss it aside. It adamantly stuck to his fingers. In his frustration at the piece of parchment, he accidentally knocked his cup of water over. He moaned, the only noise he was really capable of making, and began to lap at the water that poured over the cold stone.

"Thank you for missing dinner to stay here," the princess said as she yawned and lay back on her pillow. The sun had sunk beneath the far off hills hours ago and it had been a very trying day. Sern smiled.

"I would do anything for you, Aralé," he said and she suddenly looked sad.

"You are all I have now that my brother is dead and Nerin will soon be," she said sadly and Sern was about to speak, as if to apologize, when she put one of her white slender fingers to his lips. She started to sob hysterically. "He is innocent! Why does no one stand up for him?"

Sern held her as she cried and until she succumbed to her exhaustion and collapsed against him. Sern took her hand and kissed it gently after laying her down and covering her with a thin blanket. "Sleep well princess." With that, he quit the room.

As he walked down the hallway toward his chambers, too lost in his own thoughts to pay much attention to his surroundings, he collided with Danen who seemed to be in an unnatural rush. This crash along with the sharp pain he felt in his side sobered Sern immediately.

"I am so sorry!" Danen said quickly, seeming to be in quite a rush.

"Where are you going in such a hurry?" Sern asked as he gently patted the small tender spot on his side. It was really next to nothing, but he could not help but wonder what the younger man was carrying. The fact that it was concealed and Danen looked so guilty only fueled his curiosity. "And what exactly did you just attempt to skewer me with?"

"Do you remember what close friends Éumes and I used to be?" Danen asked. It was not painfully obvious that he was lying, but he had never been a good liar. Sern nodded. "Well, when we were friends, he gave me the keys to his wardrobe and I would borrow his clothes often. After we had our falling out months ago, I had meant to return the keys but had forgotten. I just remembered now." And he finished by taking out the keys and showing them to Sern.

That was his mistake, for even in the brief second he had seen the keys, he had recognized them as the keys to a dungeon cell and not to a closet or chest. He also knew that Éumes had been the one who lead the party of guards that had found Nerin's body on the roof.

"Danen..." Sern said quietly before tucking the keys back into the younger man's pocket. "You look suspicious running about with concealed keys." And with that, he continued on his way. Danen let out a huge breath and looked back at the retreating form of Sern. He knew and he would not try and stop them.

Danen then continued to walk, this time at a much more leisurely pace. He was known for pacing the corridors at all hours of the night so no one he happened to pass paid him much attention. He soon came to Éumes, who was standing by an old tapestry.

Danen nonchalantly passed him the keys and attempted to walk away. The bigger man grabbed him and held him back briefly.

"Does anyone know?" He mouthed.

"Only Sern," Danen mouthed back and Éumes grimaced.

"He is no threat to us," Danen pulled away and the other man still looked completely unconvinced. "Trust me," he said quietly and Éumes sighed before throwing him something square that was wrapped in a black scarf. Danen caught it and then began the very short journey to the castle wall, where he would distract the guards.

Éumes then walked toward the dungeons with the concealed keys. He walked down the stairs and through their eerie darkness nonchalantly. It was late and the dungeons were deserted with the exception of a guard who had fallen asleep while on duty and the warden who was having an argument with another man in his office. Their screaming drowned out any sound that Éumes made as he went.

As he walked down the thin hallway that separated each cell-lined wall, he gazed at the sickly and dirty prisoners who filled them. These were all murderers, thieves, and wretched men who had been nothing but a burden to society. In Éumes' mind, Nerin was not such a man. He had saved more lives than possibly any other man in history. Éumes had seen him lying weak and wounded on the roof. He had imagined that the healer had earned such a beating by attempting to thwart the actual assassin, a man who was going unpunished due to a weak and unreasonable king.

Éumes approached the cell and clasped his hand to his mouth in order to stifle a gasp. He held the lantern he carried aloft as he gazed into the empty cell several times, making sure that his eyes did not deceive him. The cell was locked and there was only a small hole in the brick only big enough to fit an arm through at the very top of his cell. Nothing was disturbed. Had they anticipated someone trying to rescue Nerin and moved him to a more secure location?

"No," Éumes breathed aloud. It was more likely that he had died, being in the condition he was in and his body had been moved before it started to smell. Then again, if anything at all had happened concerning the prisoner, it would have been known for the Laaven castle was infamous for its gossiping staff. He decided to see if the castle healer, Dorin, was awake and ask him if anything had happened concerning Nerin.

"I win!" Danen exclaimed as he pulled back the cards that lay on the wooden table in the office where on-duty guards watched over the castle entrances. The slightly older guard of a darker countenance who sat across from him scowled. "You owe me a drink," Danen added.

"I must have spent near half my pay on drinks for you this past year! You must be cheating!" The other man cried miserably and Danen smirked.

"You are simply distracted by my boyish charm. Confess," Danen replied facetiously and the man growled. He looked as if he were about to reply when his focus changed and he let out an annoyed sigh.

"What kind of sane person goes riding about this late at night?" The older man asked, running his fingers through his hair. Danen only shrugged and began to set up the cards again as the older man went out into the night to inspect the person who was leaving. Danen assumed that it was Éumes. The second the other man's footsteps were out of earshot, he filled a tall clay pitcher with water and pushed it off of the table. It created an almost ear splittingly loud crash. Danen cried out for the broken pottery had made a deep gash in his arm. The guard, who had recognized the rider as Sern and immediately signaled for him to pass, heard the crash and went rushing back up to the little room.

Éumes arrived at the guard's temporary office ten minutes later to find Danen sitting on a chair holding his wounded arm and the guard soaking up the water on the floor with a table cloth. Danen stared blankly at Éumes as he realized that it could not have been him who left. It started to rain and Éumes stood in the doorway, little beads of clear water running down his face and dripping from the ends of his long, dark hair.

"Nerin has been moved," Éumes mouthed to Danen and the young man paled. "I do not know to where."

Danen hung his head low and Éumes looked at him for a brief second before disappearing without the guard ever having been aware of his presence.

Sern sighed as he rode through the rain in the dark. He knew that it could only be his luck that would lead to a torrential downpour during such an endeavor. Then again, the rain would wash away any tracks his horse left behind and his scent, making it near impossible for him to be tracked.

"Can you hear me?" He whispered as they went past dilapidated shack after dilapidated shack. Rotting corpses lined the side of the road and a starving dog, its ribs clearly visible, lay in a puddle of mud whimpering.

"Nerin!" Sern exclaimed as he grabbed the hands that were clasped and rested against his stomach.

"So sorry," Nerin replied feebly.

"Hurts," he said as his head fell against the older man's back. He had been hidden behind Sern, under his cloak for nearly three quarters of an hour and he felt as if he were about to die. His body ached, his head spun, and his throat burned. Sern had to tie him to the saddle and then to his own body to keep him upright. This did not prove extraordinarily comfortable for Nerin but it was the only thing that kept him from falling off of the horse. He was so light and Sern so strong that he barely even noticed him.

"We will be there in an hour or so. Just hold on and keep as quiet as possible," Sern said and he felt Nerin's breath hitch in pain.

"Where are we going?" Nerin asked weakly and Sern shook his head. He had told him three times before.

"To see a very old friend of mine in The City of the Wood. She is wise and powerful. She will take you to a place where you can heal and no one can hurt you."

"Who would want to hurt me?" Nerin replied with a childlike innocence, his voice small and barely audible over the falling rain.

"Do not think about that now. Just rest. We will be there soon," Sern said and he felt Nerin snuggle against his back and was certain that he had fallen asleep. "Maybe for the first time in two thousand years she will do something for someone other than herself." He added quietly for he was certain that Nerin would not hear. They rode for a while in silence. Then Nerin awoke again. He had the same complaints and the same questions, once again not remembering anything he had been told before he had fallen asleep. After asking virtually the same exact questions again, he fell asleep once more and remained asleep as they rode for several hours along a muddy dirt rode that cut through the countryside, which was quickly becoming a swamp.

The City of the Wood was one of the few havens for artists, poets, musicians, actors, mavericks of all kinds and modern witches. It was a place that was bright and effervescent and busy during the day but dead in the early morning. Streets that were usually lined with all sorts of people doing everything from selling incense, to painting, to meditating, to playing their instruments and singing in the square for coins were muddy and lifeless in the rain. Small dark homes lined the streets and got larger and larger as they came to the end of the small city. After making several turns they came to a stop in front of one of the largest homes. On its porch sat a small child wrapped in a water darkened cloak. She did not seem to acknowledge their presence.

Sern carefully untied Nerin from him and climbed off the horse, carrying the unconscious young man. The small cloaked figure on the porch made some sort of signal with its hand and Sern was surprised to find his horse being led away. He then stepped toward the porch. Nerin sighed in his sleep.

"Mistress Maveree," he said quietly and the cloaked head of the child turned up as if looking at him. "You have been expecting me." She beckoned for him to come forward with one bloodless hand and opened the door. She held it for him as he entered her home.

It was a beautiful lofty home with large windows. Velvet divans and intricately carved wooden chests rested on colorful carpets. Weapons, pottery, armor, outfits, accessories, and works of art from every age and some places no one else had ever been covered the walls and rested on tables. One wall was almost entirely covered by maps, the oldest of these over a thousand years old. Not only did beautiful things abound in her home, but also things that were remarkably strange or macabre. Eerie fangs, ominous looking or deformed skulls of both animals and men, books of dark magic, mysterious tablets that ran with fresh blood, and devices used for torture in days long since passed could also be found in her home. Most of her more disturbing artifacts were locked away in a secret place or decorated the walls of her bedroom.

Sern had hardly noticed her busily lighting candles as he stared at the myriad things that filled her living room. His eyes had fallen upon a map of Laaven and its neighboring kingdoms when her voice interrupted his thoughts.

"You know, you only ever bother with me when you need my help," she said and Sern turned to see her stretched out on one of the divans taking almost inhuman gulps from an ancient looking goblet of wine. He could not believe it. He had not seen her since he had been a young teenager. Then she had appeared to be an adorable child with wide hazel eyes and long unkempt curls of hair so light brown that they were almost blonde. She had looked to be ten (give or take a year) apart from the unnatural intelligence, experience, and age betrayed in her eyes and the way she carried herself. She walked and spoke like a proud woman with her head held high and her steps sure and firm. Almost a decade later, she looked exactly the same, only perhaps a bit more impatient and weary. It was as if inside this little child there was someone who had aged fifty years in less than twenty.

"And I only ask for your help when I truly need it," he replied and watched Maveree take another gulp from her goblet. It had never sat right with him to see one who appeared so young drinking and smoking a pipe like a brigand. He wondered if she still kept a flask and pipe on her person.

"Indeed," she said and motioned for him to sit down on the divan opposite her. Sern did as she silently commanded and placed Nerin down gently beside him. She looked at the poor unconscious healer and then to Sern. "You are a fool," she said after another long drink.

"While some of us are only out to achieve our own ends, others will not see an innocent man executed," Sern said matter-of-factly with an almost sad smile as he gazed at Maveree. She shrugged and nodded, knowing that what he said was perfectly true.

"Sern, you forget that no good deed goes unpunished. Do you not realize that with Nerin gone you can have the princess and by saving him you are being nothing but a detriment to yourself?" This was followed by another drink.

"He will not stay here. He would not be safe here or in any of our neighboring kingdoms. He would be hunted and killed. I came to implore you to take him to your secret city, the place you go that no other can find and no one can follow him to," Sern replied somberly and Maveree was silent for a moment, before smiling broadly.

"So, you get to feel like you are doing the right thing and get your precious wench. Are you not clever?"

"Maveree, I am saving his life and I need your help to do it. You know as well as I do that to stay here is death to him. The King is mad!" Sern exclaimed and Maveree sighed.

"Very well, I will take him with me when I leave," Maveree said and as Sern dropped to his knees in thanks, she abruptly stopped him. "However, only one problem remains."

"And what is that?" He asked, the overwhelming relief he had felt seconds before abating as suddenly as it had swelled within him.

"What to tell the princess," Maveree said and, upon seeing the man's almost annoyed look at her even mentioning so stupid a thing, she rolled her eyes. "That girl keeps you on a shorter leash than even the cruelest hunters use on the most wayward of hounds. You crumble to dust in her conniving claws."

"It is not like that at all," Sern said and Maveree nodded as if to say "I'm sure it isn't," in the most mocking way possible. Sern scowled and continued, "I love her more than any other man could ever love a woman and I will do what is best for her regardless of how it affects me. Even with Nerin gone, she is not mine to have for she is a princess and I am the son of a mad old innkeeper. She will marry King Seraavran of Nallel, forming a strong alliance between our peoples to combat the threat of war that looms like a storm cloud in the northern sky. And when Phallé-Nal does call out for war, Seraavran will crush them. When she is queen, I will serve her faithfully and love her everlastingly, as I have always done," he said vehemently and Maveree looked almost incapable of speech before she took another gulp of wine and started to mockingly clap. Her usual cold acridity returned.

"You certainly can deliver a pretty speech," she said and Sern sank back down on the divan, careful not to hurt Nerin. "Although all of the eloquent soliloquies and blind moronic love in the world, and such idiocy abounds in you, cannot act as compensation for truth. At least, for long."

"You hate everyone on principle! Who are you to say anything about Aralé or about love in general?" Sern cried, angry that Maveree had insulted the woman he loved.

"That is true," she said with a bitter smile as she refilled her goblet. "But humans in general are despicable and selfish animals. I know, because I am one of you. Your beloved princess is simply one of many. You are one of a kind and are wasted on her." Maveree sighed and Sern remained silent. She then turned her cold hazel eyes to Nerin and looked him over almost disgustedly. "I do not know what she sees in him anyway. He looks more like a woman than Prince Amíen!"

"Maveree!" Sern said, appalled. "It is not wise to speak ill of the dead."

She scowled. "The dead do not care what we say about them. All I am trying to say is that if I were her and had to choose between you and Nerin—"

"You would choose me?" Sern asked and looked to the younger man beside him as if he expected him to wake up at any second and be outraged.

"Well, at least I can be certain that you are indeed a man. I think that Sir Sleeping Lovely over there is prettier than I," she said and took a deep drink.

The captain shook his head.

Chapter V
Departure

The princess awoke the next morning to the tentative whispering and gentle shaking of one of her chambermaids. The princess sat up quickly and glared at the middle-aged woman with long greying hair.

"What?" She spat angrily, tossing her covers aside violently and muttering under her breath. The chambermaid glared at her as much as she dared to.

"Your brother's funeral is this afternoon, Your Highness," the woman said and all of the color drained from the princess' face. "You will give a speech in his honor."

The princess said nothing as she was dressed in black and readied for the funeral. Her hair was tied behind her in long golden braids interwoven with black gems and her nails were painted black, along with her eyelids. It was a slow hour, but, at the same time, an hour that seemed to end as soon as it started. It did not grant Aralé much time to think. She knew what the kingdom thought of her brother. They thought he was weak and vain and would never make much of a king. He could not wield a sword or a pen or even make a tolerably decent decision. He had been known to sleep through lessons and make merry more than he would study and acquire the knowledge necessary to run a country. He was the laughingstock of the royal world and aristocracy in almost every country she could name. The princess knew she would have to stand behind the podium and talk of his accomplishments (of which there were none that she or really anyone else for that matter could have thought of), his talents (of which there were none she could think of that high society would deem actual talents), and why the country had suffered a terrible loss. She hoped that people would not laugh as she said this. Even though she personally had suffered a catastrophic loss, the country would not feel the same way. When the king's health started failing, many people started leaving Laaven, for it was practically common knowledge that Phallé-Nal would attack in the coming years and that Amíen was a poor leader in no way fit to handle anything at all. Their defenses would quickly crumble and lead to a sweeping victory for the northern kingdom. Phallé-Nal was never kind to those it conquered.

The princess barely even saw herself in the mirror as they led her over to it, making sure that she approved of the way she looked. On certain days, she would and, on other days, it would be near lunch before she left her room. On those days, people would most likely be fired or have to dodge whatever the princess threw at them in her impatience and rage. On this day, she only glanced at herself for a few brief seconds, noting how the black clothing made her look as white as a marble statue and the deep paint around her eyes as bloodless as a corpse. She looked thinner than usual for, in her melancholy, she had almost no appetite. She thought that this would have been near what her brother looked like, being that their faces were so similar. With that thought, she turned away from the mirror.

"I am ready," the princess said and was led away, down the castle corridors and out onto the castle grounds. The weather was deceptively warm and bright and it only served to darken her mood.

The king lay in his bed. He had been dressed and readied in black raiment. He had wanted it to be laden with gems as all of his old outfits had been, but, to his dismay, soon found that he did not have the strength to wear an outfit so heavy. The exertion had left him exhausted and, after being put in a simple outfit of the lightest material possible, he had collapsed. Risúrat stood beside him.

"I have nothing left to live for," the king murmured and Risúrat began to gently stroke his head.

"Of course not my lord," Risúrat said and the king looked up at him the utmost shock and anguish in his eyes. "Your wife was the real king. She was starting to rebuild a failing kingdom and she acted through you! She ruled you as a king should rule his queen. When she died, you had to stand alone and it nearly killed you. You are a coward who turned to powders and concoctions instead of dealing with your problems and your pain like a man."

"It was you who gave me the powder in the first place!" The king cried in a barely audible voice.

"And it was you who was too weak to deny me! As you always have been! When your wife could no longer rule you, I stepped in. You are useless, a puppet on my string. With your daughter in control, our country will fall and our men will become slaves and our women concubines. That is why I am leaving for Phallé-Nal tonight," Risúrat said with a smile and unshed tears shone in the king's eyes.

"You are my only friend," the king said and Risúrat laughed.

"You have only enemies. I used you to gain wealth and have been stealing from you and drugging you so that you would be easier to manipulate for years. Now that I am wealthy I can bribe the king of Phallé-Nal to give me a high position in the new government once they destroy Laaven. It was I that made sure you would not be able to attend the Enembír Festival, I who placed your only son behind the dais, and I who hired the assassin that shot him with an arrow coated in poison used to oust vermin and it was you who let me. Now your lone family member left, that monster of a daughter, would sooner be a suitable queen than weep over your dead body. She will not marry King Seraavran, for she is too wretched to ever want any man for more than a few months at a time and he was your only hope. You will never be able to escape the pain and the shame you have brought upon yourself. I will, however, do you one last favor before I depart,"

Risúrat said and he started to reach into one of the inner pockets of his robes.

"And what is that?" The king asked weakly, his body trembling.

Risúrat then took a bag out of his pocket and threw it at the king. "This is enough to end your pitiful suffering Amíen," he said before he spat on the king. "And with that I bid you farewell, *Your Highness*," the man added before departing and slamming the door behind him.

Amíen looked down at the bag and painstakingly sat himself up. He coughed and realized that he was starting to feel the sickness he would feel whenever he went too long without his powder. He looked at the bag, tears running down his cheeks and neck in rivulets, and his body trembling as he began to undo the laces that kept the pouch closed.

A quarter of an hour passed and still the king had not arrived. The princess, the prince's tutors, King Seraavran, and four other of the belated prince's closest friends all sat at the front of the crowd of other nobles, royalty, castle employees, and citizens of Laaven waiting to give their obituary speeches, or in the princess' case, lack thereof. The princess had been frantically searching the crowd for most of that time, looking for Sern only to find that he was absent. However, the captain's absence went fairly unnoticed next to the fact that the king and Risúrat, who followed in his wake like a shadow, were both absent. Two quarters of an hour later, all eyes turned to the castle doors as they opened. In place of the king, there stood Risúrat who looked incredibly distraught.

"The king has taken his own life by poison!" He wailed, his grey hair wild and matted with sweat. None moved except the princess who rose so fast that she knocked the woman who sat beside her to the floor. She knew that it had to be Risúrat who had done it. She suspected that he had been slowly poisoning her father for months. When she voiced her suspicion, her father had her locked in the tower for near a week. "Someone! Do something!" He screamed so loudly that the ground echoed. He had started to scream again when the princess stood before him and, with a snarl, struck him in the face. When he fell to the ground, she continued to buffet the older man mercilessly.

"You murdered him!" She cried. "I know it was you! My father would never take his own life! He might have been a right bastard but he would never sink so low as to end his own life! Liar!" She cried and continued to relentlessly flay him.

"He failed at it twice before, mayhap three is the magic number after all," a voice in the crowd murmured in a disparaging tone.

"No, he only tried to off himself once before," another replied with a sneer. The princess, seeing exactly who said these things, immediately sent guards after them and sentenced them to death by torture. She then turned back to Risúrat.

"You are banished Risúrat, son of Néiro! Get out or in the name of all that has ever lived and died you will be tortured to death along with those whoreson half-wits!" She bellowed and Risúrat immediately rose and began to drag his bloodied and beaten body away. "Someone get my father's carcass, we shall make this a double funeral," she continued in a more even tone. However, rage was still present in her voice and blazed in her eyes.

"You will not even have another grave dug for him will you, Your Highness?" Master Dorin said as he stood, sounding both angry and appalled. However, he was far more controlled than the young princess.

"No," she replied with a sadistic smirk.

"What about tradition? Do you not think that your brother would have wanted—" Master Dorin began only to be interrupted by the fuming princess.

"Both my brother and my father are dead! They are gone! The dead care nothing of the feckless and insignificant tasks of the living! *I* am the last of The Royal House of Vénatheln and as such it is *my* orders that will be obeyed and *my* wants that will be acquiesced to and I want to see the birds and the uncivilized flesh eating half-men that live in the deep and dark places of the world rise from their holes and feast on his carrion flesh!" She screamed and fell to her knees in the dirt. "NOW!"

Her wishes were carried out. Her brother was unceremoniously dropped into his grave where several of his closest friends remained for the rest of the day. Only one person in the world, Éumes, wept for him.

The corpse of the former King Amíen II was stripped and left to rot in the dirt at the eaves of the Ariyekk forest and the two men the princess had ordered to be tortured to death were thrown into a cell to await their fate. Risúrat, who had been banished on the very day he had planned on leaving, thought of nothing except the heavy bag of money he kept under his cloak, whether anyone would notice the absence of the horse he had stolen, and how he would gain the king's favor once he reached Phallé-Nal. King Seraavran left, insisting that regardless of outer beauty or an alliance, he refused to spend another minute in the company such a raving madwoman.

Sern returned late in the day to find the princess distraught and the atmosphere tense in the Laaven castle. He had known that he would miss the prince's funeral by taking Nerin to Maveree Eldestchild but it seemed that more had transpired during his absence than a simple funeral, something so dramatic that no one had noticed the absence of the man who was thought to have assassinated the crowned prince. The princess was certain to give the captain her incredibly skewed version of all that had happened and he unquestioningly believed her. However, it seemed that she was not so quick to believe him.

"Sern, in only four years I will be queen of Laaven. Even now I have almost no one that I can trust. I can see that you are lying to me about where you have been. After losing the only family I had in this world, a father who never cared for me and a brother who never had time for me, am I going to lose you too? Am I destined to live and die alone, with none who love me?" She said and pulled away from his embrace.

"I love you!" Sern exclaimed. "I love you more than a garden ravaged by summer's heat does the sweet water of the first spring rain."

"So you say, and yet you hide things from me?" The princess said and Sern sighed.

"While most people assume that the prison is the lowest level of the castle, in reality there is one below it. Over a thousand years ago, when this castle was built, the floor that is a prison now was a storeroom and the floor below it a treasury. When your distant ancestor King Amíen I led the revolution that made him king, he did not know of this treasure room and all who did know of it, the royal family, were killed. Amíen I changed the storeroom into the prison it is today and the treasure room was lost to all memory.

"The prison today has thirty-six cells and four set aside for prisoners who are too dangerous to be kept with the others. These four cells, due to their placement and errors in construction, can be accessed from the lower level by simply pushing up a few floorboards. It was in this way that I took Nerin from his cell and merely put the floorboards back when I was finished.

"He had an awful head injury so I carried him from the passage to its entrance, which is through one of the old mausoleums in the graveyard. I hid a large old cloak there and tied him to my back and he was hidden beneath the cloak. He stayed tied to my back as I carefully mounted a horse in the stable and then rode to The City of the Wood where I left him with my friend, the seeress Maveree Eldestchild. She will take him to a secret place where he can heal and be safe," Sern said and watched as the young woman seemed to mull all he said over. She ran her fingers through her hair.

"How do you know of this treasury? You must be the only soul alive who does," she asked thoughtfully.

"When I was a boy, I was tutored by a man named Master Virahéen. He was obsessed with histories. He probably taught me about it and I just remembered it now."

"You are friends with that unnatural witch, Maveree?"

"I was very dear to her closest friend Róethel."

"Where is she taking Nerin?"
"I could not tell you. Only Maveree knows."
"Then take me to her."

Chapter VI
What Does the Seeress Desire?

That very night Captain Sern and the princess simply walked out of the castle. In the disguise of a young student warrior with her hair hidden by the hood of a cloak and her face obscured by shadow, she followed the captain out of the castle under the pretense that she was a pupil visiting an ailing mother in the city and that they would return in a day or so. Sern's reputation of bravery, honesty, chivalry, and all good things that can be found in a man made it so that none questioned him.

The pair rode side by side on the nearly deserted road to The City of the Wood. In the first hour of their journey, two young women on a large grey horse tore past them. Then all was still for a long while except for a light rain (which lasted less than a quarter of an hour) and the scurrying of the small nocturnal creatures, which are not really much harm to anyone. It was an ultimately uneventful ride and Sern ended up making a remark every ten minutes or so just to make sure that the princess did not fall asleep on her horse. The City of the Wood was in view when a small group of men on horseback seemed to materialize quite a distance away out of the heavy darkness.

"Who are they?" The princess asked quietly. They were coming far too close for her liking and the closer they came, the more apparent it became that they were unsavory folk. They appeared dirty and were dressed in weatherworn dark clothes. Some were bald or had hair that was entirely too long to be fashionable. Many were scarred or had skin decorated with intimidating designs. Each one of them had multiple menacing looking weapons on their person.

"Bandits." Just as the captain replied, the man at the front of the group pulled down the hood of his cloak to reveal his face. He stood erect in his stirrups.

"Why did he just do that?" The princess asked and Sern did not answer. He merely positioned his horse so it was in front of hers and repeated what the bandit had done exactly only he drew his sword and held it high, the wind sweeping his dark hair behind him. The bandit came within several feet of the warrior, revealing himself to be an average looking man with a gruesome scar across the left side of his face. Greasy yellow hair was tied behind him and hung almost to his waist. It blew over his shoulder as he nodded to Sern. Sern returned the gesture and the bandit turned around and rode away. The group vanished almost as soon as they had come.

"You are a bandit-friend?" The princess queried, her eyes wide and disbelieving.

"No. I am feared among them. They do not dare provoke me," he said quietly.

"What do you mean, Sern?" The princess asked.

"I am twenty-nine and captain of an army. I am the first in the history of any country to accomplish such a feat. You are sixteen. When I was your age, I had already been a soldier for two years. Few complete their training before eighteen. I proved I was worthy by defeating twelve of their best. After becoming known for that, I became a famous warrior for many of my feats in battle."

"I know," said the princess. "I know what has been exaggerated and what you accomplished in actuality for you told me. In the Kingdom of Nallel, they say you are unbeatable. In Phallé-Nal, they think you are immortal for despite all of their efforts they could never kill you, and in almost every other kingdom I could name they think you divine or a witch."

"Thieves are cowards. If they do not know for certain that you are too weak to fight back, they will not attack you."

"But there were at least ten of them and I am useless in battle. It is almost unheard of that one man can defend himself against ten fully armed bandits."

"Yes, but in their eyes I am more than a man. If there were thirty of them together, they would not provoke me. I know that I am merely mortal. However, at some point in time, someone decided that I was something greater and told anyone within earshot and, as I have already stated, people will believe whatever they might be told," Sern finished and they did not speak for the rest of the journey.

Less than an hour later, they came to the large house of Mistress Maveree Eldestchild. She sat on the porch smoking a pipe with a silver flask resting in her lap. She wore a red dress and her feet were bare. Her hair was windblown and unkempt and so long that she sat on the ends. She appeared to be in a state of bliss as she blew a smoke ring and leaned back, taking a drink from the flask.

"Can you believe that after all of these years Eriver still will not allow pipes, pipe weed, or ale in his house?" Maveree said aloud as she took another long smoke.

"Why is that child holding a pipe and drinking ale?" The princess whispered to Sern in the dark.

"That is Mistress Maveree Eldestchild."

"In earnest, you cannot be serious!"

"Your Highness—"

"That is the powerful seeress everyone is so fixated upon! She is nothing but a little girl!"

"Appearances can be deciev—"

"And from the looks of it an intoxicated one!"

"If you insult her, you will pay dearly."

"Hark! Do not be ridiculous. I am princess of the most

powerful scepter in the land. I will say what I like to whomever I like."

"Yes, you are associated with the monarchy. In fact, you are now the ruler of this country! She openly detests the monarchy—"

"Then why is she not locked away in a cell somewhere where she can be kept quiet and be humbled?"

"Maveree is governed by no one and despises all authority. She is the Mistress of Vision and Fate. She goes and does as she pleases. The last thing in the world you want to do is get in her way. Her powers are not of this world."

"I will not fear a child."

"She is not a child!"

"Then what is she?"

"Something beyond our understanding."

"In other words, evil."

"No. Just because you cannot comprehend her does not make her a demon."

"Nonsense. This is ludicrous. She is but a child."

With that, they both turned their heads to see a composed Maveree sitting with a pipe pressed in between her pursed lips and her eyes closed. She sat stiffly, as a corpse would have sat if it had died while in prayer. The princess opened her mouth as if to speak when she was suddenly thrown from atop her horse by some invisible force. She landed in the mud left by the earlier rain and her horse leapt over her as it frantically galloped away.

"Maveree!" Sern exclaimed as he jumped off of his horse and went to help up the princess, who had remained in the mud, struck dumb. The mistress' eyes opened and life returned to her. There was a smirk in her eyes. She watched as Sern coaxed the princess to rise and then angrily stalked toward her.

"Mistress, you cannot just randomly attack the innocent!"

"She is not innocent. She insulted me and is it not my prerogative to defend my honor when I am insulted?"

"But I am the princess—" The princess began and stopped when Maveree closed her eyes and began to assume the same countenance she had before throwing the princess from her horse.

"Who your father is does not matter to me. I judge people based on their character and yours is abominable—"

"Maveree!" Both Sern and the princess exclaimed at once.

"You are insolent and shall be punished! I will be queen. I will be all powerful. You have no authority over me and need to be taught your place! As of this minute I decree—"

"I do not really have the authority to be able to waste my time with decrees but I can promise you that the next time you anger me I will raise you twenty fathoms in the air and drop you to your death."

"You cannot do that!" The princess exclaimed.

"I managed to knock you from your horse. Do you think that my power is only limited to such meager displays?" Maveree replied nonchalantly and the princess glared at her and made as if she were about to speak. "Ponder your situation," she added with a smirk and the princess fell silent. Sern sighed.

"We have come—" Sern began and Maveree interrupted him.

"I know why you have come. You can see him, but first I have a proposition for Aralé," Maveree said with a mischievous grin. The princess clung to Sern. She looked positively terrified.

"Do not worry, child. You will love me after hearing what it is I offer. Come," Maveree said and made a sign with one of her tiny hands. Aralé began to walk forward slowly, still clinging to the captain. "No, I must speak with you alone," she said and adamantly waved the man away. Sern acquiesced immediately and the princess blanched noticeably. "However, you cannot enter my house covered in mud. Wait here briefly." And with that Maveree disappeared into the night.

"Sern!" The princess cried.

"I tried to tell you not to insult her."

"What did I say?"

"In earnest, Your Highness?"

"Yes! I want to know what I said to justify her knocking me to the ground!"

"She is simply very vindictive. What you said did not merit a physical attack."

"Indeed. If she tries anything of the like again I swear I—" The princess was interrupted as she was doused with a bucket of frigid water and screamed. After the initial shock wore off, the princess looked to see a smug Maveree leaning against the railing of the porch with an empty bucket at her feet.

"I am sorry, but I could not have you tracking mud all over my floor. Follow me please," Maveree said and then opened the door to her home. A wet and freezing princess grudgingly followed her inside and Sern settled himself on one of the chairs on the porch as the door was shut.

"Sit," Maveree said as she stretched herself out on one of the divans in her living room. The princess stood staring at the ceiling, which was covered with paintings, and looked at it as she made her way to the divan, almost tripping over a small table with a necklace made of fangs and a skull of what appeared to be a human who had three eyes. She watched as Maveree took a swig from her flask. "Tell me why you really came to my abode this night. I know all, but I must hear it from you," the seeress said.

"I need to leave Laaven," the princess replied. "My life depends upon it."

"Care to elaborate, princess?" Maveree replied, sounding quite bored.

"It is a fact that Phallé-Nal intends to conquer every kingdom in this land. They have already done so in the north. It is only a matter of time before they set their eyes on a southern kingdom. Being that Laaven is the largest and most powerful, not to mention they do not like us for harboring so many of their former slaves, it would be only logical for it to be their next target. They have already destroyed kingdoms that are far superior to Laaven in the north, being that my father is an idiot and managed to bring it almost to ruin. Our military is a farce and we are crumbling from within. When they come, there will be a massacre unlike anything the world has ever known.

"Being of royal blood, I realized long ago that I would suffer a horrible and humiliating death were I to stay for it is their custom to torture the royal family of whomever they conquer to death before a crowd. I wish to be taken to the far north where only you have been. I know that you have friends everywhere and grant wishes for a price. I come to tell you that no price is too high."

"But why travel here with Sern under the pretense of worrying for Nerin? You must know how much he has risked for you."

"No one can know of my flight. If anyone were to learn of this, they would only see me as a weak woman in love, not a traitor deserting her country. Also, I want *no one* searching for me."

"So, you mean to tell me that you care nothing for either of these men who would both die for you?"

"A beautiful woman is allowed such liberties."

"You are wretched."

"I know this, but will you aid me? You will find yourself in possession of a diamond the size of a human heart if you agree."

"I am rather fond of diamonds. However, I have not made my proposition yet."

"I am listening."

"I have seen the future and I can honestly tell you that your body, being unaccustomed to the severe cold, would fail you within three years of escaping to the northern isles. Your death would be a slow and painful one by infection of the throat. You would suffer coughing and choking episodes that will grow worse and worse and more frequent until one day one is so strong that it does you in. You can run away to the northern isles and enjoy your final years or you can accept my offer."

"Which is?"

"You can join me on a long and perilous quest to The Empyrean Stairway."

"Pardon?"

"Far in the frigid lands of eternal night in the north, atop the tallest mountain there sits a shrine of ice. Within this shrine there is a fountain that runs ceaselessly with the blood of a fallen race. One draught of this fount and you are granted your deepest desire. It is ancient, unforeseeable magic and there is a grave history behind it. However, I doubt such mere details matter to you. Just know that once you serve my purpose you will forever be under my protection and the true rulers of the very kingdom you fear will answer only to me."

"Why would you need me to accompany you? I cannot protect you and would only prove a burden."

"Do you know who the first king of Laaven was?" Maveree asked and the princess shook her head. Maveree sighed. "His name was Amíen I and he was a descendant of the Ziríva, or elemental witches. It is his ancestors' blood that flows from the fount atop The Empyrean Stairway and therefore distantly yours. Spirits guard the fount that can only be disarmed by one of their blood."

"But I do not know any magic."

"It matters not."

"And I know that name. It is not associated with your foul brand of witchery."

"Of course not, his ancestors had denounced their powers millennia before he was born. The Ziríva have passed out of all knowledge and were I not a seeress of past, present, and future, I would not know of them or of your blood. The fount atop The Empyrean Stairway as well is only known to few. However, I am the only one among these few who has the means by which to enter it."

"You speak of me? I cannot be the only descendant of Amíen I. There must be others."

"There are exactly one hundred seventeen descendents of Amíen I living as we speak. Throughout all of the kingdoms, there are in this land of ours nine hundred sixty-three of this ancient bloodline. Another was just born last week in the northernmost part of the Oran."

"Then why choose me over a thousand others?"

"Convenience. I have spent millennia searching. When one such as I need comes willingly to me why waste my time in pursuit of another?"

"So, if I had not come here tonight you would have sought another?"

"Most definitely," Maveree replied nonchalantly and the princess parted her lips as if to speak when the seeress stopped her. "I grow weary of being questioned. In actuality, only these questions linger between us. Do you want to aid me in my quest and live or do you want to die young, housebound, and alone as you freeze and drown in your own fluids?" The seeress finished.

"I-I want to live!" Aralé stammered. The seeress's words rang in her ears and played like a horrid dream before her eyes.

"Then do we find ourselves in accordance?"

"Yes."

"So that none will know of our arrangement, you will tell Nerin and Sern that we are journeying for the purpose of returning your brother to our plane. You will unyieldingly swear that I told you that with a true king on the throne, Laaven would be saved."

"Everyone knows that he was a useless drunkard and an idiot who spent more on powders and in brothels than on his ridiculous outfits and feminine jewelry. They will never believe that."

"People will believe whatever they might be told, especially when told by a clairvoyant and the woman they love," Maveree finished and took a long drink from her flask. Aralé opened her mouth as if to speak and Maveree interrupted her. "Now go and see Nerin. He is on the third door on the left. I will inform the good captain of our plans and send him away. You will stay here until we leave."

Aralé rose and prepared to leave when the seeress stopped her. "By the way, this human heart-sized diamond you spoke of earlier. Do you have it with you?"

"No," Aralé replied and Maveree sighed. Suddenly, a large diamond flew from one of Aralé's pockets and landed in the seeress's grasp.

"Lying has become a habit for you. Know that there is no deception that I cannot penetrate. You would only be wasting your time," Maveree then made a sign with her hand for Aralé to exit.

She did as the seeress told her. She quit the room immediately and walked through the parlor to a hallway and directly to the door the seeress had indicated. It was a large wooden door with a large green gem encrusted with gold for a doorknob. She turned it and found herself in a large room. One candle stood on the far side of the room atop a wooden chest. It provided little light, but enough that she could make out the bed where Nerin slept and a daybed under a window near it. Soon after laying in the daybed, she realized how exhausted she was and only minutes after that she fell asleep. Her golden hair escaped its confines and poured over her shoulders as she shifted slightly in sleep.

After guiding Sern into the parlor, Maveree had invited him to sit. After she had offered him a drink from her flask and he accepted, she proceeded to tell him a fabricated story of visions, miracles, and the return of the prince from the lands beyond death. She spoke of the princess being the lone descendant of a sorceress whom her mother, the belated queen Aralevena, descended from and that made her the only one able to use certain ancient relics (which Maveree had invented on the spot) that could bring about the return of a true king. She told him that when Amíen returned from the lands beyond death he would be changed and become the savior of the south instead of its laughingstock. After she finished her monologue, Sern sat silently for a long while.

"I think that you speak falsely," he said after a while. Maveree began to defend herself but Sern stopped her. "Is whatever you truly intend to do for the best?" He asked solemnly.

"Yes," the seeress replied and Sern nodded.

"Then that is all I ask to know. You are the mistress of fate and you move in mysterious ways as it is the Great Spirit that moves you. I understand this."

Maveree gasped and fear and sadness were apparent in her countenance for only a second before she regained her composure.

The Persian Rug

"You are a true king amongst men," she finished and took a drink.

"Maveree, I am no such—"

"Part with Aralé and return to Laaven," she said quickly and quit the room. Sern followed her and, after showing the captain to Nerin's room, she entered her own chambers. She emptied her pockets of pipes, flasks, knives, several little phials, and several stones before throwing herself onto her bed.

Sern entered the room to find one flickering half-melted candle that barely pierced the darkness. He looked to see Nerin sleeping in a bed and the princess asleep in a daybed beneath one of the room's windows. He quietly walked over to her. He stood, watching her bosom swell and deflate as she breathed deeply in her sleep and the scowl on her statuesque countenance. He gently pushed a thick lock of her hair away from her forehead and bent down to gingerly press his lips against it.

"Fair well, my princess," he said and took one of her slender white hands in his calloused and weatherworn one. Even in sleep, she pushed him away. She withdrew her hand from his and turned on her side so she faced the window. Sern gazed at the girl sadly for a long while, watching the moonlight reflecting in her hair and on whatever pallid skin was exposed. She had taken off her boots and dainty bloodless feet stuck out of the dirty raiment. He attempted to wake her again by touching her shoulder, but again she pushed him away and continued sleeping.

At three in the morning, Captain Sern left the abode of Mistress Maveree for the Laaven castle. From the daybed she had feigned sleep upon as Sern attempted to say what he thought might be his final farewell to one of the only women he had ever loved, Aralé watched the captain ride into the distance. When she had lost sight of him, she rolled over and fell back into an untroubled sleep.

Chapter VII
Father and Daughter

Aralé had slept soundly on the daybed until a voice interrupted her sleep. "Awaken," it murmured and she felt consciousness returning. She opened her eyes to see the seeress standing by her daybed. Maveree was dressed richly in a tiny outfit of black embroidered with silver.

"I have people whose futures I must see to today. They come from far and wide to see what I can tell them. For the rest of this day, you must remain in this room. You will find food, fresh clothes, a washbasin, buckets of water, perfumes, and soaps about the room. Tonight we will depart."

"For The Empyrean Stairway? So soon?" Aralé asked as she sat up and looked to see a washbasin against the opposite wall with an array of soaps, oils, shampoos, and perfumes beside it.

"No, tonight we will set out for Iarnel Eremnad."

"I have never heard of such a place. It must be quite a distance away."

"It is nearer than you could imagine. It is simply *well-concealed*."

"Is it now?" Aralé said as she walked toward the basin and ran her hand along the edge. It felt cold against her skin. "How many servants will be attending me as I bathe?"

"How many would you require?" Maveree replied acerbically. The young woman either did not hear or pretended not to hear the seeress' tone.

"Well, one to dress me, one to undress me, one to wash my

body, another for my face, it should take no more than three to take care of my hair unless they are lacking in skill—"

"This is not your palace," Maveree replied. "Here I have no servants. There is but a man who looks after my horses, a cook, and several pretty young girls who I pay to clean. None are treated special here. Guests, be they royal or weary outcasts merely passing through, all wash themselves in my house." She finished and quickly departed before she could perceive the pronounced pout that had followed her final statement.

This pout quickly became a scowl as Aralé laboriously began struggling with the heavy water-filled buckets. By the time she managed to get a sufficient amount of water into the tub, the floor was slippery with it and the water that had actually gotten into the tub was frigid. Then Aralé clumsily divested herself of her dirty clothes, for she had never had to dress or undress herself unassisted before. Eventually, she sunk into the benumbing water inside the basin, hissing.

Her first instinct was to strike out at one of the castle servants for causing her such displeasure, but after looking up to see a plain white ceiling and feeling a small, hard, wooded basin beneath her she realized that the only person she had to blame was Maveree, for the seeress obviously did not know how to treat a princess.

"Wretched child," she muttered as she reached for a bar of soap and found that it had no scent, which made it common and unworthy of her. Nevertheless, she scrubbed her body with it until the unblemished exposed skin was once again clean. She then took a bottle that looked exactly like the shampoo she used at the palace. She poured a little out into her hand to see that it was the exact same. She ran it through her hair, finding it a nuisance to have to wash so much hair and an even bigger nuisance getting the shampoo out. After she finished bathing, she massaged herself with the necessary oils, perfumes, and lotions. She found that her hands cramped and ached both during and afterward.

After over an hour of trying to work a small brush through her unruly thigh-length hair, she drenched it in water again and wound it into one long loose and messy plait. Upon reaching for the gown Maveree told her she would find, she groaned. It was far too revealing for her taste and proved difficult to put on. It was a black lace bed-frock that hung off of her shoulders and clung to her body in a most undignified way. Slits in the sleeves and in the bottom of the frock left her white arms and one of her legs exposed almost to the hip.

"What is she, trying to make a lowly tavern wench of me?" She groaned as she examined herself in the mirror. She had only worn black once before in her life, to her brother's funeral, and found that she did not like it. She then looked to see Nerin still sound asleep in his bed and wondered how on earth he could have slept through all of the noise she had made. However, all of her thoughts were abandoned as she caught sight of a plate of fruit, cheese, and bread and her stomach began to growl. After devouring all of the food there, she crawled back to the daybed and fell asleep, exhausted from the morning's exertions.

She awoke again to find an elderly man standing over her, gently stroking her shoulder. Her first instinct was to scream at him for waking her as she did to almost every servant who had the misfortune of waking her up since she was two, but the unadulterated kindness in his warm light brown eyes stopped her. The old man seemed to embody light and goodness. Yellowed teeth showed through a benevolent smile that had been withered by age. Even the vain and prosaic-minded princess found something beautiful about this withered gaffer.

"I am Eriver, Maveree's father. She requests that you sup with us," the old man said kindly. Aralé was even willing to overlook the fact that he had omitted her royal title.

"Very well," she replied through a yawn and began to stretch.

"Follow me, please," he said and watched as the young girl slowly rose. He knew that Maveree had myriad friends and acquaintances from every corner and class of the world. Most of these he had never met. Quite a few of them he had never met for his own protection. Eriver knew that his adopted daughter had nothing but his best interests and safety at heart so he did not question her when she refused to tell him the girl's name or history. He knew that Maveree often dealt with criminals and the most elaborate of schemes. When he was a young man, he often assisted her, but as a man who had lived over a century he was weary and longed for an end to the excitement and only for well-deserved respite. So many years had taught him that while such knowledge could often seem enticing, it was nothing compared to happiness and peace.

All this he contemplated as he led the young woman to the dining room. Aralé only thought of what she could eat for she was ravenous. Upon entering, the thoughts of both Eriver and Aralé were interrupted.

"We leave at midnight," Maveree said unceremoniously as she poured herself tea, not even giving them time to sit.

"Tonight?" The old man and the young girl asked in chorus.

"Of course tonight," the seeress replied and Eriver unobtrusively quit the room.

"But midnight is not a good time to be about! No one dares to be out at such a time!"

"Exactly, no one will bother us," Maveree rolled her eyes at the princess' incredulity. "That is an old superstition invented… well I am sure that you do not care for the history. Regardless of the history behind it, it remains untrue. Now sit. Eat. Drink. I suggest you enjoy it now for the fare will be quite substandard on our little sojourn to Iarnel Eremnad." And with that, the seeress gestured to the many plates of food on the table.

Aralé seated herself at the table and began to gluttonously pile food on her plate. When she was halfway through her third plate she realized that Eriver had not seated himself. She looked to see Maveree idly pushing peas about on her plate. Her head rested in her hand and her wide eyes stared sadly at the tablecloth.

"Maveree?" Aralé asked in between mouthfuls of a thick milky pudding. The seeress did not reply and the princess was certain that she saw a tear trickle down one of her tiny cheeks. "Maveree," she tried again and this time the seeress looked up.

The Persian Rug

Her vulnerable and forlorn gaze quickly hardened and her lips returned to their normal almost nonchalant smirk.

"If you ever dine here in the future, I shall have to bring out the painters' tarps," she muttered as she looked at Aralé, noticing for the first time the food in her hair, on her dress, and on the tablecloth and floor around her. "What do you want? I hope not more food," she added, this time so the princess could hear her.

"Hardly," the princess said as she rolled her eyes. "I was simply wondering why Eriver does not sup with us."

"Old bones. My poor father is probably exhausted."

"Pity. He seemed to be a pleasant fellow."

"He is a gem, my old father."

"How old is he?"

"Over a century."

"Truly?"

"Indeed."

"Then how does he have a child who is as young as you?"

"For one thing he is not my birth father. My true parents passed from this world ages hence. For another, I may look a child but in fact I am even older than Eriver."

"Truly?"

"Indeed."

"Exactly how old are you?"

"Almost two centuries."

The princess looked awestruck and soon after fearful. "What in the name of all that had ever lived and died are you?"

"That is no business of yours."

"You expect me to spend months traveling by your side and will not even let me know what exactly it is I am traveling with? How can you even begin to think that I can trust you?"

"I think that the more relevant question would be how can you expect to endure in a harsh and wicked world with no talents or knowledge of how to live without a myriad of servants and guards at your beck and call? You can either trust me or live a life of misery and poverty. Ponder your options."

Aralé did not reply to this. She only carved another leg of pheasant and began to gnaw at it like a starving animal.

"Now, I am going to prepare some things for our journey. When you are finished, return to your room. You will find clothes there. I will come for you when it is time." With that, Maveree left Aralé to rapaciously gorge herself and walked to the room where she knew she would find her elderly father. She waited outside the room for several seconds, letting tears fall. After wiping them away, she knocked.

"Enter," she heard Eriver's sad voice call from within. She gently opened the door and closed it behind her to find him sitting on his bed, dressed in a sleeping gown and rich robe.

"Can you help me with my shoes and tie my robe for me? My bones are stiff from the night chill," he said quietly.

"Of course father," Maveree replied and nimbly removed his boots and tied the strings that kept his robe about him.

"Tonight we shall make our final farewells," he said after a long silence.

"Father—"

"No, I am old Maveree. I am one hundred thirteen years old. Most men are grey and sore by fifty. My bones have been failing me of late and my strength is waning. Your journey will be a long one, and I doubt I will live to see you return. You know that I will not live to see your return."

"I do not know—" Maveree said, fresh tears arising from her eyes.

"Your herbs and your magic have availed me this long. You should be thankful for all of the years we have had together. However, it seems it takes powers beyond yours to forestall nature any longer."

"You do not know how grateful I am," Maveree said as she crawled into his lap. "In all my years I have loved only twice. The first man I would have taken as a lover were I not cursed to remain a child until the end of the world. You, my father, are the second. I only...I...need to believe that this is not our farewell here."

"Even if you know that it is not true?"

The Persian Rug

"Father—"

"Maveree," Eriver interrupted. "You would scorn another for trying to harbor such delusions."

"I am not delusional. I am...hopeful."

"Your hopes are in vain. The next time we embrace, it will be beyond this world. That is my hope. I hope as well that this is not our farewell."

"So, you do not ask for love to see you through in life for you have forsaken it, but you believe that it will see you through in death?"

"I only hope, just as you do. For all of your understanding, you do not know death. I am old. I feel it in my bones and in my sleep and in the tips of my slowly weakening limbs. I have accepted my fate. You who, as you say, are destined to live on as a child until the end of the world could not comprehend me."

At this, Maveree said nothing and only hid in her father's arms as the pair wept. It was a while before either spoke again.

"Midnight approaches, you must prepare," Eriver said as he tried to remove Maveree from his lap.

"I know, but I cannot bring myself to go."

"You must."

"I know this," Maveree said quietly and, after several minutes, she rose from her father's lap and fixed her skirts and hair. "Will you see me off father?"

"If my body does not betray me," he replied darkly. With this, Maveree strode toward the door. Just as she was about to quit the room, she turned to face her father.

"Farewell daughter," Eriver said as tears streamed in rivulets down his withered cheeks.

"Farewell for now," she said and strode from the room, leaving Eriver to collapse with grief and exhaustion on his bed. She then made her way to the cook's room.

"Mélum," she called as she flung the door open. A portly middle-aged man with greying red hair tumbled from his bed, startled by Maveree's sudden intrusion. He looked up at her with frightened eyes. "Take care of Master Eriver in my absence. He will only require much…near the end," she finished quietly, her eyes glistening with unshed tears while her child's face remained stoic and cold.

"You mean…" Mélum replied sadly. He had always been fond of Master Eriver. Maveree only looked at him as if to confirm the man's beliefs.

"Of course mistress. Anything for you and dear old Master Eriver, mistress," he finished awkwardly. He had always found something about Maveree unnerving, as if she were merely waiting for him to make a mistake so she could pounce on him and make him suffer for it. While she gave him better living conditions and a better salary than almost anyone else he could name, only ever complimented him, gave him leave almost whenever he wished, almost always would tell him his future free of charge, and let his family, which consisted of a son who had just left for the Oran and a fat old orange cat, live with him, she had always seemed so cold and knowing and her eyes so penetrating.

"Good. Sleep well, Mélum. I should return in a year. Keep the house in running order. You will be master here after Eriver has passed and ere I return," she said and then quit the room swiftly, unceremoniously slamming the door behind her. Her next stop was in the room Nerin and Aralé occupied. There she found both aforementioned youths fast asleep. Nerin lay unconscious, due to a mixture of potent herbs Maveree administered to him nightly, in his bed and the latter atop the daybed beneath the window in the attire of a young man. Maveree savagely shook her awake and dragged her from the house to the porch. In the road before the house, there was a carriage.

Aralé sat groggily on the porch and watched as Maveree disappeared into the house only to return minutes later with two men carrying an unconscious Nerin. She watched as Maveree opened the carriage door and the two men placed Nerin inside. Maveree thanked them and sent them back inside.

"Who were those men?" She asked through a yawn.

"The man who takes care of my horses and his assistant."

It was then that the princess realized that she and Maveree

were the only two people remaining outside. "Who is driving the carriage?"

"I am. Get in," Maveree commanded and Aralé only sighed and got in beside the unconscious Nerin. She pushed him away from her immediately. The carriage door was slammed shut and, within seconds, Aralé felt the carriage moving beneath her. Beside her, there was a crate full of food and drink. Within seconds, she fell asleep against it.

As Maveree sat so she could control the four horses that pulled the carriage, she pulled a flask of mead out of her cloak and took a deep drink from it. Tears poured down her cheeks as she looked behind her to see Eriver sitting by his bedroom window, arthritic hands pressed against the glass. "Safe journey," he whispered through the glass, knowing that while his daughter could not hear him or properly see him in the dark, she would feel the meaning of his words.

"I'll join you soon," she replied before speeding down the road. After only a quarter of an hour, she came to the eaves of the Ariyekk forest and plunged into them. Soon she could only rely on the vision granted by her powers and the horses to guide her through the dark of the Ariyekk forest.

Aralé opened her eyes to see trees becoming one blurred scene through the carriage windows. Despite even this, her first instinct was to call for a servant to bring her breakfast. It was when the movement of the carriage and the stiffness of her body, for she was accustomed to sleeping in a soft, warm feather bed and not in a cramped speeding carriage against a wooden crate, registered that her recollection of the preceeding days returned to her. She groaned as she remembered the tiny seeress's words regarding the food for the trip. ...*the fare will be quite substandard on our little sojourn to Iarnel Eremnad...*

"Maveree!!!" She cried from inside the carriage.

"You will find some leraj n ósvera and ale in the crate. Leraj n ósvera is basically bread, only it can last for years and sustain you for just as long," Maveree yelled back. Aralé then pried open the crate and looked inside to find pouches made of rough material and water skins. She did not even think that it would matter to Maveree that she could not stomach ale and that the leraj n ósvera was so hard that you could kill someone with it if you threw it. Aralé took one of the bits of leraj n ósvera from the bag and found that it looked like a little light colored rock with blue and red pebbles sticking out of it. She hurt her teeth trying to bite into it and pulled it out of her mouth before she could realize that it tasted like chalk, parchment, and rotten berries. She then attempted to drink the ale and spit it all over the inside of the carriage.

"How could anyone be expected to eat and drink this?" She gasped angrily before shoving both the water skin and the pouch of leraj n ósvera back into the crate.

"When you are not a spoiled palace brat used to stuffing your face with sweet meats, candy, and rare delicacies, leraj n ósvera is quite good. When you are starving, it can be the most delicious of delicacies," Maveree yelled back and the princess crossed her arms and leaned back, huffing.

At around noon they came to a clearing and Maveree stopped the carriage. She dropped to the forest floor and opened the carriage door to find Aralé hungrily gnawing at a large piece of leraj n ósvera and gulping down ale as if she were dying of thirst.

"You were right. It's truly not that bad."

"Less than half a day and you are already starving. How many of those have you eaten?"

"About three pouches."

"Three!" Maveree exclaimed angrily. "There are four pieces a pouch! You gluttonous wretch! Usually one piece can last a man four times your size half a week. These are about all of the provisions we will have for a year! Give me the piece and the water skin in your hand!" The seeress commanded and Aralé handed her the half-eaten piece in her hand after taking a bite, which Maveree made her spit into her hand, and the water skin. Maveree then tossed them into the crate. Once it was closed, she placed her tiny hands on it and muttered something under her breath. She held the concentrated look she had as she knocked the princess from her horse.

"What did you just do?" Aralé asked.

"Try to open the crate," Maveree said and she slowly inched toward it. The second the tips of her fingers came in contact with the lid of the wooden crate, she jumped back, screaming in agony. She had felt as if her flesh was being burnt.

"What in the name of all that has ever lived and died was that!?" Aralé howled.

"I placed some protection around it since I obviously cannot trust you to be in the proximity of food and not gorge yourself." With that, Maveree took out a piece of leraj n ósvera from the crate and slammed the carriage door behind her. Within minutes, they were off again.

Chelsea Isadora Teich

Chapter VIII
Lord, the Steward

Captain Sern was nowhere to be found. For four hours, the staff of the Laaven castle, which had been put under the command of the steward since the princess' disappearance, had searched in vain for the man. Eventually, after nearly an entire morning of searching, they became so desperate that they turned to his closest friends, Danen and Master Healer Dorin. Danen, who had taken the advice of his mentors and became a huntsman instead of a warrior, was found playing cards with the castle guards and Dorin had been found in the only place he ever seemed to be: the healing wing. Since the steward had offered Sern his position, no one had seen him.

It was by chance that Danen came across him at all. He was walking down a deserted corridor, opening every last door. One of the last doors opened to an old library that looked as if it had not been frequented or even cleaned in years. The young man almost shut the door again without a second thought when he saw the outline of a man sitting on the window ledge through one of the pallid moth-eaten curtains. As he quietly stepped forward, a light breeze lifted and billowed to reveal a contemplative Sern sitting on the window ledge. The midmorning sunlight lent his haggard form an earthy glow.

"I cannot do this," he heard the man mutter.

"Sern," Danen said quietly as he walked to stand beside him. He watched as the older man turned to look at him and then quickly turned back to the open window. Danen placed a hand gently on his shoulder. "The steward needs your answer, Sern," he said softly.

"And I shall give him it," Sern replied darkly. He looked as if he had not slept in days.

"Sern..."Danen said softly. "If my opinion matters to you at all—"

"It does."

"Very well, then I think that there is none better than you to rule. What Laaven needs if we want to stand any chance at all against Phallé-Nal, or if nothing else die honorably, is change. I know you and your fondness for wallowing in self-doubt. You will never admit to yourself that you are the first person to give our southern countrymen hope in near a century! Stand and lift us. The steward was appointed by Risúrat because he is a tool for other men to manipulate. Beneath him, failure is certain. Beneath you there would be...hope."

"Truly?"

"Yes. And sometimes that is enough."

With that, Sern rose from the windowsill. His countenance was undecipherable. "Thank you," he said.

"I hope I can give you my thanks as well one day," Danen replied and watched Sern stride out of the room. When the man's footsteps were no longer audible, Danen sat on the windowsill where Sern had and rested his head. He let his legs dangle out of the open window and sighed, looking to the blue sky. He sat for several minutes before rising. He shut the window and then walked out of the library. He gently closed the door behind him and then made his way toward the throne room.

As Sern walked down the corridors toward the throne room, time seemed to stop.

A chorus of "Where have you been?" "We have been searching for hours!" "Are you going to take the position?" and "Please say that you are!" followed him as he made his way. However, he answered none of them. He walked steadily, his head held high, and did not hesitate upon coming to the double doors that led to

The Persian Rug

the throne room. Doors that usually took two men each to open he pulled open and shut behind him, leaving the mob that had formed behind him in the corridor.

The throne room was a magnificent and immense place of white stone. The walls and floor were inlaid with glittering gold and beautiful gems. The ceiling was of colored glass and cast slight shades of fuchsia, emerald, crimson, amber, and sapphire all about the room. The ceremonial, although occasionally battle-tried and stained with blood, suits of armor and swords of every king there had ever been since the very first king of Laaven lined the walls. In the back against the farthest wall stood the conjoined golden thrones of the king and queen high above the ground on golden platforms. Before it sat the steward in a far less impressive wooden chair inlaid with gold. Guards were strewn about the room. They idly chatted, drank, or consorted with pretty young maids.

The steward, Danút, was a balding rotund man who sat in the steward's chair dressed in simple brown robes. He looked at Sern coldly as he walked toward. "It is about time. We have been searching for you all morning."

"I apologize milord. I know that after begging for three days to make up my mind and you granting me them, the least I could have done was give you my answer at the appointed time." Sern bowed to the man.

"That is all well and good, but will you become steward in my stead? I certainly am not going to wait around for Phallé-Nal to conquer us and roast our heads over a spit. I do not see why you would want to be, but it matters not. With all the chaos of late none of the usual choices to become the ruler would even consider it. They laughed at me when I asked them. I am leaving tonight for The Isles of the Sun whether your sorry carcass is sitting on this little chair here or not."

"And what about when they come for The Isles of the Sun?"

"Then I will go to the Northern Isles."

"And when Phallé-Nal sets it sights on the Northern Isles?"

"That will, in all likelihood, not come to pass during my

lifetime. And even if it does, there are lands far beyond the Northern Isles."

"Coward! You intend to spend your life running then!"

"If it keeps me alive."

"And even if I did not take your place, you would leave all of the people here to ruin?"

"Absolutely, 'tis not my fault if they cannot afford to travel."

"Yes it is! You and your other nobles and royalty and wealthy men steal almost all that they have! They can barely afford to feed their children let alone travel!"

"Then perhaps those peasants should stop having so many of them. Last week I saw some lowly peasant woman cross the street with nine unruly little jackanapes! Just yesterday I saw another trollop dragging seven little whelps down the road behind her! I would call it almost unfashionable," Danút said laughingly. "Ah, but that is not what we have come to discuss. So, will you accept your doom or no? Although, it would be a shame to lose you to Phallé-Nal, such a strapping young man of obvious loyalty and virility and succinctly and…philosophy!" Danút added emphatically. It became increasingly obvious as he spoke that he was slightly intoxicated and had almost no idea what half of the words he said meant. "How would you like to make a heavy wage by protecting me on my travels? Are you in agreeable…?"

"Never!" Sern spat. "From this day forward I shall be Lord, The Steward Sern, son of Stavir!"

Cheers were heard from behind the doors across the room.

"Suit yourself. You must be either an idiot or completely insane. You do know that you have just accepted your death sentence? If I were you I would have accepted my offer. I have heard that The Isles of the Sun are lovely. Beautiful dark women who slink about half naked and delicious fruit! Oh! So much fruit!" Danút continued to talk idly until Sern finally took it upon himself to stop him.

"You are a despicable creature. Leave this instant," Sern said in his soft-spoken way. Danút laughed at him.

"Some steward you will make. I do not think I have ever heard you speak above a whisper."

"Guards!" Sern called and only eleven out of the thirty guards in the throne room responded to him. One fell over unconscious in a puddle of mead.

"Yes, milord?" The eleven replied.

"How many of you just heard Danút say that he would willingly desert his country?" Sern called and only eleven of the thirty said that they had.

"Now I know whose fathers have bought them their place here and those who have earned it. The eleven of you who are loyal to me, go fetch every other healer, border guard, body guard, cook, warrior, soldier, and servant in the palace and bring them to the throne room. Those who are not stay here," Sern said and the group of eleven bowed and departed. The rest stayed. Some looked at him indignantly while others looked afraid.

"As for you all," Sern said, clearing his throat. He perceived Danút slipping out of the room through a side door and sighed unhappily. "Tell your friend he has until sunset to get out of the palace," he gestured toward the intoxicated man lying prone on the floor.

The guards gasped. "But, that is Fénrin, son of Lord Fén. Lord Fén will have you punished for impugning the honor of his family," one said and the others agreed.

"I am the Steward and he is a Lord. According to cannon, he can do no such thing. Not to mention, young Fénrin impugned his own honor and that of his family by being a drunken buffoon whilst he should have been doing his duty. I will not tolerate such antics," Sern said and ordered that Fénrin be put beside his chair and the other guards stand before him. Within the hour, every last castle worker was standing before the new steward in the overcrowded throne room. Some looked happy for they knew that he would bring about change. Others looked discontented or even livid for the same exact reason.

"Hello," Sern said quietly from his steward's chair and silence spread throughout the room. "Now, I know that this entire situation is wholly unorthodox and by rights I should not be before you today—"

Several acerbic murmurs to the gist of *No, really?* rang throughout the room. *My father will have something to say about this* and *Soon anyone will be allowed to be steward. When Sern gets assassinated for angering the men who truly own this pathetic little spit of a country I should sign up* could also be heard.

Sern did not seem intimidated in the least. "As a slightly enlightened man, I believe that a man has every right to his own opinions and beliefs. You may think whatever you like of me. However, I demand that you show me respect. I wish that I could be your friend through these difficult times. However, what is needed now is the restoration of order, unity, peace, and strength. This castle is a disgrace and our poor fellow countrymen are succumbing to poverty, disease, and decay. We are a pathetic, rat infested mess of a castle in a sea of dilapidated shacks and starving men, women, and children. It will take a stalwart ruler to return to us the glory of ancient days," he said and rose from his chair. "Many of you want me to bring about change. Transition is never easy. You all know this. I will not lie to you and tell you that this will not entail a lot of self sacrifice and that it will not be a struggle. However, it will be worth it." He finished and the majority of the room clapped. They were interrupted by the waking of Fénrin. He sat up and retched all over the floor.

"How my head aches!" The young man exclaimed before looking to see Sern seating himself in the steward's chair beside the conjoined empty thrones of the king and queen.

"The castle is the heart of a kingdom and when it does not run smoothly, neither will its dominion. We must start here if we are ever to affect change. Those of you, who have integrity and have always worked hard regardless of your lineage, will only ever be rewarded by me. It is those of you who do nothing because your father had secured your place with friendships or bribes that will find yourselves under my scrutiny today. With both Amíen and Risúrat gone, those things hold no sway over me, nor will any bribery in the future. If you want to earn your way like everyone

The Persian Rug

else in any way, shape, or form, I will not only commend you but I will help you. If you do not wish to do so, then you may leave when I dismiss you. In order for things to run smoothly, everyone involved must pull their own weight. If you do not wish to have integrity and do as I have said, then those of us who do actually perform our duties, whether these duties include caring for the lawns or teaching young apprentices or cooking, do not need you here."

With that, the majority of the room began to cheer wildly.

"There are only six of you here who have no say in whether you stay or go. You are despicable creatures and I despise you for your criminal or simply loathsome acts. I also despise the fact that you have never known consequences due to the guile and riches of your fathers or by some design of Risúrat's. Today you will get what you deserve." Sern then looked down to the young man lying by his feet. "Fénrin!" he called loudly.

The people crowded in the room gasped. It was well known that Fénrin's family was the richest in Laaven.

"Not so loud!" Fénrin whined. "Whoreson dolt bastard," he added and the room gasped again.

"Fénrin, get out," Sern said calmly and the young man looked at him wide-eyed.

"Why? What?" The younger man said as he tried to stand and came crashing back to the ground.

"In the twelve years I have known you, I have only seen you sober once. As far as I know, you have fathered seventeen children by seventeen different women and have had your father bribe the women with jewels so they will deny you as the father. When you have spent all of your money on ale and mead and wine, you steal it from others in the palace and that is the hardest you have ever worked in your life. You are a disgrace to this country and yourself. Leave now," Sern said and watched as Fénrin dragged himself away and out of the double doors at the end of the hall. The crowd parted around him. After Fénrin had exited, Sern began again.

"Íerles, Ccéal, Neret, and Cíetien come forth," Sern called

and the crowd parted as the four men who had been sent to see if the assassin was still on the roof or had left any clues behind, but decided to stare down women's dresses instead sluggishly came forward. "Over the years you have been assigned various important tasks and during all of them you have caused problems or completely failed to do your duty. Neret and Cíetien, you two were only kept because your father did some secret service for Risúrat. Ccéal, you were kept because your father is a friend of their father. You three, leave at once."

"What about Íerles?" Neret asked angrily.

"I know that he has in essence been your servant for the last several years so that you would ask your father to grant him a fixed position. I know that he endured years of ill-treatment so that his wife and two children could live a comfortable life. I taught his eldest son and am acquaintances with his wife. They told me all. "

"Thank you, my Lord Steward!" Íerles said as he bowed before Sern. The other three stalked away. As they made their way through the crowd, they pushed to the ground anyone who did not move out of their way fast enough.

Sern shook his head. He jumped upon feeling the slight pressure of lips against the back of his hand. He looked down to see Íerles pressing his lips reverently against his skin.

"What are you doing?" He demanded.

"It is custom," the man replied. "I did not mean to offend you."

"Oh!" Sern exclaimed, suddenly feeling foolish. "I am sorry. You did not offend me. It is just that I am not used to such customs."

Íerles nodded and rose, still looking quite abashed. Sern then leaned toward him. "Go and be with your wife and children," he whispered.

"Thank you so much Your Benevolence!" Íerles moved to bow again and Sern stopped him.

"Once is more than enough," Sern said and Íerles quit the room, beaming.

The Persian Rug

"Now, as for the rest of you," Sern continued. "You have heard the terms and conditions. And now you can stay or you can go of your own volition."

A quarter of the room departed.

Chelsea Isadora Teich

Chapter IX
Iarnel Eremnad

"This is it?" Aralé asked incredulously as she stood before the entrance to Iarnel Eremnad.

"Yes," Maveree replied.

"It is but a little puddle!" She exclaimed almost laughingly. She then actually started to laugh. They had traveled for six days through the heavy forest, spent another two days winding their way through the labyrinthine cave system in the Golden Mountains (during these two days Aralé had dragged Nerin along behind her on a makeshift sled Maveree had crafted from the lid of the food crate and the cloth from one of her extra cloaks), and spent two nights shivering in the dirt in order to reach Iarnel Eremnad. After over a week, they stood in a little almost antechamber-like part of a cave system in almost total dark before a water-filled aperture less than half a fathom in diameter.

"That is no puddle, imbecile. This is the entrance to Iarnel Eremnad."

"No it is not!"

"I am not surprised that you argue with me."

"Why? Is it because I am logical?"

"No, it is because only a born fool with a general understanding as weighted as that of an exceptionally thickheaded mule would be obtuse enough to question one who is nearly omniscient."

"What?" Aralé blurted out. Maveree sighed and rolled her eyes.

"Let me put it in terms you can understand: I am smart. You are a brainless dolt. Ha ha...ha," she replied flatly as she leaned against one of the walls, holding her torch aloft.

"I hate you," Aralé replied with the tone of a spoiled child who is denied extra sweets or toys by their parents.

"Hmm, it would seem that my uncanny ability to ignore the whininess of the innocuous and callow will prove useful after all."

Aralé searched her mind for the meanings of the words used so artfully by the mordant seeress. Upon finding none she folded her arms and growled, "I hate you."

"So I've been told," Maveree said with a smirk.

Just as Aralé opened her mouth to respond, a great stream of water surged from the aperture. When it ceased, a man clad in silver and white and grey stood atop the water. He was tall and dark hair fell down his broad back in rivulets. His face was severe and he bore a strange mark slightly above his eyebrows: A small full moon in between intricate waning and waxing crescent moons. Pale skin made him look ethereal and almost alarming. Water dripped from his hands but the rest of him was completely dry though he emerged from the water that swirled dark and foreboding beneath him.

Aralé screamed and attempted to flee. Maveree coolly extended her foot and sent the frantic girl sprawling to the ground. There she remained as Maveree surveyed the man before her.

"Qí ajíl vócer vos?" The seeress calmly asked the man in his own language. *What do they call you?* He only echoed her question. "Adesí Domí Valdesenlías." *I am Mistress Eldestchild.* The man smiled genuinely at this. His cold exterior melted. They had become quite fond of the seeress in Iarnel Eremnad.

"Adesí Láetúre. Adesyv valdesalve deq. Páryv dele, Domí Valdesenlías." *I am Láetúre. You are most welcome here. Follow me please, Mistress Eldestchild,* he said kindly. Maveree briefly told Láetúre of Aralé and Nerin (mostly she spoke of how ill the young healer was) and he promised that they would both be retrieved later.

Aralé screamed as Maveree climbed into Láetúre's arms, begging to know what was happening and who the frightening man was. She pulled on her hair as the water in the aperture surged about them and formed a translucent barrier as it reached toward the cave ceiling. When the water calmed, Maveree and Láetúre had disappeared. Aralé fainted.

Láetúre carried Maveree down a stairway of crystalline falling water. Individual steps formed beneath his feet as he walked. The opening to the city had closed above them. They quickly descended the liquescent stairs. An arched hall that seemed to have been carved from the falling water rose from either side of the stairway. The passageway opened to Iarnel Eremnad behind a waterfall. A small silver encrusted catamaran awaited them there. Láetúre set Maveree down before standing behind her and used a staff-like paddle to propel them through the waterfall and the mist that formed where it met the water. They silently moved forward through the water. Great monsters slithered beneath the surface like leviathan serpents. Within minutes, land came into view. People could be seen standing on the bank looking out.

"Cúryv ním óssemíyr deq." *You have many admirers here,* Láetúre said kindly as they drew closer to the shore.

"Nesqí." *I know,* she said, seeing the man she recognized as the prince she had met during her last visit now wearing the ceremonial circlet engraved with the symbols of the four clans of Iarnel Eremnad and robes of the king. She sighed unhappily for she had been fond of the old king. They had been friends ever since his youth. At that moment, she regretted not returning in so many years. "Vóa enúum adesun qedivú." *Your realm is a blessed one,* she said and the man who stood behind her smiled. Within seconds, they were ashore and surrounded by the inhabitants of Iarnel Eremnad. Láetúre left with several others to gather the princess and Nerin.

"Welcome, Mistress Maveree," King Anderíen said in an awkward and strangely accented common tongue. He, along with several of his brothers, were the only people in the city who spoke any language other than Céremín. She noticed how he stared. He could not believe that she had remained a child and it was apparent in the way he attempted to school his features. "It has been many years since we have seen you here."

Maveree bowed low to him. She had come in the hopes of spending time with the former king and for this reason already she was not fond of the new king. She wondered why she had not foreseen the death of his father.

"Too many years indeed," she replied.

"Our shamans foretold of your coming and of your long journey. A great meal has been readied in your honor. Lodgings have been prepared as well."

"I will clean myself and don the necessary raiment there before coming to the feast."

"Of course. Lodgings next to yours have been made for your two companions. I must speak to you about them after you are readied."

"As you wish," Maveree replied. King Anderíen then called for Maveree to be shown to her chambers. By a small group of woman servants, she was led through the narrow streets of Iarnel Eremnad, which were surrounded by average sized hut-shaped tents of colorful woven cloth. Eventually, they came to a street that ended before a tent that was similar to all of the others, the abode of the king and queen. The only thing that made it different was the soft, silken, purple material worked into the cloth and the fact that it was slightly bigger. She was led to the left of the royal quarters.

Inside, she was bathed by two attendants and dressed in the common trappings of Iarnel Eremnad for a young girl, a tunic of soft blue that was held together at the shoulders by two small golden clasps adorned with small white preserved flowers, a wreath of flowers woven into braided hair, and bare feet. She left her quarters looking like a small cherubic being with a child's face and the eerie, empty eyes of a granite statue.

The Persian Rug

She followed the women servants silently to the festival where she was immediately taken aside by King Anderíen.

"Your one companion, the young man, has been taken by our shamans to their sacred shrines where he will be healed," the king said. "However, we must talk of the young woman."

"Ah, I thought something like this might happen," the seeress replied.

"Tell me if I am mistaken, our shamans have foreseen your princess as a young promiscuous woman of artifice and selfish ambition who uses her beauty and charm to take advantage of others."

"For the first time in fifteen years I find myself in total agreement with another."

"Good, then you will not be averse to seeing to it that she walks about our city covered. After all, it is custom for any visiting men of the world above to be covered."

"Averse? I would insist upon it. Could we gag her as well?"

"If you think it best."

"No, I think encasing her in a sack will do well enough."

"As you wish."

It was then that the king left her, making his way to the head of the table, which sat low to the ground and was surrounded by all of the inhabitants of the city who sat on cushions. The immediate royal family sat by him. A large flower with its petals sewn together served as goblets. Maveree took her seat at an empty cushion beside the king. There was another vacant cushion beside her. The table seemed to go on forever, as it sat all of the inhabitants of the city. Men and women filled every other spot. Maveree cordially greeted those who greeted her.

The general air about the place was that of peace and contentment as well-dressed and well-fed men and women slowly came to the table. All bore either the mark of a full moon with an intricate waxing and waning crescent on either side, a circle divided into quarters with triangles jutting from the vertical line and two dots on either side of the horizontal line, a flowering wand on their right hand, or something that slightly resembled a two and four combined in flowing script surrounded by dots on both of their cheeks.

Before the meal began, a shaking and muttering Aralé, with all but her eyes covered by beautiful cerulean silk was dragged to the cushion beside Maveree.

"Wh-wha-wha-"

"You are in Iarnel Eremnad. They are not fond of your kind, men from the world above, here so it is customary that they be covered. You fainted upon seeing me disappear through the threshold. You were taken here when you were unconscious. Here they speak Céremín and you speak Cancín. That is why none understand you and you do not understand them. This is a banquet welcoming me, for I am well liked here. Does that answer all of your questions?"

"Yes," Aralé replied quietly.

Soon after, a smiling young man dressed in a bright flamboyant tunic with a golden flower pattern emerged from one of the tents. There was a flowering wand tattooed on his right hand. He bowed to the king before calling "Jeqc!" happily. The people at the table repeated this merrily and the young man returned to the hut.

Aralé turned to Maveree. "What are they yelling about?" She asked timidly. She barely remembered waking in a small tent only to have fearful looking women whom she could not communicate with forcibly wash her and shove her into the ridiculous outfit she wore. She felt shaken and afraid.

"Jeqc, in our tongue, literally means *we eat*. In this situation however, he was more or less announcing that the food is ready and will be brought out shortly." Just as Maveree finished speaking, well-dressed men and women in the beautiful simple clothes of the realm gracefully came forward carrying ornate tureens of strange fruits and vegetables and pitchers of juices, milks, and teas of all colors. They poured out of nearby tents, sending and receiving obvious glances of love, happiness, and occasionally lust. After gently placing whatever they held on the table, they returned to the tents to get more.

"Why are mere servants so well-dressed?" Aralé asked as she

perceived one bend down briefly and kiss his lover's crown before returning to the tents with the others to retrieve the rest of the food. "The audacity!" She exclaimed, still thinking the servers mere servants.

"We have no servants in Iarnel Eremnad!" The king spat. "These are all beloved spouses doing their duty to their loved ones and scepter. They are just as respected as any other."

Aralé opened her mouth again as if to speak. Her comment turned into a muffled howl of pain when Maveree struck her in the knee to quiet her. "I suggest you say nothing for the remainder of the banquet," the seeress said quietly.

"I am a princess! I have to suffer none of these grievous indigni—"

Maveree struck her in the knee again and, beneath the cloth covering, tears began to stream down her face.

"You are a refugee, a deserter, a pariah. Refugees suffer whatever they need to suffer in order to survive. You are no longer a princess," Maveree spat and watched as the veiled head of Aralé slumped and the shoulders began to shake as if with silent weeping. Maveree said nothing to her and ignored her as she spent the rest of the meal eating and speaking with the inhabitants of Iarnel Eremnad. Aralé touched nothing and said nothing for the rest of the banquet. At its conclusion, she was led back to her tent where she collapsed on a small mattress.

The following morning, Nerin awoke in a small mud hut with two men in strange robes standing above him. One was an old man with long grey hair twisted into intricate braids and a similar beard. He was clad in red and a flowering wand was etched on the back of his hand. The other was a man of no more than thirty or thirty-five years. He was fair with bright blue eyes and thick hair so blonde that it almost fell silver against his slim shoulders and back. His robes were also of red.

"Podun." *He wakes*, said the younger man.

"Where am I?" Nerin asked weakly. "What happened? Who are you?" He began to shake violently.

The men only stared at him. "Aji imeniler nesqun Céremín." *I do not think he knows Céremín,* the younger man said. The elder then placed his hand on Nerin's forehead and his body eased before becoming limp and falling against the floor of the hut.

"Súmyv Nerin ja íe zethes omné Domí Valdesenlías." *Take Nerin to the abode of Mistress Eldestchild,* the older man said.

"Athím Devinqe Seré." *Yes Master Shaman,* the younger man said and then gathered others to aid him in carrying Nerin to Maveree's abode.

Meanwhile Maveree and Aralé sat in the aforementioned abode.

"I refuse to wear such a degrading costume!" Aralé screamed.

"Why must you be so impossible? We are leaving tomorrow night and from then on you can scamper about naked if you feel so inclined."

"You do not have to! Why should I be forced to?"

"After you can see past, present, and future and have spent a century as a child you might not be forced to wear *such a degrading costume.*"

"I hate this place!"

Maveree did not reply to this. She only rolled her eyes and sighed. Aralé continued to howl. Several minutes later Maveree stopped her. "Shortly Nerin will arrive here. If you cannot be quiet, then return to your own quarters."

"I do not have to listen to you!"

"Do you not understand? They already loathe men of the surface world here. They think you all warmongering, despicable, usurping, base, wastes of skin. By behaving so childishly you are not exactly helping to change that."

Aralé only sat in the corner of the tent, making an angry show of it as she did so and glared at the seeress.

At least she is quiet now, Maveree thought as she strode out of the tent to see a myriad of people, who had all obviously been listening in mere moments before, gathered within various distances of the tent pretending that they were doing something other than eavesdropping on a conversation that they could not understand anyway. Soon Nerin was brought to her and laid on a mattress inside the tent. Later that night, he awoke to see Maveree guzzling mead rapaciously out of a flask.

"Where…where…where…" he stammered before realizing that his head did not ache, his stomach did not turn, and that his limbs did not feel unbearably heavy. "I am healed?"

"Welcome to Iarnel Eremnad," Maveree said and Nerin jumped three feet in the air. "It is all right. There is no safer place to be."

"Where are we?"

"Iarnel Eremnad. It is a hidden city beneath an incredibly complex cave system in the Ariyekk forest. It is so well hidden that I can count the people who know of it on one hand."

"And by what witchery am I healed?"

"In Iarnel Eremnad there are shamans. Some have preternatural healing abilities. It depends on which elemental spirits they channel."

"Is that so?" He said dryly, obviously not believing her. "And how do they manage that?"

"You will see that the inhabitants of the city all bear marks, some on their faces and others on their hands. They are symbols that represent the elements: fire, water, wind, and earth. For the majority they simply show what clan you belong to, but few are conduits to the energies and spirits of the aforementioned elements."

Nerin stared at her for long moments. "Either I am dying and these are the last thoughts of my mind as it slowly declines, or I am lucky and the healers who are caring for me slightly overdosed me on numbing or sleeping elixirs."

"This is no hallucination."

"Of course it is. Just a while ago I was being stoned by four little boys with an endless supply of angry cabbages. Before that I had somehow misplaced my feet. I would say that I am hallucinating."

"Tell me the last thing you remember, before the little boys with the cabbages."

Nerin thought awhile before answering. "I was moving. The ground was a blur beneath my feet. I was bound to something, which must have been another person, and it was holding me upright because I was too weak and sick to keep steady. My head was spinning. I asked where we were going and a soothing voice replied but I cannot remember what it said. Then my strength failed me and in my bonds I collapsed against the person in front of me."

"You are not hallucinating," the seeress said. Then she proceeded to explain the entire situation to Nerin. She omitted the fact that Sern had been the one who had rescued him and also the true reason.

"So, you are trying to tell me that due to completely improbable circumstances, I was accused of assassinating the prince and awaiting my execution when a masked stranger saved me and brought me to you in the hopes that you would take me to a forgotten, unheard of, and enchanted city that none can find? Aralé feared for me so she came searching for me? Oh, and this is a city of *conduit-people*?

"Then, after you leave here, you intend for you, another helpless woman, and me, who in battle is just about as useful as you or Aralé, to trek thousands of miles through warring states and then through a frozen wasteland to a mountain? Then you want to climb this mountain because atop it there will be some sort of fountain type…thing that runs with blood? After you drink a cup your deepest desire is granted? Aralé is going to drink a cup and wish for her brother to be resurrected so he can save the land!? Oh, and somehow in all of this, Sern became the Steward of Laaven and Prince Amíen became competent?"

"That is about the gist of it, if you cannot perceive the whole story," Maveree said. Nerin began to chortle disbelievingly. "If you do not believe me ask Aralé," Maveree added and at this the young man stopped laughing. His face became almost expressionless but his eyes smiled.

"Aralé," he stammered, remembrance of the beautiful young woman finally returning to him. "She is here?"

"As far as I know," Maveree replied nonchalantly as she took a quick drink from her flask.

"Where? May I see her?" Nerin asked, evidently excited.

"She is sleeping," Maveree said with a knowing smile that Nerin did not observe. "It would not be prudent to pester her for she has had a very trying day."

Nerin sighed and threw himself back on the mattress. Maveree turned away and rested her head against the material that formed the wall of the tent. She momentarily worried her bottom lip between her teeth and sighed before turning again to look at Nerin, who had just about fallen asleep.

Meanwhile, an angry Aralé had ventured far from her tent. Clad in only a men's shirt that was so large it fell below her thighs, she had stomped throughout the city. The enraged young woman had continued in such a fashion until she came to where land met water. Realizing that she could go no further she kicked at the ground until her feet throbbed with pain. She then settled on a rock by the water. The mists rolled in as she sat trying to ease the tension in her weary limbs and assuage the agony in her sore feet. Her golden hair poured down her back and shoulders.

Once she was in a slightly improved state, she looked down from her large rock and realized that thick mist had set in such a way that she could not tell water from land or even see her own hand if she held it too far away. She cursed under her breath. Aralé then turned again to see a great glistening serpentine body pierce the mist briefly and delve back into it. There seemed to be dozens of others as well. She became too afraid to scream as one came so close to her that she caught the strange scent of the water mingled with its skin. She nearly fainted upon seeing the head of one of the creatures. It was a horrific fanged head with two sets of yellow eyes.

"You are brave to draw so near to the Ószerepentth," an accented voice said softly. Aralé looked to see a tall young man standing beside her. He had dark curly hair, dark eyes, and a sign that looked remarkably akin to a two and a four combined on both of his cheeks. Aralé only looked at him. He then turned to look at her. Captivated with one another, they did not speak for a long while.

"I am Prince Aravír, younger brother of King Anderíen. Who are you Lady?" Aravír asked gently.

"I am Aralé," she said somewhat dejectedly, omitting a royal title she finally realized did not belong to her. "Maveree's charge."

"Maveree? You must be great friends for you call her by her given name."

"We hate one another."

"Truly?"

"Yes, she is most unkind to me."

"I am sorry to hear that," Aravír said and they fell back to looking at one another. Their silence was broken as the Ószerepentth began breaching the top of the glassy lake.

"What are those creatures?" Aralé asked.

"They are the Ószerepentth. It is their berth to guide the dead from our world to the next. They also protect our city, for any boat that has not been blessed by our shamans that touches these waters is devoured. I am intrigued by them. Sometimes at night, I come and watch as they swim."

"How did they get here?"

"They are spirits made flesh, immortal deities. No one knows how they came to be here. We only know that they were probably here for millennia before my people arrived and we have dwelled here for two thousand years."

"Your people? Are you not men?"

"Not at all."

"Is that why you all bear markings?"

"Yes. My people are descendants of the elemental witches who lived in the world above thousands of years ago, or the Ziríva. Though very few of us still have powers, we still are members of the clans of earth, water, air, and fire. The markings on my cheeks represent air."

"Why did your people leave the world above?"

"Men attacked us and slaughtered the majority of our kinsman in cold blood. Knowing that we would have to give up our peaceful and harmonious way of life in order to survive among such beasts, we fled."

"That is why men are not well liked here."

"The old grudges do not exist anymore. Time has seen to that. However, what has happened will never be forgotten."

"Ah," Aralé replied as she mulled this over. "So, do you hate me then on principle?"

"No! Not at all!" The prince insisted. "You are lovely."

"May I..." Aralé began and trailed off, looking away.

"What?"

"It is foolish, but I have never seen such markings before. May I touch them?"

The prince nodded and leaned forward onto the rock. Aralé then lightly traced the marks with her fingers. The man's face was cold from the night breeze.

"What is the world above like?" Aravír asked as he took her hands in his, admiring the golden ring she wore on her index finger and reveling in the soft feel of her skin. Aralé then proceeded to tell him almost all that she knew. The prince sat beside her and they spent many hours exchanging tales of their different worlds and their lives. Aralé told the fabricated story of the quest she intended to embark upon with Maveree. Aravír thought it noble and offered his aid and his sword if she would accept.

Aravír, while kind, was not usually a man to take to much trouble for another. He was certainly helpful to an extent but those who knew him would never think him one to offer his aid in a heroic and toilsome quest. His true desire to aid the younger woman stemmed from curiosity, after hearing so much of the world above, he simply had to see it and experience it firsthand. For years, he had dwelled in Iarnel Eremnad: a sheltered peaceful utopian hamlet where everyone knew everyone and the most interesting thing that ever came to pass were Domí Valdesenlías' incredibly infrequent and almost always short-lived visits. Adventure did not exist there. In the prince's eyes, Aralé breathed adventure and the unknown and everything that he had ever lusted for.

"I accept and I am sure that Maveree will as well. It would be prudent for we are all but helpless. Are you well trained with a blade?"

"There is only one better in our city."

"Let us go to Maveree then."

"Would Domí Valdesenlías not be asleep?"

"She never sleeps."

"Still, it would be most disrespectful to bother her at such an hour."

"I could not agree with you more," Aralé said and rose before starting to walk away.

"Where are you going?"

"I am going to see Maveree."

"To her private dwelling?"

"Yes."

"Will she not be angry with you for showing such insolence?"

"Almost definitely. Luckily, it would be almost impossible for me to care any less. Now, will you join me or no?"

"O-of course," Aravír replied with a slight smile. He felt nervous but also incredibly wicked. He had never deliberately been disrespectful or deliberately disobeyed the customs of his land.

"Show me the way, my prince," she said and he led her through the city to Maveree's tent, holding aloft a lantern full of glowing insects. The second they reached their destination, Aravír pulled the top off of the lantern and let the bugs free. He watched, dumbstruck, as Aralé unceremoniously strode into the tent. Maveree sat inside, smoking a pipe.

"Bring him in," she said flatly and Aralé pulled the older man inside. He looked pale and almost sickly. He stood a head taller then her.

"Do not fret," Maveree said to Aravír. "You look as if you have committed a crime. You have not and you may join us. However, first I must ask one question of you and if you answer dishonestly I promise that you will suffer for it."

Aravír turned pale but nodded.

"Aré aq edíre?" *Love or lust?* The seeress asked and briefly eyed Aralé.

Aravír smiled, "Éa adesun elú pélú, t adesí imeqúra omné Éa." *She is living beauty, but I am* not *her fool.*

Maveree grinned at this. "Originally I had planned to leave tomorrow night, but I believe Nerin needs to regain his strength. We will leave in one week. Now get out, both of you," she said and the pair left to return to their respective dwellings.

Maveree then went back to smoking her pipe and watching Nerin sleep. "Your precious princess did not even see you," she remarked after a while, shaking her head sadly. He began to moan and whimper in his sleep. Obviously, he was in the midst of a nightmare. "It is a cruel world in which those with such inner light and love in them are denied and beaten beyond recognition." She then strode over to him and placed her hands on his forehead. She was given several brief flashes of a younger Nerin in a dark room, screaming as various methods of torture were enacted upon him.

"They cannot hurt you anymore," she whispered and smoothed back his hair. "Such horrors are past you now. Here you are safe. Sleep in peace." She moved her tiny hands over his forehead as if pulling the horrid thoughts from his mind. It would seem that she had succeeded in doing so for he calmed greatly and returned to a semi-peaceful sleep as she did this. She removed her hands. "Whilst you can, child," she added gravely as she returned to her corner of the room and resumed smoking.

Chelsea Isadora Teich

Chapter X
Kerúx and Risúrat

Risúrat loathed the cold. Often upon waking, he would feel the painful chill in his bones and wondered at the stupidity of northerners. To him, it seemed that they lived in a cold unmeant for human life. Having spent his entire life in the south, he was used to it being warm enough to swim even in the winter. Also, being accustomed to loose fitting robes of thin material made thick and heavy robes of fur, especially two or three of them being worn at once to stave off the cold, a nuisance. Not to mention that the rich flamboyant color and spirit that thrived in all things in the south was completely absent in the north. Stark-looking men and women in dark clothes, frozen dark green and murky brown earth, and blindingly white snow were all that was to be seen.

He constantly reminded himself that if all things happened as he intended, he would soon be back in the south and he would return as a rich government official of Phallé-Nal. *Soon I will be out of this wretched wasteland,* he thought as he looked out of his carriage window. A beggar had frozen to death on a street corner during the night and the corpse still sat, staring blankly. Risúrat felt as if the eyes were watching him and disdainfully shut the carriage window. He gathered the fur-lined hood of his cloak about his face and shivered.

"I hate this damned cold place," he muttered, rubbing his painfully cold face with gloved hands. He pulled a flask of hot drink out of one of the pockets within his robes to find it empty and scowled. He hated the northern flasks for they held less than southern-made ones. He grumbled about this as the carriage came to a stop.

"Master Risúrat, we have arrived," the driver said as he opened the door for the older man. He too was dressed in a similar outfit, only his was obviously more weatherworn and of a lesser quality. Risúrat unceremoniously dropped several small silver coins in the snow before the young man and stalked away. The driver sighed sadly before picking up the coins.

They had arrived at one of Phallé-Nal's many palaces. This one in particular was the palace belonging to the second oldest prince of Phallé-Nal and his wife. Unlike the beautiful and bright palaces of Laaven with their many colored windows and beautiful gardens, this was a four-tiered palace of cold grey stone. The lawn was covered with snow so high that it rose to Risúrat's waist. Several paths just wide enough to allow two thin men to walk abreast had been carved into what seemed to be sheer ice. It was one of these he walked along until he came to the castle door, which was lowered and raised, like that which provided a walkway over a moat, by thick black chains. Imprints could be seen from when it had last been lowered in the snow.

As he stood, shivering, he perceived the guards standing on the second tier looking down at him to see if he could be identified and allowed to enter the abode of their master, or killed on the spot. Men with readied bows could be seen lurking in the shadows if one knew where and how to look. Risúrat glared at them. Within minutes, the door was lowered and Risúrat was quickly ushered inside by sickly and fearful looking servants. They smelled terribly.

"Risúrat, old friend."

Risúrat looked to see a man slightly younger than he, with thin yellow hair worn behind him in one long braid and a slight beard of the same color, descending the stone steps that led from an upper level to the grand hall. Weapons and all sorts of horrid devices beyond mention lined the walls and candles burned with a gloomy subdued brilliance. The silver and metallic hues of the weapons along with the yellow candlelight reflected in the man's grey eyes. He was broader and taller than Risúrat. He radiated confidence as he walked toward his old friend and there was something tolerably handsome about him.

"Kerúx," Risúrat said. "It has been years."

"Come with me to my study," Kerúx replied. "We have much to discuss."

Risúrat then followed his friend up the stairs and through the second level of the house. Soon enough, they came to a large door of dark wood. Kerúx unlocked it and opened it. He bade Risúrat enter first. The second after the door was shut and locked and several candles were lit, they embraced almost wildly.

"I have not met with a friend in years," Risúrat said.

"I look forward to having a fellow conspirator once more!" Kerúx said, grasping him by the shoulders. "It will be as it always should have been, you and I defeating all that stands in our way!"

"Undoubtedly," Risúrat replied with a genuine smile. "Now, what is this little bit I hear of you overthrowing your brother?"

"He will not attack Laaven!" Kerúx cried as he unceremoniously shed his outer robes and threw himself back on one of the animal skin sofas in the large room. His study was an enormous room with two desks and several divans. Pelts of various animals covered the floor and furniture. Bookshelves, stuffed animal heads, maps, and various other objects covered every inch of wall.

"Why ever not? Did Danút make some sort of deal with him? Perhaps I underestimated Danút."

"Danút? What are you prattling on about?"

"The Steward of Laaven."

"So you have not heard then?" Kerúx asked, astonished. He was used to Risúrat informing him of all things that went on. Risúrat shook his head. "Sern, son of Stavir, is now the Steward of Laaven!"

"No!"

"Yes."

"Damn that bastard! He will destroy everything I have worked for! We must do away with him!"

"Easier said than done, my friend. I cannot count the number of times various governments have tried to do away with him. It cannot be done."

"That is preposterous! Anyone can be killed. All you need is the right amount of money and the right people."

"As for the right amount of money, my father almost exhausted our funds trying to kill this man when he was king. Seventeen failed attempts. As for the right people, you will not find someone willing. Every assassin sent has failed and then suffered some sort of hideous freakish death or punishment. That seeress has her eye on him always, protecting him."

"Seventeen attempts? In earnest?"

"On attempt number seventeen, we sent twenty fully armed hired swords to attack him as he walked out of an inn. He had only his daggers on him and killed them all. They say he escaped without a scratch and was half-intoxicated at the time."

"That is impossible! Have you tried poisoning him?"

"Eight times. It always happens that he is either not thirsty, all of the sudden no less, or someone spills it as they bring it to him. Once a man elbowed him just as he was about to take a sip and he spilled it all over the poisoner, who had miraculously misplaced the antidote. By the time he had gotten some antidote, the poison had already taken his legs."

"The protection of the seeress could be the only explanation."

"Speaking of Mistress Eldestchild," Kerúx said. "We believe that she is somehow involved."

"How so?"

"Do you remember the spies you aided?"

"Yes, I was paid well for it. I used the money to purchase more powder for that imbecilic King Amíen."

"That was admirably done by the way. And still, no one knows!"

The Persian Rug

"That was by no guile of mine, but the stupidity of everyone else."

"Even so, I do not possess the mettle to even consider doing something of the like! In any case, those very same spies were returning to Phallé-Nal when they saw Mistress Eldestchild enter the Ariyekk forest in a carriage. Guess who was with her!?"

"Nerin and Her Royal Highness."

"How did you know, Risúrat? How do you always know?"

"I have some information that you do not. You see, it was the little woman who advised me to send for an assassin that murdered the prince on the exact day I did. She told me that the guard, being so well disciplined, would have engaged in a drinking game and our man would have been able to slip by unhindered if he arrived at nine. She was right!"

"The only question is what she would gain from the prince being assassinated."

"It looks like she needed Aralé and Nerin to come to her and no one to search for either of them. Only the little witch herself knows what for," Risúrat said as he looked at the white snarling wolf head mounted above the fireplace.

"However, you did not let me finish. The spies said that the last thing they saw was Mistress Eldestchild and the princess dragging Nerin into the caves within the Golden Mountains. When the spies were asked why they did not follow they had this to say: *It is a place of evil. Those who enter are never seen again.* However, spies have seen her enter thrice in the past."

"I do not like this. It would seem that the seeress is at the heart of all the political intrigue, revolutions, monarchies, and social change there has ever been."

"Oh! You do not even know the half of it! She certainly has left her mark on us northerners!"

"Truly?"

"Yes! Have you ever heard of The Year of the Uprising?"

"Briefly, that is when that blind slave named Zetth tore across the land with some makeshift army liberating slaves and what not. Correct?"

"Ah, but you do not know the whole story. You see, this is the only account of Mistress Eldestchild's early years that exists and almost none remember it now."

"Come to think of it, I know absolutely nothing of her past or present. She is quite a singular creature. Pray tell."

"Very well," Kerúx said and cleared his throat before beginning again. "It was during the rule of either my great-grandfather or great-great-grandfather, about a hundred or so years ago, that Maveree surfaced for the first time. Visitors from the Northern Isles were presenting the king beautifully woven rugs as gifts. They unrolled one and out fell a little girl. She insisted that she was the seeress reincarnated and the king laughed at her and threw her in the dungeon. 'Maveree Eldestchild, daughter of No Man' she called herself.

"As she was about to be executed with the others of the night (after dinner entertainment was so barbaric in those days), she halted her executioner by telling him his entire life story and almost everything he had ever thought. Then, in the arena as they held her head down and readied the axe and asked if she had any last words, she looked the king in the eyes and began to rattle off myriad ridiculous things about the king that she would only know if she were him or a seeress. Rumor had it that she even told the king things about himself that he had forgotten.

"Needless to say, she was not executed. The next day she was made his advisor. As every government official, she was offered her own personal slave. The king was fond of her and brought hundreds to her, but she denied them all, saying that when she saw one that she found suitable, she would take it. A year passed and she had taken none, although she had become the king's favorite. He loved her more than even his own children.

"One night, after about a year had passed, the after dinner entertainment was about to commence. It was a night of torture, for these were incredibly wretched criminals. First was a slave named Zetth who had been caught with the oldest daughter of his master. For it, he had first had his eyes gouged out with hot metal. After this, he had become virtually useless so they decided to make him part of the entertainment.

"Just as he stood naked awaiting the whip, it is said that Maveree stood and said that she ordered him to be spared so he could serve her. The man whose daughter had been deflowered by Zetth attempted to argue but the king succored Maveree, as she was his favorite.

"Over the year, she trained him in secret. No one knows how, but she taught a man without eyes to see and to fight like a knave. I believe it was by the same witchery that makes Sern indestructible. The next year, Zetth and Maveree led the rebellion that almost destroyed our country. After all of the rebelling slaves fled south to beg Laaven for help and Laaven refused, they were destroyed. Zetth along with all of the other slaves were slaughtered with the exception of Maveree, who was not seen or heard of until she settled in The City of the Wood about eighty years later. She has remained unchanged since The Year of the Uprising."

"That was an interesting story," Risúrat said after a while. "But I believe there is business to attend to."

Kerúx nodded, "I know that when we conquer Laaven you want to act as resident king. Since I cannot be in two places at one time and I trust you that would only seem fitting, but what can you give me in return?"

"What kind of business would you be dealing in if you received no compensation for your pains?"

"Not good business I can assure you. Now, it is nothing personal but I do not grant anything for free. I know that you have come here with an offer in mind and knowing you it will be one I could not possibly refuse."

Risúrat smiled, "You know me too well indeed. Obviously, your brother fears Sern like a fool, so as long as your brother is on the throne, Laaven, with all of its beautiful land and resources, will remain just out of reach. However, unlike your brother who is a shiftless, ambitionless and overly superstitious man, you do not fear battle. You need the means to kill him in such a way that you would seem the last person responsible even if everyone knows you were obviously behind it. After all, it does not matter what anyone knows, as long as they cannot prove it."

"You can do such a thing?"

"Yes. All it will take is a few drops of poison."

"Hardly, he has been made immune to nine out of ten poisons. All kings are in this day and age. Even so, how would you intend to get it to him?"

"You forget who my brother is."

"You have a brother?"

"I am Risúrat, son of Néíro. My brother, Néírn, son of Néíro, prefers to be known as Master Healer Dorin of the Laaven castle."

"No!"

"And Dorin, as he prefers to be called, has created an untraceable and incredibly potent poison that none other than him and I know of. Therefore, there is no antidote and no way could he have possibly built up immunity to it."

"How do you know of it?"

"A decade ago, when I mentioned something about killing Sern to him (and from what I remember I was really only being facetious), he threatened me with it. He explained all of its effects, how it functions, and even showed me a phial of the foul substance in order to frighten me. His threat was empty, of course."

"So, exactly what makes this poison so remarkable?"

"It is tasteless, odorless, and virtually invisible once added to food or drink. Once imbibed it takes at least a week to affect the victim, making it near untraceable if you are clever. According to my brother, there is something in the body that fights sickness. This poison obliterates that something so it will appear that the poisoned person died of an illness. Since all cures work by helping that something that fights disease, when it is nonexistent, no cure will work. Now, Dorin never made an antidote. Also, every king is given a myriad of poisons in small doses, so he can build immunity and not be done away by any typical poison. The singularity and obscurity of this wretched concoction would make such a thing impossible. One bit of this in the king's food and he will be dead in less than a fortnight."

"Brilliant! But, how to get it to him?"

"Simple. Promise one of the royal food tasters their freedom if they do you a favor."

"I have but one last question," Kerúx said and Risúrat made a sign for him to continue. "Do you possess such a poison?"

From one of the hidden pockets in his robes, Risúrat pulled a phial of something clear and almost jelly-like. He held it up to the light and it gave off a sickening green hue. Almost as soon as he had taken it out, he hid it again.

"It simply does not make sense," Kerúx said and Risúrat looked at him questioningly. "What would Dorin be doing brewing toxins that just beg to be used for dark purposes? He is almost inhumanly righteous."

"Even Dorin, or should I say Néírn, has his secrets. I would wager any amount there are many things about him that even I do not know."

"Well, your brother's secrets are not of much importance. I will bring the poison to the royal food taster tomorrow eve," Kerúx said and Risúrat shook his head.

"I will see to it. You know me. I prefer to do things myself. However, if you betray me—"

"I will not."

"Then you understand that there will be consequences, if you do."

"Of course! We may be among the greatest of friends, but there is no such thing as unconditional friendship in such dealings."

"Then it is agreed," Risúrat said and began to leave. Suddenly, he turned to face Kerúx.

"What is it?" The other man asked.

"I have truly missed you," Risúrat said and Kerúx smiled slightly.

"All of the time in the south has made you soft."

"Ah, but not entirely," Risúrat said as he held the phial of poison aloft for a second and hid it away again. With that, he exited the room.

Chapter XI
An Interlude in the Ariyekk Forest

She has seduced you! King Anderíen's voice rang in Aravír's ears as he sat, staring out into the night. He smiled as he remembered his reply.

I could not care less for her if I tried. She is too young for me. It is her world that I find attractive. I have lived by the same routine for twenty-four years!

It was then that Anderíen had banished him, but Aravír cared not. The only things he knew he would truly miss were the Ószerepentth. They had always truly mystified the young man and he had been assured that on the surface there was not a creature that even slightly resembled them. He sighed. That night as they settled, he had fallen into a deep and perfect dreamless sleep, only to be wakened after midnight by Nerin, who had been having a nightmare and howled as if he were being murdered. After Maveree calmed him, Aralé and Maveree had fallen back asleep, but Aravír could not. He sat staring at the sky, which he had never seen before.

In Iarnel Eremnad, there had been enchantments that had turned light to dark and then dark again to light as long as their people had dwelled there, but living beneath the caves had denied him ever seeing a sunrise or a moonrise. He had never perceived the stars before or the endless night sky. He lay on his back in the grass gazing at them, amazed.

"Men or no, how could my people have lived their entire lives without experiencing such beauty?" He mused and ran his hands through his hair. "Everywhere I glance, a thousand eyes peer back at me, cold yet piercing like living phosphorescent gems." He stayed awake for the rest of the night, staring at the stars and then watching the sunrise, as he had done almost every day since they had left Iarnel Eremnad.

As the sun rose, he whispered *six* quietly. Ever since his first sunrise, which he had seen on the fifth day of their journey, he had counted them. He still lay on the ground, relishing the last quiet moments he would have before Maveree awoke and forced them to resume their trek to Oran Itae. While Aravír was excited to enter his first city of men, he had never had to walk so far before and found it tiring. The sword he wore about his waist seemed to grow heavier with every passing minute.

"You are an early riser Aravír," Maveree said quietly as she stood beside him. Aravír had not seen her wake or even come toward him. He only nodded. "Your name is too old-fashioned for a young man of today, Aravír. You must change it if you do not want to draw attention to yourself."

"I do not know of any modern, common names."

"Niithéum, Aranth, Varin, Léorn, Féian, and Amarant are quite common these days."

"It is between Léorn and Féian then. What do they mean?"

"Lé means inner light and Fé: spirit."

"Féian it is then."

"Very well," Maveree said and then stood. She stretched slightly and took breath. "AWAKEN!" She bellowed so loudly that the forest around them shook. Nerin jolted awake and landed on his feet. In a panicked frenzy, he attempted to flee but failed to notice the fact that they were in a clearing surrounded by trees and ran headfirst into one.

"I promise you that if there is reason to flee you will be the first to know," Maveree said as Nerin rose, looking utterly blank, and returned to the others. He sat beside Aralé, with the intention of resting his head on her shoulder, but the second he sat beside her, she rose.

"How much farther do we have to walk on like this?" She asked, as she took a drink from one of the water skins. "I am weary of this constant journeying!"

"By the end of the week, if we walk quickly, we will come across some old friends of mine and they will aid us," Maveree said. "This afternoon we will come across a river. There you will all bathe and we will refill the water skins. Enjoy it, for once we leave the forest we cannot waste water on bathing anymore."

"That is disgusting!" Aralé moaned. "My hair is already nearly impossible to manage—"

"Then cut it off. We cannot waste time caring for it."

"Never!"

"Suit yourself. Ere long you will beg me to rid you of it. I warn you that it will only prove a nuisance."

"I will never cut my hair!" Aralé said indignantly. Maveree shrugged nonchalantly.

"Féian, Nerin: eat and drink. We will not stop until we come to the river this afternoon."

"I thought you said that his name was Aravír," Aralé said as she pulled a piece of fruit from a low-hanging branch of a tree. She sat on a log and bit into it. The past few days had taught her not to wait to be fed and also that dirty fruit and vegetables, leraj n ósvera, and stale water were better than hunger pains.

"We changed it to something more common, as to not draw attention to ourselves."

"Interesting," Aralé muttered acerbically, obviously too unhappy at her situation to care much. The group sat in silence for several minutes as they ate and drank. Soon Maveree had them up and walking again. She strode in front, leading them, with Féian behind her, Aralé trailing behind miserably, and Nerin behind her. He could have walked faster than all of them. However, it seemed that trailing behind at an absolutely ridiculous pace was the only possible way to get close to Aralé.

Maveree and Féian would speak to one another, in Céremín,

occasionally. Almost everything filled him with awe and curiosity and he was full of questions. When Maveree would no longer suffer his incessant questioning, he would turn to Aralé, who eagerly answered him. Nerin would attempt to talk to Aralé, but she would always ignore him or was cruel in other ways. Even after Aralé began walking faster for the sole purpose of being closer to Féian, the healer lagged behind.

Late in the afternoon, just as Maveree had foretold, they came to a river. It was a river so clear that one could see the brown and grey stones that rested at its bottom. It cut through the foliage for miles. Maveree ordered that the men bathe and wash their clothes first. Nerin would not be unclothed in front of the others, so he disappeared upstream. Féian quickly bathed and washed his clothes and handed them to Maveree who laid them out to dry.

"I do not want to get out until we need to leave. I have never felt such water before. Do you mind if I stay in with you?"

"Not at all," Maveree said with a strange smile and dove gracefully into the water, still in her clothes. Aralé swiftly stripped and jumped in, her golden hair floated behind her on the surface of the water.

"This water is frigid," Aralé said, shivering.

"Move. It will make you warm," Féian said as he glided by. She took his advice and, before long, the pair was splashing one another merrily. Maveree floated under the surface of the water, relaxing. Even with her eyes closed, she still looked stern and conscious. They stopped as they heard someone walking along the side of the river. Nerin was standing there. He was dripping wet to the extent where he left a trail of puddles behind him.

"It is time we begin walking again. We have wasted over an hour here. Tonight we will have to make up the time," Maveree said as she climbed out of the river. Féian and Aralé moaned but reluctantly followed. After they were dressed in their wet clothes and their water skins were filled, they journeyed late into the night. Near midnight, they climbed into trees and slept there, for they were deep in the woods and they were safe from wolves and most other carnivorous creatures in trees. Maveree and Nerin slept in one tree. Féian and Aralé slept in another.

The next day they awoke, ate and drank, and walked on until dark without a single rest.

"I would kill for a leg of pheasant. We have been eating nothing but apples and that hideous whey bread for ages," Aralé said as they sat down for the night.

"I do not know about pheasant, but this forest is near overrun with other game," Maveree said.

"You hunt?" Féian asked, horrified. "You kill animals and *eat* them?"

"You don't?" Aralé asked, astonished.

"I survive," Maveree said. "If that means I have to kill, then I kill without hesitation."

"That is rather doltish. They are just animals," Aralé said, completely ignoring Maveree's comment. Féian became furious.

"They are living things with souls and hearts and minds, just as we are!" He bellowed.

"Both of you bite your tongues. Yes, I agree that animals are living things with hearts and souls, but they are also delicious. Besides, I would not be considered human if I had a weapon and did not kill or destroy something with it."

"What weapon do you have?" Féian asked bitterly. Maveree then pulled the sword around her waist from its scabbard.

"This one," she said and disappeared into the dark of the forest. Féian let out a frustrated hiss and sat down on a rock. Aralé placed a hand on his shoulder.

"Maveree is an awful little wretch," she said and Féian glared at her.

"So are you, you are a murderer. You will feast upon the carcass she brings back like some lowly beast. I will not have it. It is sick!"

"Your sword is taller than she is. How can you expect her to pick it up let alone kill with it? It is almost unheard of to kill an animal with a sword in the first place."

"You are a foolish little girl," Féian replied coldly. "She can bewitch anyone, animal or man, to bludgeon itself to death if she feels so inclined. Her powers are untold. Once one of my own countrymen tried to attack her and he fell dead at her feet."

"I am not a little girl! I am a woman!" She bellowed.

"You are what, sixteen? You are an innocent, a child."

"I have watched men be tortured to death. I have sentenced men to death! Great men bow before me! I lost my innocence at fourteen!"

"Then you are a foolish little girl lacking in morals and decency who has been given too much. Now leave me be. I must ask for forgiveness, for it is my weapon that shall tonight slay an innocent creature." He then closed his eyes, let his arms fall beside him so his open palms faced out and tilted his head toward the sky. With his eyes closed, he began to mutter prayers and beg for forgiveness in his own language. After coming to the conclusion that she could not regain his attention, Aralé stomped over to Nerin.

"Talking to me now are you?" He asked coldly. She let out an angry howl and stomped away into the dark.

With her feet planted firmly in the ground, she became one with the forest. She could hear the wind whistling through every tree, the quick movements of even the smallest animals, and their breathing.

Come to me.

Deep breaths: in through her nose, out through her mouth.

Hear my voice.

Deep breaths: the crisp and natural scent of the forest, in through her nose, out through her mouth.

Come swiftly.

Deep breaths: the scent of a stag, the beating of his heart, the strength of his step. She opened her eyes to see him standing before her. She nodded and began to walk toward where she had left the others and he followed. When she was only a short distance from the camp, she looked at the stag and he knelt before Maveree.

"I am sorry for this," She said to him and he seemed to nod, understanding her meaning. She stroked his neck. Maveree then plunged the sword into his neck.

Féian retched as the sounds of the stag's suffering reached them. A tear escaped one of Nerin's eyes as he sat clinging for dear life to the rock he had been sitting upon.
"What kind of men are you? You, Nerin, afraid of the smallest sound and you, Féian, sickened for the sake of a mere animal!"
"What kind of a *girl* are you? You, who are callous, cruel, and cries for no one?" Féian asked as he drank from a water skin.
"A strong woman!"
"No," Féian said and went to comfort Nerin, who readily accepted it.
"Pathetic," Aralé snorted.
Soon, Maveree returned with the dead stag. She skinned and prepared it herself. She made a fire and cooked it herself. She only cooked a small amount of it and after her other companions, with the exception of Féian, had eaten and fallen asleep, she dried the rest into strips. When she had finished cooking the stag and only had its bones and organs, skin, and antlers left, she set to work scraping the skin so it could be used as a blanket later on. Using rocks, she sharpened the bones and antlers into long and short knives. She ate the heart and the rest she left for the wolves to eat. Less than an hour before sunrise, she fell asleep and awoke at first light. She awoke the others then and, after they quickly ate, they were off and supplied with the weapons Maveree had made. Féian left his sword with the remains of the dead animal. Instead, he had twin knives made of antler that he carried for the rest of his days.

Chelsea Isadora Teich

Chapter XII
The Letter

Danen panted heavily as he sprinted down the castle corridor. He had run all the way from the kitchen to Sern's chambers (across four levels of the castle) to convey to him important information. He had nearly fallen against the door as he wildly pounded against it. He was reminded of the lateness of the hour when Sern opened the door, dressed only in leggings and a shirt so old that it nearly fell off of him. He looked utterly bedraggled. His hair had grown, falling far below his shoulders in messy locks

"Do you *know* what time it is?" Sern asked, but, upon seeing the younger man's petrified countenance, he let him into his chambers. He felt the younger man's heart beating wildly. This worried him greatly.

"Here, sit, my friend," he said and led Danen to his bed where he almost collapsed.

"Something terrible has happened!" Danen gasped, so short of breath he could barely talk.

"What has happened, tell me all," Sern said as he poured his friend a glass of wine and sat beside him. Danen refused it and put his head in his hands. "Nen, please, is it something you have done? I promise that I will not be too harsh with you."

"This is worse…far worse than anything I could have ever done," Danen said and gently took the wine glass from Sern's hand and pressed it to his lips. He nearly drained the glass.

"When you are willing to talk, I will be willing to listen,"

Sern said and Danen sat in contemplation for several minutes before taking a breath.

"The last thing I want, milord, is to upset you but…earlier I was pacing the corridors when I became thirsty. I went to the kitchen and was enjoying my third or fourth mug of ale when I heard footsteps and voices approaching.

"'*Do you really think the kitchen an appropriate place for this?*' One said and I did not recognize the voice.

"'*Yes, no one is in the kitchens this late. It is early morning.*' This was the voice of Master Virahéen. '*So, in your mind there is logic behind dragging a man from his bed in the dead of night to the kitchen in order to discuss classified matters of state!*' The other man said.

"'*There is terrible news from the north and you are the only other council member I trust well enough to convey such information to. You were one of my students. I know your mind,*' Virahéen said and the other begged him to continue. Virahéen then proceeded to say that he had received a letter from his cousin in the north, which he had received a week ago but not had time to open until last night! He said that in the letter his cousin told him that the king of Phallé-Nal had died of the worst fever any had ever seen and his brother had taken his place upon the throne! Then Virahéen bent very closely to the man and whispered *you do know what that means do you not?*'

"'*Our doom will be upon us,*' the other said and after a while he said, '*Call an emergency council in the morning. Give the poor steward at least one last night of pleasant sleep. We all know he deserves it,*'" Danen then cast his eyes down. "I am sorry to have disturbed you. I do not even understand but I just felt that it…"

"I must see Dorin!" Sern exclaimed angrily and then looked to Danen. "You were only being loyal to your steward and your friend, and there is no shame in that. Forget all that you have heard. Do not tell a soul. You may even spend the night here if you like, for I shall not return."

"Where are you going?" Danen asked quietly as he sat back on the bed. He watched Sern rise. He had rarely even seen Sern act as if he were annoyed. However, at that moment, he had never seen so much anger and unadulterated rage exhibited by a person before.

"To kill Dorin!" He snarled and stormed out of the room without putting on any shoes, proper clothes, or fixing his unruly hair. He stormed from his bedroom to the healing wing. Once there, he ferociously pounded on the door. One of the apprentices who had been forced to watch over the patients and the healing wing itself at night answered the door. He cowered upon seeing Sern so furious.

"Take me to Dorin!" He said in an even tone that was even more terrifying than a screaming, bellowing tantrum would have been. The apprentice complied immediately and led Sern through the healing wing to Master Dorin's apartments. Sern marched directly into the man's bedroom and shook him awake wildly.

"Take me to the place where you keep your poisons!" He bellowed. Dorin was still not conscious enough to completely comprehend the man.

"Sern? What are you doing here?" He half mumbled.

"Take me to the place where you keep your poisons!" Sern said again and, when Dorin began to question, Sern grabbed him by the collar of his sleeping gown. "Show me *now!*" He ordered and a completely dumbstruck Dorin rose and led him to a door with five locks hidden behind a tapestry in the back of his apartments. After he had finally gotten the door opened, Sern burst in.

"The poison you invented, The Perfect Poison you called it, how much did you concoct?"

"Seven phials. Never used any of them," Dorin said through a yawn. "Why?"

Every wall was covered with tables holding a myriad of phials and containers filled with different colored liquids. All were labeled. Sern stopped upon coming to a drawer labeled *TPP*. He opened it to find six phials.

"Really? Well, there are only six in here," he said darkly and Dorin's eyes became wide. He then moved forward and frantically counted the six phials over and over again.

"Do you think it is a coincidence," Sern began, "that both

your brother and a phial of the most dangerous poison ever created have miraculously disappeared at the same time?"

"No!" Dorin moaned, putting his head in his hands.

"Risúrat, you, and I are the only people in this world that know of it. And certainly it was not you or I who stole it. And how about another coincidence, your poison causes a person to die of fever, which has not happened in a hundred years for medicine had improved, and isn't it just the strangest thing? The king of Phallé-Nal, the only man who stood between Laaven and complete cataclysm, just died of such a thing and his younger brother, Kerúx, who just happens to be one of Risúrat's many old acquaintances, is now king. And is it not a coincidence that this all surfaced in just about the exact amount of time it would take someone to travel from Laaven to Phallé-Nal?"

"No!"

"Oh yes, and he is a vindictive man who feels we should suffer for harboring their country's slaves for so long! It is a wonder his troops are not gathered on the outskirts of the kingdom as we speak. And you know that Laaven has no hope of defeating Phallé-Nal."

Dorin did not reply.

"So, it would seem if someone had taken my advice, and not wasted their breath on empty threats and braggadocio, a million people would not die at the hands of the merciless northern battalion!" Dorin fell to his knees with his head in his hands.

Sern stepped over him on his way out and walked quietly back to his room where he found Danen asleep in his bed, shivering. He shut the bedroom window and then settled himself in a chair. The childlike innocence Danen seemed to evince as he slept helped to assuage Sern's anger slightly. Before realizing how overwrought he was, he fell asleep sitting upright in the chair.

He suffered several hours of uneasy sleep only to be awakened a short time after dawn by frantic pounding on his bedroom door. "Lord the Steward!" They called. As Sern awoke, he fell off the chair. From his uncomfortable position on the floor, he answered them.

"I will join the council in exactly one quarter of an hour," he mumbled sleepily. "Now go." He stayed sitting on the ground until their retreating footsteps were no longer audible. He then rose and woke Danen, who he asked to aid him with tying several of the more obnoxious knots on his simple yet stately black robes. Even after combing his hair, he found that it was still unruly and decided to leave it be. Danen quit the room through the back entrance and Sern through the main double doors.

The haggard appearance of the steward worried all who he passed in the hallway. The other eleven council members looked almost afraid as he walked steadily into the room and then collapsed gracelessly into the chair at the head of the table in the deliberation room. "I know why we are gathered here this morn. Are you all aware of the circumstances surrounding this meeting?"

All said no with the exception of Master Virahéen and a younger man named Ccarad. "Then explain what has happened Virahéen," Sern said to the slight old man who then stood and not only confirmed what Danen had said with his words, but then gave Sern the letter his cousin had sent. Sern read it, noting that Virahéen had failed to mention the fact that in the letter his cousin also begged him to flee to the north before it was too late.

"You do not intend to flee, then, Virahéen?" Sern asked, placing the letter on the desk.

"To whatever end, I will remain steadfast in my loyalty my lord," he said and bowed.

"To whatever end," Ccarad murmured as he stood and bowed low. The others followed in short order. A subdued yet radiant smile, which was more evident in his silvery-green eyes than in his countenance, brought hope to the hearts of all the men who stood before him. The very essence of self-effacement, beneath his joy was comprised of not only pride but also gratefulness and disbelief.

"Captain Sólien," Sern said and a man in his fifties, a man

whom Sern had personally chosen to lead his armies in his stead, stood. "Begin recruiting, exhaust every last option."

"Yes milord," Captain Sólien replied.

"Virahéen, I call for assemblage. The people of Laaven deserve to know what will come to pass."

"I will see it done," the old man replied. "Would His Highness wish for assemblage this aft?"

"No, that would prove most disadvantageous to the workfolk and it is not as if Phallé-Nal will attack tomorrow. This Saturday at noon, which is only two days from now, will be acceptable."

"Is it mandatory that every man, woman, and child attend?" Virahéen asked and Sern chuckled.

"Every speech of the king has been mandatory since I can remember, and yet no one has ever attended aside from the nobles who would have killed their own children to gain his favor. Those who want to will and those who do not wish to will not, mandatory or no."

"Aye, my Lord," Virahéen said.

"I believe this meeting is dismissed," Sern said and the council members dispersed.

Sern helped himself to an apple sitting atop a pile of fruit within a basket a pretty maiden was carrying as he walked by her, on his way to the gardens. She blushed a deep shade of red and bowed in his presence. Her hair was blonde and, while it was not golden like the princess', it still reminded Sern of Aralé. As he made his way through the garden, he found himself wondering how she was, and rather gloomily missing her as he prepared to climb one of the many trees. At the last second, he realized that he could not in his proper attire. Instead, he resignedly sat on one of the many benches, his head in his hands.

Chapter XIII
Róethel

Three days earlier, Maveree had virtually walked off.

As the others had sat around the fire eating, she had risen. "I am leaving. I will return in three sunsets. Unless you have a death wish, do not venture far from here during the day, and do not venture at all in between dusk and dawn."

"You cannot simply abandon us in the middle of the forest!" Aralé had insisted as Maveree tore through her pockets, emptying almost everything. A large intricately designed silver ceremonial knife, two flasks, a pipe, small bags, crystals, rocks, small phials of various shapes filled with substances of every color and consistency, pendulums, small statues, locks of hair, several little books, various common knives, syringes, a flint, a small blowgun, and small incredibly sharp projectiles were all laid on the ground before her.

"I am not abandoning you. As I have said before, I will return in three days, at sunset." With that, Maveree picked up several handfuls of crystals and rocks and put them in her pockets, along with a statue of less than a finger's length tall that looked like a rough rock carving of a nude woman.

"But why must you leave us?" Aralé tried again indignantly. Her hands were on her hips.

"My friend is... difficult. I must prepare myself for any dealings with it."

"It?" Aralé asked suspiciously. "Do you refer to all of your friends as *it*?"

"No, just this one. And it would serve you well to inquire no further about it." With that, the seeress departed, leaving three confused young people and almost the entire contents of her pockets behind. Aralé began to follow her but found that she was thrown back upon reaching the spot where the firelight faded into the darkness of the forest. She let out an angry howl.

"Would you stop being such a child? With all of the noise you are making, it would be a wonder if wolves do not set upon us!" Féian called from the tree he and Nerin occupied. Aralé let out another angry howl before stomping over to a tree on the other side of the fire. Nerin turned to Féian as she struggled to climb it.

"I have an ill feeling about this friend of Mistress Eldestchild's," Nerin whispered to Féian as they lay on the tree branches of a tall tree. Féian rested on his stomach on a branch a short distance above the one Nerin had draped himself across.

"Really?" Féian replied.

"Yes, I recognized some of the stones Maveree took with her. My old healing master, Master Anív, used to utilize crystals for their healing powers and also for personal use. I do not like to use them, but he used them for everything. He taught me of them. With her, Maveree brought amber, jet, lodestone, obsidian, chrysoberyl, dravite, amethyst, and another black stone that I think may have been tourmaline."

"From this distance you could tell?" Féian asked.

"Before you can work as one of Anív's healers, you must be taught about crystals and their uses for exactly one year. It is brutal and almost painfully thorough, but I digress. All of the stones she brought are for clearing, cleansing, and protection from bad forces and energies. Anív used to use jet and obsidian to aid dying patients with the transition."

"And?" Féian asked through a yawn.

"From what you have told me, she has—for lack of better words—nearly unlimited power. Anyone it takes her three days and numerous stones for dispelling malevolence and protection to encounter that she refers to as 'it' worries me," Nerin said and they spent the rest of the night in either silent contemplation or a deep sleep.

The first day brought nothing unexpected. Féian and Nerin talked and ate merrily, enjoying each other's company. They also explored, but never strayed too far. Aralé sat and sulked. The second day brought the same and the third passed similarly. As the last rays of light disappeared on the third day, a drawn and gaunt Maveree returned to them. She looked thinner and weaker, almost as if she should have been an invalid. Her ashen complexion glowed eerily against her dark clothes and the night sky. She stiffly walked over to the place where the water skins were kept and quickly drained two of them.

Aralé began to accost her for this, but Maveree quickly silenced her with only a look. She held the look of a rabid wild animal ready to pounce.

"Everyone, go to sleep. We start early tomorrow," Maveree commanded in a tired voice.

"Where have you—" Aralé began but was quickly interrupted by a shaking Maveree.

"Sleep!" She cried as she attempted vainly to ease her shaking by pressing another stone against her chest. Nerin, Féian, and Aralé climbed into their respective trees for the night. Maveree fell unconscious in the dirt and remained there until morning.

Nerin awoke early the following morning to the sound of footsteps. He peered through the leaves below him to see thick, dark brown hair and a fairly broad back encased in the long top of a swordsman, with long billowing sleeves.

"What has happened here?" A feminine voice asked as the figure bent over Maveree. Nerin then saw standing beside her a grey translucent young woman with unseeing eyes, holding out her arms to reveal the deep bleeding lacerations that ran from her wrists to her elbows. They poured with blood. He screamed as she began to howl with pain and misery at him. He screamed shrilly, falling from the tree and waking the others. As he hit the ground, two other ghostly figures, one who bore a knife through its torso and another whose head hung halfway off of its shoulders, had their cold hands on either of his shoulders. Snarling faces surrounded him as he let out a final shriek before falling unconscious on the forest floor. The last thing he perceived were the unnatural silver eyes of the mysterious woman who had brought such demons with her.

As Nerin lay unconscious, Maveree stood. "Féian, Aralé," she said and they both looked at her. "My friend, Róethel."

Before them stood a broad, fairly tall woman of no more than thirty-five years. Her swarthy complexion had been weathered by the sun and wind and her thick hair was so dark brown it was almost black. It fell past her thighs. She was not the epitome of feminine loveliness nor did she appear ethereal as Aralé did, but she held an earthy beauty. She was dirty and could have passed for a man if her raiment did not show her full figure. She wore two swords about her hips and there was a knife case across her back. Daggers were attached to her boots. Her eyes were unnatural silver and absorbed little flecks of whatever color surrounded her, which in that instance was the deep green of the trees and foliage of the forest.

Aralé nodded, completely unaffected by what had just happened and reached for a water skin. Féian on the other hand stood angrily, glaring at Róethel.

"What have you done to him!?" He bellowed.

"I will never tell you to do this again: follow Aralé's example—" Maveree began caustically, but was interrupted by Féian who demanded to know what Róethel had done to his friend. Maveree ignored him. "Do you see how she is not bothering me?" Maveree said as she placed two large stone pendants around his neck. Féian growled unhappily and then sat beside Maveree.

"I would suggest some silver," Róethel said to Maveree and Maveree then put a silver chain around Nerin's neck.

"My apologies," Róethel said to Féian after a while.

"He will recover?"

"Yes," Róethel replied.

The Persian Rug

"Then I will forgive you, only after you explain what has just happened to my friend."

Róethel took her hands from Nerin's hair and clasped them in her lap. She became pensive for a long while before looking back up at Féian.

"Do you know what an eidolon is?" She said and Féian shook his head. "Sometimes when a person is murdered—"

"What is *murdered*?" Féian interrupted and Róethel looked at him strangely.

"You do not know what murder is? Where do you hail from?"

"Iarnel Eremnad."

"Ah, that explains it. Murder is when one person kills another—"

"How wretched! Why would anyone do such a thing?"

"There are many reasons. However, the myriad reasons behind the infinite number of murders that occur everyday are not relevant to this conversation. Now, you are aware that in every person there is an immortal soul that leaves the body eventually and this eventual departure is commonly known as death, yes?"

"Yes, theÓszerepentth guide the souls from our world to the great light."

"Of course they do," Róethel replied, obviously lost as to what he referred to. "Now, often if a person was murdered, their soul will be separated from their body but they will remain."

"Why?"

"Some are confused or angry. Some seek vengeance or closure. Others may be waiting for their loved ones so they can depart with them. Often, they do not even know that they are dead and spend an eternity thinking that they are living still. Occasionally, there are tasks that they must complete or they have been left behind for some other purpose. There are many, many, many reasons. The angry, confused, or vengeance-seeking tend to congregate around me."

"Why?"

"I am cursed."

"But why?"

"It is retribution."

Just as Féian was about to ask what she had meant, Nerin awoke. He took one look at Róethel and began screaming. It took both Róethel and Féian nearly a quarter of an hour to calm him. He then explained what he had seen to the best of his ability. Róethel, in turn, told him exactly what she had told Féian.

"Aralé, Féian, and Maveree did not see them. Why did I?"

"Only those who know pain can conquer it and only those who understand true suffering can feel another person's. Just as sight and smell come naturally to me, sensing pain comes naturally to you and it is that which has made you both a renowned healer and the only one to see the rather unfortunate wraiths surrounding me."

"Then why can I not see them now?"

"Maveree and I have placed protective stone pendants around your neck, black tourmaline and amber. As long as you wear them, they will not bother you again," Róethel said and Nerin looked down to see a silver chain, a black almost reflective stone and a yellow stone with a large insect trapped in the very center of it. Both stones were mounted in silver.

"Thank you," he said. Róethel placed a hand on his shoulder.

"What are you even doing here in the first place? It is not common that people take midmorning strolls in the middle of the woods," Aralé asked and Róethel looked at her really for the first time that day. Her eyes became wide. She clearly thought that she recognized her. Róethel suddenly looked rather downcast. She ran her hands through her hair and spoke quietly.

"Maveree and I are old friends. Years ago we had an argument for I was being petty. When I tried to apologize, she said that she did not believe in apologies, but if I wanted to earn her forgiveness I would meet her here at the appointed time and do her a great favor."

"And what exactly is that?" Féian asked.

"To protect her and her companions on a journey of the utmost importance," she replied.

"I thought that that was what I was here for," Féian replied.

"It is just as I suspected, you have no real use here," Aralé muttered aloud and Féian glared at her.

"Do you think that I wear these weapons for show? If I felt so inclined, I could have you disarmed and struggling beneath me before you had a chance to tell me that a woman has no right to wield a sword," she seemed to state this as merely fact.

"I doubt it," Féian replied heatedly. "There is only one better than me in my homeland."

"And I could best him easily," she replied with a slight smile. It was not a confident smile or a scornful grin, but rather a barely noticeable amused grin. She was a dangerous adversary. If one were even slightly observant, one would feel it upon first meeting her. She knew this very well and therefore did not feel the need to prove it to anyone. This knowledge made her imperturbable.

"Do you see these markings on my face? They represent the clan of air. A man of air is a man born to wield a sword!"

"Do you see this sword? It is older than you. More men than you will ever meet in your entire life have met their end by it."

"Is that a challenge?"

"Féian," Maveree said flatly. "As much as I love seeing an idiot suffer, this is really not the time. We must be going—"

"No," Róethel replied. Unlike Féian, who was getting incredibly excited, she had remained calm and detached. She sheathed her sword. "If you want to do battle later, I would be glad to, but now as Maveree said, we must be leaving."

"Just forget it Féian. If Maveree trusts her enough to protect her life then she must fight like a knave. Here, have an apple," Nerin said as Maveree gathered the remaining provisions and put them in bags. Féian only stared at him slightly for a good minute, the change in topic so abrupt that it took his mind a moment to comprehend it. When he realized that Nerin was offering him food, as he had taken to doing during the past several days, he scowled.

"All the apples in the world will not change the fact that I have been insulted."

"No, I suppose not, but as a healer I cannot allow you die of malnutrition."

"I am capable of taking care of myself."

"Yes, but you are hungry are you not." It was not a question. Féian grumbled and took the apple. "You vex me," he said eventually.

"Thank you," Nerin replied. Féian was about to respond when Maveree called for them. Róethel stood in front of Maveree and Aralé behind her.

"We have lost much time. However, we should make it to Oran Itae by midnight if we hasten," Maveree said.

With Róethel leading the way through the forest, they resumed their journey.

Chapter XIV
The Revenge of Lord Fén

It was days like the one in question when Sern wondered why he kept Garil in the council. He was a man who everyone had sworn was on his last leg and would die tomorrow (for approximately the last decade). While he was shrewd, unquestioningly loyal to Sern, and knew nearly everything there was to know about running a country properly, he was also incredibly long-winded. While occasionally he would do something to remind everyone exactly why he had been chosen as a council member by the past two kings, the rest of the time he was only a long-winded old man who spoke long after everyone else had stopped listening, if only to hear his own voice, which was cracked and dry and raw from decades of smoking.

"...now that I have said my piece, milord, I present you with the letter sent by King Kerúx," Garil finished and sat down. He then passed Sern a large sealed envelope. Sern thanked him and opened it. He let out a gasp of frustration after his eyes briefly scanned the document.

"It is written in Känakee. Master Virahéen, can you translate it?" Sern then passed the letter to Virahéen who perused it for a long while and then looked up at Sern.

"Phallé-Nal has declared war."

"We are not ready! We do not have enough men or enough weapons! The new recruits are not prepared!" Captain Sólien cried. "We cannot win this war. Boys as young as twelve have been ripped from their mothers' arms and men who have weathered far too many summers to see another battle stand at the ready. We haven't even enough weapons and armor for them all!"

"Do you think I do not know this Sólien!?" Sern yelled. "What do you expect me to do!? War is upon us! We are at a horrid disadvantage!" He then sank back down in his chair. "Have you exhausted every possible option as I told you to?" He finally said.

Sólien nodded, "Yes milord."

"Do not lie to me. If you had, the armies of the Sea Cities, Nallel, and The Isles of the Sun would be here. Possibly even the men of the forest tribes of the Ariyekk would stand with us."

"Nallel and the men of the forest tribes refused to come to our aid. They say they are too busy fighting each other—" Sólien was interrupted.

"Fools!" Virahéen exclaimed. "They have been warring for centuries!"

"Did you tell the men of the forest tribes that we would become their allies and fight Nallel with them in return?" Sern asked.

"Yes, and they say that monarchs are not to be trusted and that they want nothing to do with us and our doomed war. The king of the Sea Cities will only do it if we give him some of our land by the coast, and the Castle of Féniú. He has coveted it for years."

"Then let him have it!" Sern cried.

"We will have to take that land from one of our more powerful nobles. Lord Fén's family has owned that land for centuries," Sólien replied.

"If he is loyal to Laaven, he will relinquish it. If he refuses to yield freely, then we will not give him a choice," Sern said and Virahéen groaned.

"Lord Fén already loathes you for dishonoring his son as you did. Do you really think that he will want to be of service to you? And he is an infamously stubborn and foul-tempered man to begin with."

"Like I said, either he will cede of his own volition or he will die a traitor, rotting away in the catacombs of the castle. Such a thing has been done to peasants for less," Sern reminded them. None in the council argued.

"I will personally go and see Lord Fén. This council is dismissed," he said and left. He then stormed back to his chambers to get his sword, daggers, and an apple for his horse. He kept all of his weapons hidden in dark corners and beneath furniture. He pulled one of his daggers out from beneath his pillow, his sword out from its hiding place in the midst of a large vase of blue flowers, and his other dagger from the back of his desk drawer. The small daggers he kept in his boots were hidden in the middle of a hollowed out book. He then took an apple for his horse out of one of the fruit bowls, which was only supposed to be for decoration. Just as he walked to the door, he heard loud knocking.

"Milord, it is I, Virahéen." Sern opened the door to see the man standing before him. "You were not planning on visiting the most powerful noble in the realm looking like that were you?" He said with a sad smile.

"What is wrong with the way I look?" Sern asked honestly.

"Lord Fén will not take you seriously if you arrive looking as if you are ready to spend a fortnight in the wild, milord. Your clothes are weatherworn and look as if you have even repaired them yourself on occasion, your hair is a mess. When is the last time you washed it? You are not clean-shaven. You are wearing all black (you are not going to a funeral). Kings do not carry weapons for they have their guard to protect them, and you even smell like the woods. You *smell* like the woods! How is that even possible when you spend almost all of your time in the castle?"

"I slept outside last night."

"Why? What in the name of all that has ever lived and died is wrong with you?"

"After you spend years in battle sleeping on the ground in a tent (on occasion you do not even have a tent), you cannot fall asleep in a bed."

"You are going to have to learn. You are not a warrior or a wayfarer anymore. Now, I am calling the servants and you will be groomed properly. Fén already thinks that you are unfit do to circumstance. You can be exceedingly regal when you wish to be so. Change his mind."

"I suppose you are right. I need to present myself in a more ceremonious way if I wish to be taken genuinely. However, I will never go clean-shaven."

"Why ever not?" Virahéen replied with a groan.

"Practicality. It keeps out the cold."

"We are in the south. It is never cold here."

"Please send for the servants to *groom* me," Sern replied and quickly shut the door. Within minutes, an entire host of servants had arrived to bathe and dress him. He lacked the patience for it and ended up hurrying them through the majority of the preparations. When they attempted to get him into a more brightly colored ensemble, he refused and ended up wearing an outfit that was almost entirely black with the exception of an extremely minimal amount of silver. He found that he could not fit his daggers in the boots and from that moment on detested it.

After deciding only to bring his sword, he let a small entourage guard him on his journey. They rode for nearly an entire day to get to the coast and arrived late in the night to find no guards at the gates. The lawns were overgrown and there was an eerie silence about the place. The stone statues and fountains, which had formerly decorated the place, had been deliberately demolished. The windows in the house were broken and glass lay scattered on the lawn. The land for miles around had been scorched and destroyed.

Upon entering the house, it was obvious that it had been set fire to. Everything in it was destroyed. The rotting cadavers of household pets were scattered about. Anything of value had been defaced or marred beyond recognition. In places, the staircase had been blown apart so the upper levels could not be accessed. Parts of the walls were missing. The castle had been demolished. There was no possible way to restore it.

"We are condemned to die," Sern said quietly after a while, falling to his knees in the rubble.

"Milord?" Several of the men of the entourage who were within earshot turned toward him.

"The king of the Sea Cities will not trade the lives of his men for leagues of fallow scorched earth and a castle that has been destroyed. His armies will not come to our aid."

"We still have the armies of The Isles of the Sun. Their queen loves you. She has already agreed to send her armies," one of the bodyguards replied.

"Even so, the southern army is outnumbered five to one."

"But we have you."

"Me?"

"Yes," a different bodyguard replied. "Our leader is Sern. Men from the other southern armies are coming of their own free will just to fight beside you, hundreds of them. More slaves than ever before are risking their lives escaping from the north, so they can risk their lives fighting for you. Do you not know this?"

"No," Sern replied. "I did not."

"You serve the commoners, who are the most underserved of all people. In the short time you have ruled, you have done much for us. If there is anyone we would fight for it would be you," the bodyguard said and Sern remained silent for a long while.

After almost an hour, he stood. "Have the horses been watered and rested?" He asked.

"Aye milord," the bodyguards replied.

"Then we return to the castle," he said and the others nodded. They departed.

Chelsea Isadora Teich

Chapter XV
Oran Itae

O ran Itae was a settlement of fair size, hidden in the Ariyekk forest, with a scandalous reputation. Murderers, thieves, criminals, brothels, and every illegal activity imaginable thrived in the city. While only Maveree and Róethel, who nearly lived there, had been there before, both Aralé and Nerin had heard of it and what they had heard left them near shaking with trepidation. Nerin was sure that they were going to be killed upon entering. Aralé did her best to explain Oran Itae in its quintessence to Féian, who only seemed excited to view more of the world.

They had arrived at the end of a long road lined with almost dilapidated looking buildings. The streets were packed with men and women, all in various states of decay. There was so much noise that one could scarcely hear themselves think and everything was scented with pipe smoke, ale, wine, and unwashed bodies. Aralé nearly vomited from the putrid aroma as they made their way along the road. Several times, they had to dodge flying mugs, bottles of ale, bodies, and even swords. Quite a few men shouted rude licentious comments at Aralé. They seemed too afraid of Róethel to say anything.

Finally, Maveree came to a stop in front of one of the better looking buildings. Not that there was much to say for it. Two of the windows on its façade were boarded up and there were holes in the door. The porch in front of it was splintering. On the porch sat a sickly thin and haggard old man with a long neglected beard and thin, greasy silver hair. A pipe was placed in between cracked twisted lips.

"Old Fogey!" Maveree said as if she were waking him up. He seemed to jolt awake and then looked at her.

"Well, if it ain't not the li'l mistress!" He said, his voice barely a scratch but his eyes shining. "Been awhile since you came 'round th'Grave!" He exclaimed, gesturing toward the building behind him.

"This inn is called *The Grave*?" Aralé blurted out disbelievingly.

"Yes lady, Th' Queen's Grave. That not 'greeable t'you?" He asked with contempt.

"Forgive her, she's a southerner," Maveree said and Old Fogey nodded as if that explained it.

"Then again northerners jus' s'bad. Th'snobbery!" He said with a sardonic laugh. "In any case, yer rooms ready, juss as ye said the last time y'were about."

"You remembered," Maveree said with a smile.

"I may be old but I ain't gone...yet."

The pair shared a laugh. "My thanks," Maveree said and entered. Féian, Nerin, Aralé, and Róethel followed. The outside of the building may have appeared neglected but the inside was not much better. There were only mismatched pieces of what might have once been fine furniture indiscriminately strewn about what appeared to be the bar and lobby of the Queen's Grave. Men all well-dressed but either dirty or just classless were strewn about the room as well. While these men did not shout rude things at Aralé, they were most certainly not ignoring her or averting their eyes politely. She sighed miserably and looked at Róethel pleadingly for it seemed that the men would not dare say such things to her. Róethel, in turn, placed her hand on the hilt of her sword and glared at them. They stopped immediately.

They walked through this lobby to a staircase. There was blood on the outermost railing near the bottom and the stairs were old and splintering. The wood floor of the upper level was in a similar condition and lined with old wooden doors. Many had chunks taken out of them in various places. Maveree led them to a door that had a knife sticking out of it. She bent down and pulled it free from the wood, examining it.

"Pure gold, very nice," she muttered before turning to Nerin, Féian, and Aralé. "You three will share this room. Róethel and I will be in the room across from yours." She gestured toward the two rooms and then opened the door to theirs, nearly shoving them inside. "Do not leave this room. Rest. We will spend no more than three days here and then there will be about a week before we reach the city of Merend Faaj."

"Rest well," Róethel said and, with that, they departed.

They entered the room to find it of a fair size with nothing in it but a window and two beds. Neither had sheets, but each had a thin old blanket. Only one had a pillow. The walls were white.

"I am taking the bed with the pillow," Aralé said as she pounced on the indicated bed. "And I sleep alone." She then kicked off her boots and all of her outer clothes and threw them on the floor beside the bed. Nerin and Féian grudgingly took the other bed. Féian stripped himself of everything but his leggings and collapsed on the bed. He was exhausted. Nerin slid in beside him.

"You do not even take your boots off before you go to sleep?"

"No."

"Why not?" Féian asked

"My feet are cold," he replied flatly and rolled over. Féian sighed and went to sleep.

"It has been a long time," Maveree said after a gulp of ale. She and Róethel sat at one of the tables in the lobby, each with a drink.

"Seventeen years," Róethel replied. They sat in a comfortable silence for a while before Róethel spoke again. "She looks exactly like her mother."

"What?"

"Aralé, looks exactly like her mother."

"You miss her," Maveree replied. It was not a question.

"Those were good years with you and her. I even have missed you on occasion," Róethel replied quietly. "Even though I know that you cannot say the same."

"I have thought about you often. Now that Eriver has passed, you are the only friend I have left here."

Róethel's eyes became wide. "No."

"Yes."

"Maveree I—"

"Eriver, son of Doveetth: born January tenth eighteen sixty-four, died April twenty-sixth nineteen seventy-seven."

"But, that was yesterday!"

"Yes," Maveree said sadly, resting her head against the table. "He held on and suffered for weeks in the hopes that he would see me again and I wasn't there."

"Maveree I—"

Maveree silenced her by slamming her fist into the table.

"You could have stayed with him."

"No, life does not care if your loved one is dying or if you yourself are dying with them. It moves along regardless of whether you are able to move along with it or not. If you do not, then you are left behind. The opportune moment presented itself and I had to grab it even if it meant leaving my father to his death bed alone. Nor had I the time to grieve. There were things I had to and still must do."

"There are always *things you must do*. As long as I have known you there have always been *things you must do*. What are these *things* this time?"

"They involve traveling through the south and then through the warring north to a desolate wasteland of ice. Where this wasteland meets the sea, there is a mountain and at the top of this mountain there is a sacred shrine that runs never endingly with blood—"

"You intend to make a wish at the blood fount atop The Empyrean Stairway!" Róethel gasped as quietly as possible. "Have you lost your mind!? Men have died seeking it in the past!"

"Ah, but they did not already know where it is."

"And how do you intend to survive the thousands of leagues of storms and ice that separate the outskirts of Phallé-Nal from The Empyrean Stairway?"

"Merend Zetth."

"Merend Zetth? They actually let you in? They kill outsiders on sight."

"The lord of the city is fond of me. He will grant us respite for as long as we require, and even give us supplies. He always has a gift for me."

"How do you intend to survive Phallé-Nal? One does not simply walk in and out!"

"Incognito."

"As what?"

"You will be a young man transporting slaves. You will ride a horse and they will all be tied and walk behind you."

"That is ludicrous!"

"No. It really is not."

"What do you want so exceedingly that you are willing to put yourself through all of this?"

"I will not be putting myself through that much in earnest. I will be riding in front of you, hidden under your cloak."

"So you will make them walk, but you will not?"

"Yes, but it is not only because it is more convenient for me."

"Oh, really? Enlighten me."

"Northern spies saw Aralé, Nerin, and I enter the caves within the Golden Mountains."

"So, they think that you are trying to protect Aralé and are having all in their kingdom keep an eye open for you, for where you are she will be."

"Yes, and I cannot afford to lose Aralé now. I need her. While the dirt of the road, hunger, and exhaustion have made her almost unrecognizable, the same cannot be said for me."

"Of course not, you are Mistress Maveree Eldestchild. You are the most recognizable face in the world."

"Which is only an advantage most of the time," Maveree replied and Róethel nodded.

"Maveree, I still do not understand why you do this."

"You know my story correct?"

"Yes, you were cursed to remain a child after the Year of the Uprising because as Zetth died you gave an oath that you would grant his last wish to free all of the slaves in Phallé-Nal and see to it that their empire fell. Then, even after you promised you would do this great thing in his honor, you decided your time would be better spent laying on a table in the Queen's Grave drinking yourself to death."

"Naturally," Maveree added through a gulp of ale.

"So, you are cursed to remain a child, for only a child would be as fickle, until you fulfill his final wish and your oath…you are going to wish for the fall of Phallé-Nal," Róethel finished and Maveree nodded.

"More or less."

"What do you mean *more or less*?"

"I mean that what you say is more than true but less than accurate."

"What does that even mean?"

"That you have not unequivocally predicted me."

"Has anyone ever been able to?"

"No, I am fairly unpredictable."

"That is the biggest understatement of the last ten thousand years!" Róethel exclaimed and they both took a long drink. The conversation then turned to lighter matters, such as the past escapades they had shared and adventures they had while they were apart.

"Féian, what in the name of all that has ever lived and died did you do to him?" Aralé bellowed. Nerin had sat up in the middle of the night as everyone slept and let out a shriek so ear piercing that even the people in the adjacent buildings had been awoken. Aralé had been having a lovely dream about a table piled high with food and was absolutely furious at being disturbed and reminded of her hunger.

"He did not do anything," Nerin replied sheepishly. "Just go back to sleep," he said and rolled over.

Aralé rolled her eyes and let out a disgusted snort before throwing herself dramatically back onto her pillow. Féian watched her though half-lidded eyes until he was certain that she was asleep. He then turned over to find Nerin awake and shaking violently.

"Nerin," Féian whispered and Nerin did not respond. He stared blankly ahead as he shook. The scars on his neck and arms showed. Suddenly, his tensed muscles relaxed and his body collapsed. "What happened to you?" He asked as he traced one of the scars with his finger. It was deep and looked as if it had even gotten infected. They sat in silence for a long moment.

"Would you really like to know?"

"Of course," Féian replied. Nerin then looked pensive for several minutes before beginning.

"Do you know what a slave is?"

"No."

"Do you know how in Iarnel Eremnad the men and women who own a home take care of it and cook themselves and do everything themselves?"

"Yes."

"Well, in the north you can buy a person, just like you can buy a hound or spices, and force them to do or be anything you want until either the day they die, the day you sell them to another master, or the day they are no longer useful. On that day you kill them."

"That is horrible...you were a slave?"

"Yes. I was born to a peasant hunter and weaver in a small village outside of Phallé-Nal. I had nine brothers and sisters. I only remember the name of one of my older sisters, Aamahla. I have always been of very slight build for a man. I was the littlest boy in my village. In the village, they needed men only to hunt and protect the women and children. I was not strong enough to fight or fast enough to hunt therefore my parents saw no use for me. They were sure to let me know.

"When I was seven years old, they sold Aamahla and me to a man who kept us locked in a room with a number of other slaves for months. They sold her because not one man in the village wanted her for a wife. She killed herself in that room. I watched them throw her corpse into the street, like it was garbage!

"First, I was sold to a man whose name I cannot recall. I cleaned. One day, I accidentally broke a window. This angered him so he sold me to a lonely old widow named Veerah. She was very kind to me and loved me like a son. She taught me how to read and write and whatever she could about healing. When I was eleven, she died and I was sent to an auction. One of the royal princes, a man named Avarat, bought me. He was a cruel man who ignored his young wife, Jaeah. Rumor had it that he was home less than a month out of the year.

"She and I were friends for she was only four or five years older than I was. We grew fairly close over the years that I lived there. However, I had lived there for three years before I had even seen her husband. She was not beautiful, but nor was she ugly. She was very slight and short and had a mess of red hair that hung down past her knees. She bought me all of the books on healing and any ingredients I ever needed. I cleaned in his house as well.

"When I was fifteen, Jaeah became with child by one of the wine stewards. I don't know his name, but I know that she was in love with him. When Avarat came home and found his wife a number of months along, he not only nearly beat her to death, but wanted to see the man who had done it to her punished. Jaeah could not bear the thought of the man she loved suffering as she knew he would be if he were caught, so she told Avarat that it was I. At the time, I had no idea what she had done.

"One night when I was asleep in one of the slave houses, his men came and dragged me to the dungeons where I was tortured with whips, brands, knives, spears, swords that had been left in the fire, maces, chains, sticks and manacles. Many times, I was

The Persian Rug

tied down and the most brutish warriors that they had would beat me. The entire time a bag was kept over my head so I could not see and only feel, which intensifies sensation.

"Every night, my wounds were salted, the bag was taken off of my head, and I was thrown into a dungeon where there was a piece of stale bread and water. I do not know how many nights or days this went on, but by the end I felt nothing. I remember that one day they branded welts that had been made by a large man bringing metal chains as hard as he could down on my back, and I knew that it hurt. I just did not feel it. Perhaps I did not even care. It was then that Avarat said that my punishment ended. As I walked back up from the dungeons to the main level of the house, he told me that the child Jaeah had told him was mine had been born deformed and was left for the wolves, like all undesirables are in the north.

"The next thing I knew I was thrown outside, in the middle of the winter, naked by the eaves of the forest. The baby was there, lying frozen. It had only one eye. I couldn't stay there with it. I could not *die* with it. I ran until I came to one of the ports of the city. An intoxicated man was loading rugs onto a raft that he said would float downstream to the Oran. Thinking I was a hallucination, he laid me in the middle of the rugs.

"I do not know for how long I floated downstream. All I know is that I do not remember arriving in the Oran. There, I was cared well for and my wounds were properly treated because they abhor slavery and always aid escaped slaves. By my sixteenth birthday, I had arrived in Laaven with the intention of seeing if I could become an apprentice to Master Healer Anív. He took one look at me and made me an apprentice. I studied and practiced everyday and before long I was second only to him—"

"Would you mind? I am trying to sleep!" Aralé snapped.

Nerin only glanced down at the bed beneath him. Féian glared at her. "You are unbelievable!" He said coldly.

"And you two are suddenly incredibly chatty! Unless you are planning your wedding, I suggest you cease your prattling!"

Féian jolted out of the bed, looking as if he could kill her.

"Féian please—" Nerin began.

"Yes, you should listen to him. If you do not, he will make you sleep on the floor," Aralé replied with a smirk and Féian lunged at her.

"Every time you open your mouth, I just want to kill you!" He cried.

"Hmm, you are not enough of a man. You became upset when Maveree killed that worthless deer."

"You are lower than an animal! I would not lament driving a sword through you!"

"Oh, really?"

They both stopped upon hearing the door slammed shut.

"Look what you have done! You upset him!" Féian cried.

"What an awful wretch I am," she replied flatly. "How shall I ever live with myself?"

"I thought that you loved him!"

"He loved me, I needed entertainment. And trust me, if I would have ever seen how deformed he is, I never would have wasted my time."

"He was tortured!"

"It does not matter *why* he is hideous."

"You are despicable!"

"What an awful wretch I am. How shall I ever live with myself?"

"It is people of your race like you that convinced my people to hide away!"

"Do I really have to say it again?"

Féian fled the room in an angry rage. Aralé sighed and grabbed the blanket from Nerin's and Féian's bed and laid it atop her blanket. She then crawled back into her bed and went to sleep.

Féian left the room to find Nerin sitting against the wall in between two of the doors. His head was in his hands.

"I am sorry," he whispered as Féian approached.

"You do not have to be. Aralé is one cold, cold woman. That is by no fault of yours."

"I am pathetic Féian. I am afraid of everything. Even in my dreams I am afraid. I live in fear."

"You are not pathetic. After going through what you have gone through…I would have killed myself. I would have lain in the snow next to that dead child and frozen to death. I would have given up," Féian said and Nerin did not reply, but he visibly relaxed somewhat. "Come, you need to rest," he said and dragged Nerin back into the room to find that Aralé had taken their blanket.

Chelsea Isadora Teich

Chapter XVI
Queen Erié

Sern and the rest of the palace officials stood behind the gates of the palace awaiting the arrival of the queen of The Isles of the Sun and her battalion. They had been reported within view of the castle and, soon after, the sounds of countless heavily-armored warriors on horseback tearing through the city overpowered every other sound. Almost as soon as it had commenced, it ceased.

"They have arrived, milord," one of the watchmen called from atop one of the watchtowers and Sern signaled to him to open the gate. "Open the gate!" The watchmen called and the gate was opened to reveal hundreds of glorious swarthy warriors in gleaming mail and armor reminiscent of nightmarish animals and hellish creatures. Ferocious bears, eagles, foxes, wolves, snakes, hawks, raven, and demonic fanged and winged creatures could be seen for leagues holding their dreadful weapons aloft. They looked positively fearsome, as if they had just crawled from the darkest corners of the earth. In front of them stood a tall lean figure in darker armor and a fanged helmet, which had black scales and yellow eyes upon it. It climbed off of a golden horse.

The figure then removed its helmet to reveal the beautiful face of a woman. Her wide, dark eyes smiled at Sern as her full mouth remained even and expressionless. She of dark countenance stood nearly as tall as he. Her dark hair had been woven into intricate braids and tied in a knot behind her. Standing erect, she held the presence of a goddess of war. "Hail his immortality, Sern, the

Steward of Laaven!" She bellowed and her entire army echoed in chorus and bowed.

"Hail her eminence, Erié, Queen of The Isles of the Sun!" Laaven's army, along with all of the others in the courtyard, repeated and bowed. Then the foreign warriors departed. They had camped in the woods, refusing to accept any hospitality aside from two meals a day. The queen came forward toward Sern.

"My men wish to rest, for we have traveled for the past three days and two nights without more than several pauses in our journey to water the horses. I think that you and I, however, have some lost time to atone for," she said quietly so none could hear but him.

"I think that you just may be right," he replied. He then turned to Virahéen. "Her royal highness and I have much to discuss. We shall be in my study. Please have food and drink brought to us. Other than that, see to it that we are not bothered."

"Yes, milord," Virahéen replied and walked away. Sern took Queen Erié respectfully by the hand and led her through the castle to his study. The old friends spoke of simple friendly matters and arrived at Sern's study to find a bowl of fruit, cheese, bread, meat, and two different types of wine were waiting for them.

"How lovely," Queen Erié said with a smile as Sern locked the door behind them.

"Indeed," Sern replied as he finished locking the door. Within seconds after the door was locked, they were locked in an embrace.

"It is so great to see you again!" Erié exclaimed.

"Yes, we should never go four years apart from one another," Sern replied.

"It is a shame that we have to meet again under such wretched circumstances," Erié replied as she broke from Sern's embrace and began to shed her armor. She left it lying on the floor as she sat next to Sern only in her long underclothes. She poured them both a goblet of wine.

"Did you know that it is not only the armies of my country that came to your aid? As we passed through the Oran, an army of over half a thousand men asked to join our cause. Some were renegades from Nallel and a surprising amount were escaped slaves from the north. Nearly one hundred warriors from the Northern Isles left with us from The Isles of the Sun."

"I knew of the renegades and the escaped slaves but I knew nothing of the men of the Northern Isles. I am surprised that they would concern themselves with our war."

"You forget that my husband, Oenír, may his spirit be at peace, was one of their people. Two of my children live among their father's people now. Your war is my war and my war is their war."

"Ah, I see," Sern replied and they sat in silence for a long while, eating and drinking heartily.

"So, what happened to Danút?" The queen asked after she had eaten her fill.

"Who?"

"Danút, the appointed steward."

"He did not want to be steward because he was certain that we would lose the impending war. Any other possible candidate for the position held the same view. Someone told him that I would be the only man fool enough to accept my doom so he asked me. I accepted and he fled along with the majority of the aristocracy," Sern replied sadly.

"Your doom…if you are so certain of failure then why not simply surrender or attempt to make a deal with King Kerúx?"

"Kerúx is in league with Risúrat. He is an evil man and cannot be trusted. He is the adversary of all that is good in the world. It is better to die a fool in battle than a coward hiding wherever you may find room."

"So then for you this is not about victory, but a lesser degree of defeat."

"If you are one for semantics—"

She stopped him and clasped his face gently in her hands. She looked almost heartbroken. "There is no hope in your heart?"

"Eríé, I—"

"Could you not have just told me that there is hope!? Could

you not have just led me to believe that I am not about to sacrifice the lives of hundreds of my people? Could you not have made this so obviously our final farewell?"

"You are an intrepid, profound woman and I respect you. I would never lie to you."

"You find hope when there is seemingly none. If you cannot find hope, then this must truly be your doom."

"It is."

"If I were selfish, I would ask you not to fight."

"But you are not."

"You think too highly of me."

"Eríé, there are some battles that must be fought and there is not one battle more important than your last."

"So you cannot be dissuaded."

"I do not see you trying to dissuade your countrymen. Do you not love them as well?"

The queen dropped her empty wineglass. It shattered all over the rug. "If you were of royal blood, I would have married you instead of Oenír. I did not hate him, but nor did I love him when he shared my bed and even now as he lays dead I cannot truthfully say that I love him."

"As a monarch, you are first bound to your country and tradition and duty and not me. You should weep for your countrymen and not for one insignificant man."

"Emotions rarely coincide with reason. You are only so logical because your heart does not hinder you. That wretched imp of a princess tore it out still beating," Eríé finished and shed silent tears. As she grieved, Sern took her hand. When he took his hand away, a little round red gem on a silver chain rested in her palm.

"What is this?" The queen asked.

"It is a gift from an old friend. It grants the wearer wisdom and vision."

"But, why would you want me to have this?"

"Where I will be going wisdom is irrelevant and where you will be going it is incredibly relevant."

"Where are you going?"

"To whatever lays beyond death."

"And where am I going?"

"Back to your homeland as soon as possible before their armies come, where there are still thousands of people in need of you."

"I know this," she said sadly. Sern then placed the gem and chain about her neck. She collapsed against him.

"When do you leave?" He asked quietly as he held her, carding his fingers through her hair. He did not speak of his own grief for it was not his way, but it was writ in his face.

"Tomorrow morning," she replied.

Chelsea Isadora Teich

Chapter XVIII
Merend Faaj

Aralé had sat down on the ground. Her legs were crossed as were her arms.

"Get up and stop carrying on like a dolt of a child. We are less than an hour from Merend Faaj," Maveree ordered and Aralé only glared at her. "Aralé, now or I swear that I will kill you in the most painful way possible." Maveree tried again, overexertion making her even more impatient and misanthropic than usual.

"You run us ragged. I am going no further without a rest!" Aralé said as she rolled her eyes and muttered something about how ridiculous Maveree was.

"You can rest in the city."

"I want to rest now!"

"It would be impossible for me to care any less about what you want!"

"I want to rest *now*!"

"Maveree...." Róethel said as she looked around, suddenly wary. She was ignored.

"If you do not rise, I will have Róethel drag you to the city!"

"At least I will not have to walk."

"You will walk!"

"Maveree..." Róethel attempted to get her attention and was again ignored.

"No, I will not!"

"Yes you will!"

"No I—" Aralé stopped, nearly fainting as a knife flew through the air and a man, whom none had seen approach, fell to the ground. The knife jutted out from his shoulder and blood gushed from it. At that second, an arrow was fired at Róethel from the trees and she deflected it with one of her swords.

"On the ground," she demanded of her companions and they immediately did as she said. Narrowly dodging all of the arrows that were fired at her, she made her way over to the wounded bleeding man she had hit with one of her knives. She held his weak bleeding body against her and dug the knife into his shoulder slightly to make him howl in pain.

"With the next arrow fired, I cleave your man's arm. Show yourselves," she demanded in a deadly, even voice, and her sere eyes flashed angrily. Immediately, over a dozen men stepped out of the shadows and out from behind the trees and foliage that lined the road. They were dressed in earthy colors and had no armor. Some were archers while others carried swords or long knives. They surrounded Róethel.

"Who are you?" One of them asked.

"I believe that you are in no position to be asking questions," she said and shook the knife in the man's shoulder slightly. He screamed in agony as she crushed his limp body against her. Several of the men surrounding them gasped. "Now why did you attack us? Are you renegades or slavers?"

"Neither Lady, we are the guardians of Merend Faaj."

"Then why attack us?"

"You are intruders. Only one of our own or a northern spy would know this way into our city."

"Then why not simply—" she stopped upon hearing a sword being unsheathed. She looked to see a man holding Maveree against his chest with a sword across her throat. Róethel grew pale and immediately dropped her sword and pulled the knife from the man's arm. They completely disarmed Róethel and afterward bound, blindfolded and dragged Maveree and her party the rest of the way into the city. Once there, they were thrown into an old cellar that had become a place where those awaiting trial from the town leader, an older man named Evrynd, would be held. Unfortunately, Evrynd was away on errands for his wife and would not return until the following day.

"Maveree, how on earth did you not see this coming?" Aralé demanded as she lay on the floor of a makeshift prison bound and blindfolded.

"What kind of a seeress are you?" Féian asked as he tried to move onto his side, to ease the pain in his ribs from lying on his stomach for so long, and almost rolled on top of Róethel's hands, which were bound.

"Féian," she growled angrily. He had been jabbing and rolling on top of her for hours.

Maveree did not answer. She had long ago escaped her bonds and was sitting atop one of the many crates in dungeon drinking wine from an old bottle she had found. "Did you know that this was a wine cellar before the rebels overran the city?" She said as she took another long drink. She looked at the damage the tight ropes had done to her wrists. They were an angry red and raw to the touch.

"How *very* interesting," Aralé muttered and attempted to move. She kneed Nerin in the side and he didn't respond. "Is Nerin alive?"

"He fainted," Maveree stated. "Does that really surprise any of you?"

"Not particularly," Aralé replied and Féian began to grumble at her. The young woman was about to respond when suddenly she stopped. "Why do I smell wine?"

"This used to be a wine cellar. I was trying to escape my bonds when I jostled something and wine spilled all over me," Maveree said as she sat on one of the old empty wooden crates and tilted her head back so she could see out of a small hole in the cellar door. It provided one ray of light into the dark cellar. This light grew fainter and fainter until it faded all together. Moments after that the cellar door sprang free and two cloaked men climbed into the cellar. One held a lantern before him.

They looked at Maveree, who sat on the crate before them unbound and drinking wine to her heart's content. Suddenly, they recognized her. "Mistress Eldestchild?" The one who held the lantern gasped as the light of it illuminated the cellar and revealed the small form of the seeress.

"Yes?" She said flatly, lighting a pipe. He only gaped at her. "Untie my friends," she ordered.

"Yes. Yes. Of course, mistress," he muttered and immediately began untying Nerin. The others followed in short order. The man then led them out of the makeshift prison and out into a lush green lawn before a house of fair size. The men gasped as she emerged.

"Where is Evrynd?" She asked and immediately two men volunteered to take her to him. She then beckoned for Róethel, Nerin, Féian, and Aralé to follow.

She led them into the large house behind him to find it dark and seemingly empty. They were led through the dark foyer to a large old tapestry that hung against the far wall. One of the men leading them pulled it aside to reveal a wooden door. He rapped his gloved knuckles against it four times.

"Enter!" A sharp voice called from within and one of the men opened the door to reveal a well-lit study. The walls were bare and there were only several bookshelves of moderate size and a desk against the far wall. A tall man with long greying hair and piercing blue eyes sat behind it. He was absorbed in his work, which was writing in a large book. His long skeletal fingers were stained black with ink.

"Evrynd," Maveree said after several minutes and he looked up from his work at the sound of her voice, finally perceiving all of those who stood before him.

"Maveree?" His beady eyes widened in surprise as much as they could.

"Yes Evrynd?" She replied with a smile.

"I apologize for my men attacking you. It is just that you have not been here for nearly twenty years and since then nearly all of our guard have been replaced. They did not recognize you."

The Persian Rug

"It is nothing," Maveree answered. "The loss was yours."

"So I have heard," Evrynd then looked to Róethel and placed a myriad of knives and swords on his desk. "I believe that these are yours."

Róethel nodded and took them, quickly putting her swords back about her hips, her knives on her boots, and her long knife across her back. The others were hidden in her traveling cloak or in her sleeves. Evrynd watched her suspiciously. "You look familiar," he said finally. "From whence do you come?"

"Any place will do, yet I belong to no country. I am a wanderer," Róethel said as she finished strapping a small knife to her wrist beneath one of her sleeves.

"Indeed," Evrynd replied before turning back to Maveree. "What brings you, and your most singular company, to our city?"

"We are merely passing through," Maveree said. "We seek The Empyrean Stairway."

Evrynd began to laugh. "That is ridiculous! No one has ever even seen it!"

"Then how do we know it is there?"

"We do not. It is a myth, and a dangerous one at that. Men have died seeking it."

"Evrynd, do you think I would go after it if I did not already know it was there?"

At this all mirth drained from the man's long weathered face. He seemed pensive for quite some time as his long fingers drummed a soft beat against the old wooden top of his desk. "Maveree, I need to speak with you privately."

"Will my companions be given shelter and food?"

"If it is what you desire."

"It is."

"Then it would be my pleasure."

"Indeed," Maveree replied and then Evrynd called for one of his assistants. He gave the man orders to see to it that Féian, Aralé, Róethel, and Nerin were sheltered and fed properly. They were then led away. Evrynd locked the door behind him and returned to his desk. Maveree shoved some of his papers off of his desk and then hopped up onto it.

"Are you out of your mind?"

"No."

"Then what could you possibly want that is so important that you are willing to…"

"Willing to *what*, Evrynd?"

"Maveree, nothing is for free. You must drink a cup of witch's blood from the fountain for your wish to be granted, but first you must give exactly what you take."

"I know this."

"So, you want something badly enough that you are willing to drain a cup of blood from another's veins! You are willing to kill!"

"Absolutely."

"Maveree, it is suicide! There have been accounts of men who have even found the blood fount and made their sacrifice and even so they were killed. Some accounts state that their bodies or bones were spit out of the cave or that angry spirits emerged and devoured them. In the past, thirty-one documented parties have left in search of it. Ten of these thirty-one parties were never seen again. In seven cases, the majority of the party never returned and the few who did returned telling of the horrible poltergeists that guarded the fount and the mountain and how all of their comrades were killed in front of them. The rest made it only a portion of the way and had to turn back."

"Yes, but the seven who returned telling of the wrath of the guardians of the fount did not possess one crucial piece of information."

"And what is that?"

"That not any old blood will do. The Ziríva believed in balance. An eye for an eye, a good deed for a good deed. The pure and hallowed blood of an ancient and the profane blood of today's mortal man are no where near equal. You must give exactly what you take in order to achieve equilibrium. If you take the blood of the divine and spiritual, then you must give the blood of the divine and spiritual back."

"That is all well and good, aside from the fact that you are the closest thing to a living witch there has been in thousands of years! The Ziríva are an extinct race."

"While there has not been a person able to make rain or levitate or heal others at will for centuries, the old bloodlines are far from extinct. You, yourself are of such blood."

"I am?"

"Yes."

"Well, I refuse to be your sacrifice."

"Come, I could never ask such a thing of you."

"I do not think you would hesitate to if there was no other."

"It is a good thing for you that there are nine hundred sixty-five others I could choose from."

"How do you know this?"

"I am a seeress. I can know anything I wish to know at will."

"Whom do you intend to sacrifice?"

"There are two with me who would suffice."

"And how exactly did you convince them to come along?"

"One was planning on running away to the Northern Isles and I told said person that their body would not be able to handle the cold. I told them that they would die a slow and painful death, coughing and choking on their own fluids until one day their throat eventually gave out—"

"Is that the truth?"

"Yes, I had a vision of it. I saw it as clearly as you see me sitting before you, Evrynd. The other thinks we are going on a noble quest, which is rather comical when you think about it," she said with a few quick chuckles.

"You are utterly wretched...but clever," Evrynd said as he shook his head.

"If my survival and happiness depended upon me being sweet and kind and naïve, then that is what I would be."

"I doubt it."

Maveree opened her mouth to reply and instead yawned.

"Are you tired my dear?"

"Yes," Maveree said through another yawn.

"Will you be staying with your friends, or would you rather take my bed and I will sleep elsewhere."

"Do you not share a bed already with your wife?"

"She will not sleep in the same room with me. She says that I snore. But it matters not. She has made me so miserable over the past years that I do not ever want to see her again, let alone share a bed with her."

"I suppose I shall take your bed then," Maveree answered quickly.

"You are so sympathetic."

"What do you expect me to say to comfort you, Evrynd? You are not exactly a wonderful husband but now is not the time for that. Show me to your chambers. If I remember correctly, you have the softest bed in the north."

"Very well," Evrynd replied and led her from his study to his chambers, where he left her to a peaceful night's sleep.

Chapter XVIII

Sahena

The sun had barely started to rise as a lone figure made its way up the heavily guarded gates of the Laaven castle. It was a tiny cloaked figure without a horse or carriage, walking barefoot through the dust and dirt of the street. The bottom of its light green cloak was stained brown with the dust of the roads.

"Who goes there?" One of the guards called from atop the wall that separated the palace grounds from the outside world. The figure stood erect and a clear calm voice pierced the silence of the early morning.

"I am Sahena, daughter of Stavir."

"What business have you here?"

"I wish to speak with my brother, Sern, son of Stavir, the Steward of Laaven."

"Show yourself!"

Sahena then let the hood of her cloak fall to reveal a face not identical, but similar to her brother's face. Her skin was pale and her eyes were a stormy grey green. Unruly dark hair poured down her back. A slight smile spread across her face as the gates opened to reveal two men in uniform standing side by side. One was tall and broad and the other taller and lankier.

"We will escort you to the steward, Lady," one said and the other nodded. They led her along the path that cut through the green of the palace grounds. When the castle was only a short distance away, they sharply veered off of the path.

"Are we not going to the palace?" Sahena asked, perturbed.

"The Steward is in his tree. He wanted some time to think undisturbed before the next council meeting. If he recognizes you as his sister, then you are clear. If he does not, then you have been sent here with an agenda and it will be beaten out of you by our jailers."

"Are we clear?" The other chimed in.

"Yes," Sahena replied quietly, paling a bit.

They walked the rest of the way in silence, eventually coming to a large tree.

"Milord," the taller man called.

"Yes," Sern's voice came from the tree. He could not be seen through the leaves and he was glad of it, for while he could keep the annoyance out of his voice, he could not manage to keep it out of his eyes or face.

"There is a situation, milord."

"Is it a dire situation? Is anyone's life or safety in danger? If not, then tell the head guard and he will voice your concerns today during council," Sern said and rested his head back against the tree, closing his eyes.

"What are we supposed to do with her, then?" Sern heard one masculine voice ask.

"I really do not think she is lying," another masculine voice. "But we were told by our superiors to lock her up, if nothing else but for safety's sake. We cannot trust any stranger with war so near."

"I am not going into any dungeon!" This one was a woman's voice, a frightened one that Sern found eerily familiar. "Come down from that tree this instant! After all of the pain you have caused me, the least you can do is see to it that I do not rot in a dungeon!"

Sern still could not place the voice. He swung down from the tree, surprised at being spoken to in such a way. The second he hit the ground, he looked up and into eyes so similar to his own that he gasped. "Sahena?" He walked toward her and the guards let her go. "It has been twenty years!" He exclaimed.

The Persian Rug

"Indeed," she replied with slight smile. "I feel as if we should embrace," she said more to herself than to Sern and he sighed. They then looked at one another for a long while, studying each other. While Sern was recognizable even though Sahena had not seen him since he was ten, Sern would not have recognized his sister if it were not for her eyes. She had grown from an ungainly podgy child into a fairly beautiful woman. Finally, Sern broke the silence.

"I have less than an hour before the council convenes, so we can speak now or after if you need more time."

"More time?"

"It has been twenty years. You did not just appear on a whim. You either need or want something."

"I would have come to see you if I could."

"What stopped you?"

"Our father, one bastard of a husband, three children, one dying husband whom I had to care for, and another husband who took me to the Northern Isles with him have prevented me from coming back to Laaven since I was thirteen years old. Why did you not even attempt to find me?"

"I have spent nearly half of my life at war. The other half I spent wherever I was needed."

"So be it," Sahena said matter-of-factly. "Do you know if our father lives still?"

"I was hoping that you would," Sern replied.

"This is the first time I have been in Laaven since I was thirteen or fourteen. I left only three or four years after you did and intended to never return."

"How did you escape our father?"

"I seduced a carpenter and he took me back to Nallel with him, but the past is not to be dwelled on. As you rightly said, I did not come on a whim."

"What is it that you want?"

"I want to help."

"What?"

"With the war against Phallé-Nal: I long to help. My husband

and my only surviving child have come from the Northern Isles with a small party."

"Does your husband know that you are here?"

"Does it matter? Only in the Sea Cities, Nallel, and Phallé-Nal does a woman need her husband's or father's permission to live her life still."

"I know this. I just thought that if you were not hiding from him, you might want to see him and your son one last time."

"You would do that for me?"

"Of course. It would mean that you did not come all this way for nothing."

"Sern!"

"You are a woman. Women do not go to war."

"Ah, I see you are a typical man in at least some respects. War does not only affect the men who fight in it. When the soldiers depart, they leave a different war, the one fought by the women, children, and elderly left behind. To help them is as noble an effort as any."

"How is it that you intend to help them?"

"Has it not come to your attention that the Sea Cities, while they would not send their armies, are secretly harboring those of the upper class who could pay enough?"

"Yes, I know this and while I do not think it is right, there is nothing I can do to stop it. How do you know of this?"

"Larjus, my husband, told me. In the Northern Isles, men and women are equal in every aspect."

"Ah."

"While the rich will be safe, far away from the chaos, the common people will be caught in the midst of the crossfire. Phallé-Nal will destroy them."

"You know of a stronghold?" Sern asked, incredulous.

"Not exactly."

"Then what do you speak of?"

"The Golden Mountains: the women, children, and elderly can take refuge in its caves."

"And you want to lead them?"

The Persian Rug

"Yes."

"You know the way?"

"Yes, I came here from the Northern Isles on my own."

"Without shoes?" Sern said, suddenly smiling as he looked down at his younger sister's dirty bare feet.

"I was accosted by thieves!"

"Shoe thieves?"

"No, other thieves had already taken all of my money. These thieves just wanted to teach me a lesson."

"And what lesson was that?"

"That if you haven't any coins left, you had better have nice shoes."

Just as she finished, Virahéen appeared, beckoning Sern to the council meeting. "Come with me little sister. You will tell the council of your plan," Sern said and Sahena looked at him incredulously. Her eyes blinked blankly.

"I will tell them?"

"If it was my idea I would tell them, but it was not."

"What should I say?"

"Exactly what you told me."

"What if they do not listen?"

"Then I will overrule the council."

"You will?"

"Yes, it is my prerogative as steward, but I doubt that will be necessary. The council is made up of decent men and your idea is a noble one. I made sure of it when I chose them."

"You are still the same person who you were when you left all those years ago," Sahena said with a smile. Sern was about to reply when they were interrupted by Virahéen, who they followed to the council room.

Chelsea Isadora Teich

Chapter XIX
Phallé-Nal

"No!" Aralé cried. "No! No! No! No! No!"

"You *will* do this Aralé," Maveree said as she reached for a piece of rope. "We have gone as far as we can undisguised. Do you wish to be caught and killed?" Maveree said matter-of-factly.

"I will not walk across a kingdom half-naked and tied to the back of the horse!" The princess fumed.

"Do you think any of us want to do this?" Féian mumbled, massaging his temples with dirt-encrusted fingers.

"I am a princess! I refuse to be—"

"You are no longer a princess. You are a deserter. Now stand behind Féian and put your head down." Aralé began to whine. "Now!" Maveree bellowed and Aralé did as she was told. Several minutes later, Róethel appeared with a white and grey horse, dressed like a young man of Phallé-Nal. She wore a long fur-lined cloak that cast a shadow about her face, men's winter leggings and long high boots. There were winter boots and cloaks atop the horse.

"Where did you find a horse and clothes in the middle of the woods?" Nerin asked, looking at the creature with inquiring eyes, as if he did not quite trust it.

"There are men in the business of taking horses from the south and selling them in the north—" Róethel began.

"So you purchased them from them?" Nerin said, still looking at the animal suspiciously.

"It depends on your personal definition of the word *purchased*," Maveree said as she put on the smallest pair of boots, which almost doubled as leggings.

Róethel sighed. The wind blew back the hood of her cloak to reveal dried blood on her cheek. "The rest of you put these on. It may be midsummer but it is cool here almost all year. In the far north, there may still be deep snow," she said and then tossed a pair of boots and a cloak to all of them with the exception of Maveree.

"I will tie them together and you can hold them about your waist. I will sit in front of you, hidden under your cloak."

"So she does not have to walk!" Aralé spat indignantly.

"Of course not! Do not be foolish," Maveree said and then tied the end of one long coil of rope around Aralé's wrists tightly. The same rope was tied around Féian's and Nerin's wrists. Little space was left in between the three unhappy youths. Róethel then helped Maveree atop the horse and tied the rope about her waist. Once Maveree was settled in front of Róethel, they set of at a slow pace. After two hours, the first of the many little hamlets, which surrounded Phallé-Nal to the south, came into view.

"Remain silent. Keep your eyes cast down and your shoulders hunched, as if you are broken and afraid of the world—" Róethel began.

"So, we should pretend that we are Nerin, in other words," Aralé said and Féian muttered something angrily under his breath.

"Basically," Maveree interjected. Nerin sighed miserably. "Now, do not speak unless you are spoken to. Róethel and I will stop to water the horse at the town well." She finished and they rode in silence through the cold hard ground in between small, windowless wooden shacks. In the doorways of many of these shacks stood fearful children and grim-faced adults in rags who all seemed to have Nerin's thick sable hair. The majority of the town seemed to have gathered around the few hovels that had porches.

"Why are they all looking at me as if I have just sprouted

several extra heads? This town has even sold slaves to traders on occasion. This should be considered perfectly common to them," Róethel whispered tentatively to Maveree.

"You misinterpret their stares," Maveree replied so quietly that none but Róethel would hear. "Look again."

Róethel did. She saw three little, pale, dark-haired girls sitting huddled together by a larger group of pale, dark-haired men and women of all ages watching them from the porch. When she looked close enough, she could see that for the most part they had grey eyes or clear azure eyes, like Nerin. She then realized that they all resembled him, all in coloring and some even bore features similar to his. She then realized that their gazes were directed at Nerin, whose hood had fallen away from his face. He looked as if he were ready to break.

"I cannot believe you would humiliate him like this! You are dragging him through the village of his birth like a slave, tied to the back of a horse!"

"Are you sure about that?"

"Sure about what?"

"That this is, in fact, the village of his birth."

"Northern villages are so small and isolated that almost every villager is related to every other villager by blood or marriage. Here they all look almost exactly like him and they seem to recognize him."

"Ah, but there are nearly fifty northern villages and the majority of them are full of dark-haired pallid villagers, especially those that live on or in the shadow of the Golden Mountains. They may be mistaken."

Róethel did not respond as the village well came into view. With Maveree clinging to her middle beneath her cloak, she dismounted. She let the horse drink and rest for a short while before Maveree told her that it was time to move on. Róethel mounted the horse and they rode late into the night and far away from any village. Féian, Nerin, and Aralé collapsed in a pile, huddling for warmth on the cold ground. Róethel and Maveree spent the night beside them wrapped up in Róethel's cloak, drinking heartily from one of Maveree's many flasks, hoping that it would stave off the cold. While it did make them warmer than they would have otherwise been, it also caused them to awake feeling rather ill.

Nevertheless, they awoke first and prepared for the coming day. They awoke the others and saw to it that they were tied up. They drank and ate a small amount before they started again.

By the second day of this, Aralé's wrists were bleeding and sore to a point where if a slight gust of air brushed against them she would be brought nearly to tears. After a week, Féian was in a similar state. It took nearly two weeks before they found Nerin's wrists, the skin almost eaten down to the bone. Every day it grew colder despite the fact that it was nearly summer. Every day there was less sun and more wind and eventually even snow.

Due to the fact that Nerin had collapsed of exhaustion and Féian had to carry him for almost two days, they had taken their first break of more than one night in over a month. They had taken respite in the house of a deaf man who had only allowed them to stay with them because Róethel was able to convince him that she knew his belated wife and could communicate with him using hand signals. Aralé, Nerin, and Féian were given the one spare room he had, while Maveree and Róethel slept in the main room by the fire. He shared what little he had with them.

"This will be our last real respite until we reach Merend Zetth," Maveree said as she ate bread and drank steaming broth.

"This is insane Maveree. They will never survive such a trek."

"All will be well, you'll see. It will be like none of this even happened."

"I highly doubt that," Róethel replied. She shivered and wrapped the wool blanket she wore, instead of her wet clothes, more tightly about herself.

"Trust me," Maveree said through a mouthful of bread. "It will all be worth it in the end. You do trust me, do you not?"

"Of course," Róethel said and they sat in silence for a while, watching the vermillion flames lick at the logs in the fireplace.

The Persian Rug

"I will not travel to Merend Zetth with you. The Lord and Lady would never allow me entrance to their city. My journey with you ends here."

"Of course," Maveree replied. "Will you stay until we depart for Merend Zetth or have you urgent business elsewhere?"

"I will spend the rest of the week here. Then I will depart for the Northern Isles."

"Very well," Maveree replied and lay down on the rug before the fire. As soon as Róethel was sure that she was asleep, she crept over to Maveree's traveling cloak, which hung by the door, and searched the pockets for one of Maveree's pipes, pipeweed, and matches. Upon finding it, she sat again and began to smoke, her long dark hair hanging over her face in strands so long she could almost sit on them as she smoked and gazed into the fire.

Chelsea Isadora Teich

The Persian Rug

Chapter XX
The First Battle

Darkness had enshrouded the Laaven encampment. For weeks their army had trekked away from the heart of the kingdom until they came to its outskirts. A week ago they had halted within distance of the Golden Mountains. It was well known that the army of the Northern Empire could arrive at any time, making every day possibly the last one a warrior might live. However, after a week of their absence, some men began to grow careless, while others grew restless.

It was at the end of week one that the leaders of each of the factions of the southern army met in Sern's tent for the second time. Sitting on a large woven rug sat Sern and Captain Sólien, dressed in the lighter and almost beautiful armor of Laaven with bands of purple and crimson and crimson tunics beneath the silver armor. Tiny, fanged four-legged creatures with long tails wrapped around a lit, double-edged candle decorated their shields and a fire motif decorated their helmets and armor. Each had a pair of long knives strapped to their back in a case along with a short sword and a long sword sheathed about their waists.

The captain of the army of The Isles of the Sun, Grytales, sat beside Sólien dressed in the nightmarish dark spiked armor all the warriors of his country wore. His helmet, which rested beside him, protruded to make a fanged snout. Two long curved swords with jagged edges and handles inlaid with black gems rested by his side in their sheaths. A club lined with colossal pointed teeth hung from his belt.

The captain of the army of the Northern Isles, a mountain of a man named Larjus who may have very well been one of the tallest men who have ever lived, sat with his back against the center beam that held up the tent. Thick red hair poured down his back and a short beard of a similar color covered his chin. His armor looked heavy, as it was not only thick but covered with gems and symbols, which all served a purpose. Small animal horns jutted from the silver armor that covered his shoulders, as they did from his helmet.

With these young men, gleaming in silver and grandeur, sat an older man in plain armor that seemed to be made more of leather than mail or steel. It was worn and looked as if he had had to repair it himself on occasion. It did not match his boots and his helmet did not match his armor or his boots. His sword was bloodstained and strands of dark, unkempt hair framed his face and hung in his bright green eyes as he polished his sword with a rock. This man was Amarant, leader of the rebels and escaped slaves who had decided to aid Laaven.

"My men are growing restless," Amarant said, his voice barely above a whisper. "And it grows increasingly difficult to ease them."

"If they were trained properly, there would not be a problem," Captain Grytales muttered aloud with a condescending sigh.

"Perhaps if you were *raised* properly, you would not be so rude," Captain Larjus replied.

"How dare you! You do not even care for Amarant's makeshift recruits—" Grytales began and was interrupted by a loud annoyed grunt from Larjus.

"Enough," Sern interjected. "Phallé-Nal is the only enemy and we should save all of our enmity for them."

"I agree," Amarant said coldly and the others nodded.

"We are still well-supplied, yes?" Sern said and the others nodded or voiced their agreement.

Just as they were finishing their council, the sound of chaos broke out. They left the tent to find four men holding another dressed in black. The black clad man had an arrow through his foot.

"There were spies sent by Phallé-Nal. Three of them are dead, one is dying and we have captured this one," one of the men who held the spy said.

"Were there any more?" Sólien asked.

"We had men chase one into the wood where they captured and killed him. We have his head if you would want it, sir," another said and Sólien only looked at him strangely.

"Have it taken to my tent," Captain Grytales said with a strange smile and the man nodded. Captains Larjus, Sern, and Sólien only looked at him strangely.

"Were there any others?" Sern asked nonchalantly.

"Not that we saw," the man replied. "Maybe *he* can tell us."

"*His* name is Medéen-Phíor." They all stopped upon hearing the condescending, accented voice of the black clad emissary. "And *he* will tell *you* whatever *you* want to know as long as *you* will not kill *him*."

"He will?" Captain Grytales asked, seemingly enjoying himself entirely too much. All except Amarant glared at him. He seemed preoccupied with the arrow jutting from his foot.

"Oh, and you must mend *his* foot," Medéen-Phíor said and Amarant strode toward him and knelt before him. He gently touched the arrow.

"That's not your place. Let one of the healers deal with him," Larjus said and the others were quick to agree.

"So, Medéen-Phíor, you are completely willing to volunteer information?" Amarant said quietly as he ran his fingers through the dark fletching of the arrow.

"If it keeps me unharmed," the man replied. "The way I see it I have two options: Either I am *completely willing to volunteer information* or you torture me until I am *completely willing to volunteer information*."

"Well, I have one question for you, then, and if you answer honestly you can walk free," Amarant statement was followed by groans of protest and insults from the other captains. However, he only glanced at Sern and Sern read the plan and understood the imploringness in the other man's eyes. He quieted the others immediately.

"You are awfully kind. Do you forget that I am the enemy?"

"Not at all," Amarant replied. His voice grew colder and somehow more resonant. "I only want you to answer this question without favor: Who shot you?"

"What?" Medéen-Phíor asked. All of the others beside Sern looked just as confused as the emissary. "Not only was it dark, but I do not know the names of your men. I could not say."

"This arrow is of a rare make: northern make," Amarant tried again. "Can you explain how one of our men shot you with an arrow that is only used by the army of the Northern Empire?"

The man then glared at Amarant and spit on him. Sern unsheathed his sword and drove it through the emissary's throat. In that instant, numberless northern warriors crashed through their encampment in terrible black armor, like death itself. Some wielded large hammers and the larger men wielded black broadswords already stained with blood that were the length of a grown man. Any they caught unaware were immediately massacred, leaving the remaining men to wallow in blood and the wreckage of their encampment as they fought for their lives.

Everywhere men lay dead and the sounds of the dying filled the air along with battle cries and howls. Sern had been caught in the thick of the fighting, along with Amarant and Grytales. As quiet and submissive as Amarant had always been, not one of the enemy soldiers had come within a foot of him and survived long. He had not even suffered a scratch and, were it not for his ensanguined appearance, none would have guessed he was a killer. He did so with ease, precision and a deadly calm, even as he killed he was the very picture of self-effacement. He seemed to ask forgiveness for every man he killed even as he destroyed another. Beneath the light of the moon and stars, he looked ancient, every line etched in his face by time and suffering betraying the fact that he was decades older than the other captains.

The Persian Rug

He and Sern had formed somewhat of a team, watching one another's backs and even working together to outnumber men with heavier, more cumbersome weapons on occasion. While Amarant seemed to do battle more with a principle of using his opponent's force against them, Sern could destroy three men with one thrust of his sword if circumstances permitted. Several of his toes had been crushed when a hammer-wielding northern warrior that Grytales had slain fell before him, but he fought through the pain, barely even noticing it.

Grytales, on the other hand, fought like a man possessed by bloodlust. His eyes had become the wild eyes of a madman as he stabbed and slashed at anything within reach (even some of his own men every now and again). He seemed to take some perverse joy in killing, and did so with such skill and precision that he could even choose the places he would strike, which were often the places that would cause his victims the most misery as they succumbed.

Toward the edges of the fighting were Larjus and the majority of his men, crushing their enemies beneath large hammers and bludgeoning them with spiked clubs that were often dipped in poison. They were the loudest of all, screaming curses and battle cries and the names of their gods of war, dedicating each great strike to someone or something as they turned any northerner within reach into pulp.

Sólien, the Laaven warriors, and the majority of those who had come with Amarant were fighting to where the battle had spread, beside the encampment in the grasslands. Here the southern army had managed to encircle a small amount of northern warriors and had destroyed them with very few losses, leaving a pile of broken bodies and gruesome severed limbs behind them as they went back to the encampment where war still waged. Flies gathered around the corpses and other scavengers feasted hungrily as they left them where they lay.

As the sun rose, battle ceased for not one northern warrior was left standing. Men screamed their victory, many preparing to celebrate their triumph. As their cries echoed throughout the last of the lingering twilight, Amarant stood before them. Sern looked grave.

"Do you not understand!?" He cried and the others stopped their merriment. For many, the sound of him talking above a whisper was a shocking occurrence for it had never happened before. "This is only the beginning! Less than a third of their men were killed here today and it will not be long before the rest of the Northern Empire's army is upon us! We haven't the time to make merry now!" He said and it seemed as if all of the power and passion he had shown had drained him and he fell silent.

Sern then began. "First we pile and burn the corpses. Take whatever weapons of the other army appeal to you. You may take their armor but do not wear it, for the northerners made it and know its weaknesses. While at war, we cannot afford to make merry. However, you should all be proud! IT IS THE BLOOD OF OUR ENEMIES THAT BATHES THE EARTH THIS MORN!" He cried and the men howled in response. They then set about piling and burning the corpses. Many of the men from The Isles of the Sun could be seen pulling eyes from the heads of the slain. Grytales said it was a tradition but refused to divulge exactly what his countrymen did with them.

Later that night, after whatever of the tents was salvaged could be reassembled, Sern sat in his tent unable to sleep. His body may have been exhausted but his mind raced. He had seen Danen briefly during the middle of the battle but they had been separated and duty had kept him from seeking his young friend for the rest of the day. He would have been worrying for Dorin as well had he not seen him shortly after the battle so he could amputate his three small toes on his left foot. Anyone else he might have been particularly worried about he had found well or at least alive. The fact that he had not seen Danen made him think that his young friend had been burned in a pyre with the other slain. As far as he knew, slightly less than a quarter of their army had perished. The faction of The Isles of the Sun had been the only one with no casualties.

Due to the lack of tents, he shared one with Amarant who

was fast asleep on the ground beside him and Sólien who was standing watch. When he heard a man enter the tent, he was certain it was Sólien and paid it no heed. However, he tensed when he heard the footsteps stop and breathing above him. The second he felt a hand on his shoulders, he grabbed for his daggers and flipped the person he assumed to be attacking him over and pinned him to ground. He was shocked to find a wide-eyed Danen with a deep wound across his left cheek beneath him.

"Would you two be quiet? I am not going to spend the last nights of my life kept awake instead of...sleeping," Amarant moaned as he rolled over, his hand closing about the hilt of his sheathed sword and his eyes closing.

"Pleasant fellow," Danen muttered and Sern rolled off of him.

"I am very sorry."

"Don't be. After last night's surprise attack, everyone is a bit changeable, and rightly so."

"Despite the greeting you received, I am truly very happy to see you."

"Really?"

"Of course! What kind of a question is that? You have been like a son to me! The last time I saw you, you were between a man three times your size and another with a broadsword nearly as tall as you! I have been worrying myself to death all day!"

"Well, while I am very happy to see you I am sorry to have caused you such pain," Danen replied jokingly and Sern sighed. "Actually, I have come...there is something I must tell you," he said, leaning in closer.

"Is it something bad?" Sern asked, reading the anxiety in the younger man's eyes.

"Yes," Danen said quietly and began after several minutes. "Captain Larjus has left camp to go see his wife one last time and he told me to inform you."

"What!?"

"He said that the Northern Empire will most likely not attack again for at least a week and that should give him plenty of time to see his wife one last time."

"That is incredibly irresponsible! He may even draw the enemy to them unknowingly. Not to mention the fact that we are in the middle of a war!" The pair remained silent for a while before Sern spoke again. "I just want to know how a man taller than most of the houses in Laaven with a head and beard of hair brighter than a blazing cornfield slips away unnoticed."

"He can move as stealthily as a cat if he feels so inclined. As can almost all of the men of the Northern Isles and the smallest man in their faction is bigger than I," Danen said and suddenly looked rather downcast. "It seems that I am always the bringer of bad news. I am surprised that you are not furious."

"I am. I could positively kill Larjus!" Sern whispered heatedly. "But what would screaming at you about it accomplish? You are simply the messenger."

"I suppose I should return to my tent."

"Who are you sharing with?"

"Ilmaren, Ejdis, and Valörn from the Northern Isles and Inurío from The Isles of the Sun."

"Five in a tent? That must be horribly cramped."

"We make do," Danen said quickly. "He also said that he would bring you news of your sister." After bidding Sern goodnight, he departed, leaving the older man to toss and turn next to a snoring Amarant for the rest of the night.

Chapter XXI
Cold

Aralé groaned as she opened her eyes to another frigid morning: white snow and grey sky as far as they eye could see. While the overcast sky meant that sunlight would not beat down upon the snow and make it almost blinding to look at, no sunlight meant an even colder and drearier day. She could not decide what was worse as she attempted to curl up into an even smaller ball in her cloak, which had served as her bed for the nights they had spent in the frozen wasteland that lay to the north of Phallé-Nal. She knew that it could not be long until Maveree awoke her. Maveree used to only scream or pull her out into the snow, but when Aralé started ignoring her or simply refusing to get up, she resorted to throwing snow at her.

"I cannot believe that I was amazed the first time I saw snow," she muttered aloud as she covered her ears with her hands to block out the sound of the winds rushing all about her.

"Everyone up!" She heard Maveree cry and groaned, only rising because she did not like the feel of cold wet snow. Beside her sat a tousled looking Féian gently shaking Nerin awake whilst trying to convince Maveree not to drop a lapful of snow on his sleeping friend.

"What food is left?" Aralé asked in the midst of the commotion and Maveree sighed.

"One piece of dried deer meat and some lint."

"Lint?" Aralé moaned.

"Yes, pocket lint to be precise." Maveree said. "And unless we can find a way to make one strip of dried deer and a generous amount of pocket lint last nearly another week, we will starve to death long before we reach Merend Zetth."

"I am not going to die out here!" Aralé screamed. "Everyone get up! March!"

"As you command," Maveree said with a smirk. "You heard her. *She* is not going to die out here. Rise boys." She then took out the one piece of dried deer meat out of her pocket, brushed some lint off of it and broke off four small pieces off one of the ends, all nearly equal in length. Féian refused.

"Either you eat this, or you die Féian. Please, Féian, just eat it," Nerin said and Féian did as he was told.

"This tastes like frozen smoked boots," Féian groaned as he chewed on his piece.

"For once, I actually agree with Féian. This has got to be the foulest thing I have ever eaten," Aralé said and Maveree started walking. They followed.

"Maveree, what have we to drink?" Aralé asked after several minutes.

"Snow," the seeress replied.

"We cannot drink snow!" Aralé protested.

"Yes you can. It is only frozen water. It melts in your mouth," Nerin said as he took a handful and put it in his mouth. Aralé followed his example.

"Maveree, I am hungry," Aralé said around noon and Maveree did not respond. "Maveree!" She tried again.

"We are all hungry, but this is not your palace where sweet meats, stuffed pheasant, and a plethora of puddings can cover every wooden surface if you like. There are four of us and nothing but less then one strip of dried deer meat, pocket lint, and snow."

"We could always kill Nerin and eat him," the princess replied. "Though I fear there's not much meat on him."

Féian rolled his eyes and Maveree did not respond. Nerin

only drew his cloak tighter around him, the fact that he was the thinnest of the group only making him colder. He shivered miserably.

The sunless day quickly turned into a pitch black night. They attempted many times to start a fire using wood from the few trees they had seen but the wind had picked up, blowing any spark that took away. Maveree passed out more little bits of the dried meat to her weary companions. Nerin had fallen asleep before Maveree had a chance to pass out the bits of food so he went without.

Nerin awoke the next morning to a hunger so strong that it almost pained him. He looked to see Aralé's pallid hand glowing against the snow. From the looks of it, the sun would start to rise soon, but dark clouds were moving toward them quickly. He knew that if she kept it out much longer it would become frost bitten so he rose from his cloak, beside Féian and gently crept along the frozen ground as if he were afraid of making footprints and disturbing the snow.

He then took her hand, only with the intention of tucking it back into her cloak. However, despite the cold, the familiar touch of her skin set him burning. Memories overtook him. Just as he had begun to familiarize himself with her delicate fingers and smooth palm, it was taken away from him. He looked up to see Aralé glaring at him.

"You are pathetic! Do you do this every night while I sleep?" She spat and rolled over. Nerin walked back to his cloak that lay beside Féian. He sighed sadly and lay awake until Maveree called for them to resume their journey. On one side of him lay Aralé who rested cocooned inside her cloak several feet away. On the other lay Féian who was so close he could feel him breathing and on the other side of Féian lay Maveree, who Nerin could not see over Féian. Above him was a slowly lightening starry sky that would turn the snow from a brilliant white to either blinding white or a monotonous maddening grey. He watched the last of the faraway stars, evanescent as dawn approached.

He sat silently, eating his little bit with the others as they all awoke and shivered and suffered the cold silently as they walked. Aralé's constant complaining, Féian's angry mutters and curses at the wretched princess, Maveree's occasional scorching remarks, and the constant sound of clumsy boots trudging through snow and pushing through cold wind played around him endlessly. It was all he heard until all sound faded from him, as did his vision, which turned to a blank grey. He felt nothing, hardly even hunger, just the numbing cold. He ate and he slept silently. Dark circles formed about his eyes and one might have thought him dead. Féian would occasionally wake him at night when he thought his friend had stopped breathing. For all Nerin knew, he might have.

One day as they trudged through a light snowfall he collapsed, forcing Féian to carry him. To this, Aralé had only this to say "Can we kill him and eat him now?"

Maveree hit her hard and they continued.

The seeress seemed to promise daily that Merend Zetth was only a day or two away. Meanwhile, Aralé had lost the energy even to complain and Féian could barely hold himself up let alone Nerin. Maveree near crawled across the snow.

One morning, they all awoke to find Maveree kneeling in the snow, deeply concentrating on something.

"Are we not journeying on?"

"No," Maveree replied quietly. "Now we wait." With that, she took a beautiful flower with a viridian stem and petals of brilliant shades of crimson and fuchsia from her cloak and stuck the stem in the cold hard ground.

Chapter XXII
The Golden Mountains

Larjus could not help but smile as he came to the Golden Mountains. He walked past the many cave entrances of the mountains until he came to one where the dirt floor had been disturbed by footprints.

"I will see my Sahena," he said almost gleefully as he entered the dark of the caves. He walked for nearly a quarter of an hour in such a state before the eerie silence began to worry him. He walked for nearly another ten minutes when he was assaulted by the foul reek of rotting corpses. In that second, he realized that Phallé-Nal must have come and they very well may have killed his wife.

"Sahena!" He cried over and over again as he ran through the cave, lifting up every corpse to see if his beloved wife was among the slain. After nearly an hour of this, he came across the corpse of a dark-haired woman in the same green dress Sahena always wore. Her face had been crushed and the majority of it lay beside her in a rancid pile of rotting blood, skin, and muscle, making her almost unrecognizable. Her hair was the same color and length and her dress was similar in the dark, but Larjus knew that there was only one sure way to tell if the cold dead body before him belonged to his wife.

In the Northern Isles, spouses bore marks of one another. His and Sahena's were two black serpents with green eyes, entwined about a silver chalice, which was etched on their palms. The tails of the snakes wrapped around and ended on the back of their wrists. He then turned over her left palm to find no mark there and muttered thanks to whatever gods he could name before looking at the rest of the bodies. None belonged to his wife. The majority of those who lay dead were infants and the elderly.

"Phallé-Nal must have taken prisoners," Larjus decided and then lit a torch. He followed the tracks in the cave floor left by heavy boots with spikes protruding from the toe ends and feet of the women who had been harshly dragged along by their captors. There was a good deal of blood on the ground. He could almost see his wife fighting and screaming as she was dragged away. He followed the impressions in the dirt to one of the back cave entrances and into the forest.

For three days and nights, he trekked through the dark forest, on the fourth morning finally hearing the high-pitched screams and wails coming from the woman captives. He could smell fire and burning animal flesh on the wind as he crept along in the shadows cast by trees and shrubbery. After nearly half an hour of walking, he came across the most harrowing sight he had ever witnessed.

Through the leaves of the trees he could see a beaten, hoodwinked woman tied to a large wooden staff. What was left of her dress hung about her broken and bleeding body in tatters. Her dark hair had been torn out in places and what was left was rank with dirt, sweat, and tears and caked with blood. Her eyes were swollen as were her lips. The remnants of dried blood covered her face and cheeks. Where her skin was not blue, black, crimson or yellow with bruises, it was almost grey. At first, he thought the woman dead until she opened her eyes slightly.

"If there was mercy in the world, I would not live still," she murmured softly in a voice devoid of emotion. It was a voice hoarse from screaming. Wounds left from being viciously lashed were visible on her grey-tinted, translucent skin. Most had become infected and turned an angry red. There was an inflamed burn mark on her left cheek, one on her collarbone, and others on her torso and legs. Her bosom rose and fell weakly with almost non-existent breaths.

The Persian Rug

Her hand, which had held what had remained of her dress together about her, fell weakly. Through the splinters of wood and rope, there was an ensanguined chalice with two black serpents enwreathed about it.

"Sahena!" Larjus cried as he leapt from the dark of the forest and stopped before the bound and tormented woman.

"My love..." Sahena croaked in the language of the Northern Isles as her blindfold was removed. She knew the voice and the touch of the man before her. She groaned in agony weakly, as the cloth had been glued to her face with her own blood and sweat. The skin surrounding one was violaceous and the eye itself swollen shut. There were tears in her eyes. When he moved to untie her, she stopped him.

"I led these women and I failed them. I deserve this," she said.

"No one deserves this," he replied.

"I must. Why else would it have happened?"

"I told you to stay back in the Northern Isles, where you would be safe!" Larjus replied weakly, his voice shaking. His hands ghosted over hers, afraid to touch her lest he cause her even more pain.

"I told you the same," she replied quietly. "At least now, we will meet again soon. Phallé-Nal will win this war and conquer all. At least we will be spared."

"You have been spared nothing," he said as he lightly ran his fingers against her unmarred cheek. "There is truly no mercy in the world."

At this, Sahena smiled as much as her battered lips would allow. She then slowly lifted one of her arms, her hand coming to rest in his beard. "No mercy? I will spend my last moments with you..." she trailed off, her hands weakening.

"Sahena!" Larjus cried, and she seemed to awaken slightly.

"Larjus, will you do something for me?" She asked and he nodded fervently.

"Yes, anything—"

Larjus stopped as Sahena let out a pained gasp. He felt his wife's hands growing cold.

"Sahena!" He cried as he took her other hand in his a bit too forcefully and she let out a pained gasp.

"Sahena!"

No answer came from his wife. She let out one last pained cry before her hands grew slack and the lingering light in her eyes diminished. "Sahena..." he muttered tearfully and gingerly ran his fingers along the burn mark on her cheek.

He stood there for what felt like hours, gazing at the body of his belated wife. So struck with grief was Larjus that he did not hear two armed enemy guards approaching. They called to him in their own language but he did not hear. After recognizing the make of Larjus' armor and realizing who he fought for, they readily attacked the poor grief-stricken man who was powerless to retaliate. Larjus was slain beside his wife, an arrow protruding from his throat.

Chapter XXIII
Merend Zetth

"Maveree, Nerin is freezing to death!" Féian cried as he sped over to the seeress who sat on her knees in the snow, an enchanted flower rising from the ground before her. Her eyes were fixed on the grey sky and her hands were clasped. She was obnoxiously unresponsive. The ends of her hair were frozen.

"Maveree!" He called again to no avail and then shook her.

"Don't!" She hissed. "Our lives depend on the Lord and Lady receiving my message!" She cried.

"Message? I did not see you send one," Féian replied and Maveree rolled her eyes.

"Of course not, they speak through the mind. Now return to Nerin and attempt to keep him warm," Maveree said as she quickly returned to her prayers. Féian acquiesced immediately. He returned to Nerin who lay still and wrapped in his cloak, not one inch of him visible.

"Nerin..." Féian whispered as he placed his hand on what he thought would be Nerin's shoulder. It had started to snow again and Féian had to brush it away. Nerin remained still.

"Nerin!" Féian began to panic. He feared that his friend had frozen to death. "Nerin!" He cried again, this time shaking the younger man even more violently. He sighed with relief upon hearing a muffled "What?" come from beneath the cloak.

"Just making sure that you're still alive," Féian said as jovially as he could muster.

"You should not have woken me," Nerin said sadly. "In my sleep I feel no hunger, nor do I feel the cold."

"I am sorry," Féian replied softly.

"Do not be. It is not your fault that I am so wretchedly fragile," Nerin said after a while. Féian shook his head.

"Nerin, not all men are born to be warriors."

"And yet we all must fight," Nerin said and after a few minutes he poked his head out from the cocoon he had formed of his cloak. His face was a sickly grey. "I am tired of it all Féian."

Féian's eyes grew wide. "Aid is coming! Maveree said that she is calling to the Lord and Lady of Merend Zetth and—"

"Yes, so they can save us? And then what? Nothing is left for me. I have struggled all my life, and for what? Nothing. I have nothing and I have no one. Give me one reason why I should keep denying death her latest conquest?"

"You are so young..." Féian blurted for he was unable to think of any other feasible reason for Nerin to linger on.

"Ah, and tarry for another sixty or so years of misery?" Nerin mused. "As a healer I know the signs of a failing body. My suffering should cease by dawn."

"You mean..." Féian trailed off, looking utterly forlorn.

"If aid does not arrive by dawn, you three will continue on without me. I was too frail to begin with," Nerin replied and Féian only looked at his hands, which were folded in his lap.

"Nerin, I just want you to know that I completely support your decision." They both looked to see Aralé wrapped in her cloak. Matted dank hair stuck out of the tightly drawn hood of her cloak and two of her teeth had broken from incessant chattering. Féian glared at her.

"Of course you do! It is all your fault that he's given up!" Féian cried.

"And the family that abused and abandoned him, the sister that he watched kill herself, the various slave owners who victimized and tortured him, and being both imprisoned and then made an outlaw by the very people whose lives he had saved had absolutely *nothing* to do with it," Aralé replied dryly.

"You are one cold evil harlot!" Féian exclaimed angrily.

"And you are one incredibly observant ogre."

"Don't you care that he may very well not live long enough to see another sunrise!?"

"If I am as you put it *a cold and evil harlot*, why would you expect me to be overly depressed at his passing?"

"Are you completely devoid of human emotion!?" Féian screamed.

"I suppose," she replied flatly. "I have never really thought about it that way before."

At this, Féian let out an animalistic howl and lunged at her, savagely pulling her hair and striking her with all of his strength. She screamed and fought back weakly. This continued for several minutes before Maveree finally intervened.

"ENOUGH!" She bellowed and Féian immediately climbed off of Aralé and returned to Nerin's side. Aralé was lying on her side, breathing heavily. Blood gushed out of her nose and her lip was split, allowing rivulets of blood to flow freely down her chin. They then looked to see Maveree still sitting by the flower, composed and concentrated. It was almost as if she had not let out a cry loud and harrowing enough to shake the earth.

"Please hurry," Féian murmured as he looked to the overcast sky and then turned to Nerin who had fallen back asleep. He placed his hand on Nerin's back to find that his breaths were disconcertingly shallow.

It was night and Maveree still sat by the flower. It had gotten so cold that Féian and Aralé put their differences aside and had decided to huddle in the midst of all of their cloaks and share their body heat. Each lay on one side of the slumbering Nerin.

Night had fallen hours before and the ashen moon had been obscured by clouds when suddenly Nerin began to scream. Aralé flew from the pile of cloaks and bodies and accidentally took Nerin with her. Féian followed and took him into his arms, attempting to wake him up.

"Wake him up and tell him to shut it!" Aralé yelled as she

crouched in the snow, flinging her mass of matted, neglected hair behind her and crying out as the bitter cold bit into her flesh.

"Nerin..." Féian said gently and he shook him. Nerin only continued to scream. Féian tried to call to him again but to no avail. Suddenly, the moon was revealed and cast an eerie light, nearly making it as bright as day. In this light, Féian beheld Nerin's blue lips and jaundiced eyes. His entire body seemed to spasm as he screamed in agony. He suddenly began to choke and Féian knew that he was about to retch. He rolled the convulsing man onto his side and immediately thick yellow bile poured from his mouth and coated the ends of his hair.

"Nerin..." Féian said and Nerin only looked at him with a pained expression and made little mewls and whines of displeasure before he began to vomit again. Féian cried, powerless to end his suffering as Nerin grabbed his stomach and let out a howl of agony. He then gripped Féian's hands, his nails digging into the other man's skin deep enough to draw blood as he cried out.

Féian watched in horror, powerless to help his friend as he let out one final whimper and fell limp against him. Féian could hear and feel him breathing faintly. He looked to see his frighteningly yellowed eyes rolling about in his head. As his evanescent heartbeat finally ceased, Féian laid him on the snow. While agony contorted his features, there was also relief in his eyes. Féian looked to see Maveree unmoving and still on her knees by the flower. Aralé was only staring curiously at Nerin, with detached observation as if his passing was some kind of experiment she had been studying.

Tears flowed unchecked as Féian sat beside Nerin's corpse.

As the sun rose, two figures appeared on the horizon. Several black specks hovered in the sky above them. "They're here," Maveree whispered happily and looked behind her to see Aralé curled up in a ball of dark fabric off to the side and Féian sitting beside Nerin, weeping. She sobered immediately upon realizing what had happened. She walked beside Féian and took his head in her hands, allowing it to rest against her.

"The Lord and Lady have arrived," she whispered and Féian

did not respond. "They will take us Merend Zetth," she said as she stroked his hair.

"They are too late," he replied quietly and Maveree let him go before stalking over to Aralé and giving her a quick kick in the stomach.

"The Lord and Lady have arrived. We're saved. Get up," she said in a deadpan voice and Aralé rose. She was clutching her stomach and there were tears and anger in her eyes. Her lip was swollen from when Féian had punched her.

Slowly approaching were a naked man and woman with wild golden hair that fell past their calves and haunting sere eyes. Their skin was darkened from the sun. The woman wore a wreath of flowers and the man one of leaves with horns. They were equal in height and almost in build. Only while the man was muscular and solid and moved with a sensual grace, the woman was soft and voluptuous and love poured from her. Both wore joyous smiles. The woman walked before the man and flowers and greenery bloomed about her feet as she walked. The wreath about her head was adorned with silver and amber. All of the phases of the moon, carved in amber, hung from her wild curls of hair. The sun, quartered circles, and arrow-like pieces etched in gold glittering red adorned the locks of her counterpart.

In their wake followed two men with neat gleaming dark locks that fell to their waists. One was old and the other no older than twenty. They were fair and dressed in layers of translucent material. On one perched a number of stunningly colored butterflies. On the shoulder of another, there was perched a great white bird. Their faces were serene and expressionless but contentment radiated from them. While they were the very picture of self-effacement, they seemed confident and merely observant. The third person who followed them was a woman with light brown hair and eyes of the same color, whose hair fell in gentle flourishes to her ankles. She was not as pale as the two men and she was dressed in a flowing, woven green gown of material so light that it almost looked as if parts of her body had become green. She wore a radiant kind smile.

The party stopped before the party, standing on the sea of greenery and life that the Lady had had evoked from the dead frozen earth. The Lord's arm was draped about the Lady and her head rested on his shoulder. Auric hair mingled and caught the sun, gleaming like pure light between them. Their hands were clasped and they smiled lovingly at one another. They were ethereal and beautiful.

"Welcome to Merend Zetth," the Lord said in a sonorous voice both quiet and commanding. The Lady nodded and smiled kindly, obviously surveying them. Tears came to her eyes as she beheld the dead body of Nerin. She gracefully walked past Maveree and Aralé and beside Féian. She gently tilted his chin so he looked at her. She then peered deeply into his eyes.

For you, one of the only remaining children of Time Immemorial, I will grant the gift of farewell.

Féian only blinked. Her lips had not moved. She then lightly pressed her lips to his forehead and stooped to pick Nerin's body up out of the snow. She cradled his body in her arms as she returned to the Lord.

"Our children will take you to our city," the Lord of Merend Zetth said and the men and woman who had stood behind him came forward. The old man took Maveree into his arms, the woman wrapped herself about Féian and lastly, the young man apprehensively strode over to Aralé. He wrapped his arms about her.

The next thing they knew, they were hovering hundreds of feet in the air, the wind tearing at them. Aralé tried to scream but was muffled by the young man's sleeve. Féian seemed to be in shock. Maveree, on the other hand, seemed to be enjoying herself immensely.

Soon, they landed in the midst of a lush green clearing. All traces of the bitter cold had disappeared. Flowers bloomed and sweet scents lingered in the warm spring air. The Lord and Lady had vanished, as had what remained of Nerin, but the three others who had accompanied them stood beside them. Butterflies immediately fluttered over to the young man, clinging to his shoulders and hair. One flitted around merrily on his outstretched palm. The same white bird that had been perched on the old man's shoulder before landed gracefully again. The old man happily stroked its feathers.

"Welcome to our city, travelers," the woman spoke and the other two nodded. "I am Aleá, and I pay homage to the element of air. My bound, Ccyden, and my bound's father, Relíj, pay homage to air as well. You may dwell in our abode as long as you would like, friends." Aralé stared blankly at Aleá and Féian with amazement. Maveree smiled broadly.

"Thank you Aleá," the seeress said. "It is good to be back." Aleá nodded once exaggeratedly and beckoned Aralé, Maveree, and Féian to follow.

"What did that woman just say?" Aralé asked a forlorn looking Féian as they followed the three witches over even more lush terrain.

"That the old man with the bird is her father, the young man covered in butterflies is her husband, all of them have the ability to manipulate air, and that we will be staying in their house," he replied dispassionately as he tepidly glanced at all of the beautiful frondescence about him, not really capturing any of it.

"Oh," Aralé replied. "So that is why they could fly, then."

Féian only nodded as they walked through high grass only to come to a large clearing. In this clearing sat a myriad of large woven blankets with a countless number of merry, scantily clad people resting or partaking in various activities atop them. Aralé's eye caught two children utilizing their abilities with the element of air to viciously fling fruit at one another over long distances. To her surprise, an alarming number of people of all ages were taking part in the same activity. Young couples could be seen kissing. An old man and woman were using their combined powers of water and air to make clouds in the shapes of dogs, gourds, and dancing women for a group of happily cheering adolescents. A number of young girls ran past them merrily scattering flower petals about.

They walked through all of these to one blanket in the very middle of all the chaos where there sat a little dark haired toddler hissing playfully at a snake that was wrapped around his leg. A woman who was round with child sat beside him and stroked his hair absentmindedly. A young man and woman curled about each other lovingly as they slept, hovering feet above the ground. A middle-aged man was sitting on the very edge of the blanket talking animatedly to a group of other men.

"My family," Aleá said proudly with a gleaming smile. "My sister by blood and her child," she said as she gestured toward the pregnant woman and the little boy whispering to the snake. "My younger brother by blood and his bound," she gestured toward the happily sleeping couple who hovered in the air. "And my bound's father's brother by blood," she gestured toward the middle-aged man who had obviously just said something very funny for the others in the group were all cackling madly and rolling around on the ground. "The rest you will meet at the eventide feast, for they are about now."

As Maveree engaged in conversation with Aleá, Aralé roughly elbowed Féian.

"What?" He asked quietly, still looking quite forlorn.

"What did the witch just say?"

Féian sighed. "She introduced us to her sister, her nephew, her younger brother, her younger brother's wife, and her husband's uncle. This is only a small part of her family, she doesn't know exactly where the rest of them are, and we will meet the rest at supper."

"Why couldn't she have just said that?" Aralé asked and Féian sighed again.

"Look, I understand, you are depressed because your friend died. However, if you are going to do nothing but sigh like your head is completely vacant for the rest of your life—"

"He died last night. I think I should be allowed some time to grieve."

"Yes. And I think I should be allowed some time not go completely mad. Maveree's not much for conversation and I obviously cannot communicate with any of these people. I'll have to resort to talking to myself shortly."

The Persian Rug

"Oh, how much I pity you," Féian muttered and watched as Aralé turned toward the small child with the snake. The snake disappeared into the grass and the small child backed away in fear, clinging to his pregnant mother for dear life. Aralé glared at him for a few seconds before turning to watch three handsome witches send fire signals to one another from afar.

Soon after, the majority of the place cleared, leaving only children who appeared to be under fifteen, some mothers, some fathers, and the elderly in the clearing. The pregnant woman had left, leaving her child with the man who they assumed to be the father, as he looked just like him. The two hovering sleeping lovers had left, as did the middle-aged uncle and his friends. A little boy, a little girl, and three elderly married couples came in their place.

"Why is everyone leaving?" Aralé asked Féian and, when he did not respond the first time, she elbowed him in the ribs.

"In Merend Zetth, I am assuming that it is much like Iarnel Eremnad. In the morning you wake up and you do your assigned task, which may be anything from picking food, to weaving, to cleaning, to teaching children, to cooking, to looking after the children. Then there is a long rest in the afternoon with which you can do whatever you wish. After that, you go back to do your assigned task. After that, there is a big dinner for the entire village and then the night is yours to do with what you wish."

"So, you are telling me that that pregnant woman just left to go to work and left her *husband* to look after all of these children?"

"Yes," Féian replied flatly, obviously finished with the conversation. This did not really matter to Aralé.

"That's odd."

"Not really."

"How is that not odd? If I were the man, I would be ashamed of myself."

"Here men and women are equal. One is not higher or stronger than the other and either can do any job efficiently. When a child is born, it will take to either the mother or the father. Occasionally, it will not take to either and might prefer an older sibling or other family member. In any case, whoever the child chooses is the one who will look after it the most. Obviously, this young witch chose his father. This would never embarrass the father, but make him very proud and happy."

Aralé then looked to see the little boy giggling madly as the father used his abilities to lift him many feet into the air and then float gently back down onto his lap. Once the boy landed, he used his very small unrefined ability to lightly blow his father's long raven hair about. The father obviously encouraged his son.

"Are not only women witches?"

"It depends on your definition of witch. In your culture, you were taught that they are dark warty things that conjure plagues and do harm to people. The truth of the matter is that you are far more evil and have done a lot more harm in general than any true witch would ever even think about doing."

"Then what of warlocks or sorcerers? Are there any of those?"

"There is really no word for either of those terms in Céremín, but there are óssegader. A Segader is one who has been banished for breaking important rules or doing harm to others. I would be considered one by my people in Iarnel Eremnad for I, more or less, ran away."

"You are a witch?"

"My people follow the old ways for we originated here but few of us can do anything like they can anymore. Yes, I suppose I am," he said and as soon as Aralé opened her mouth to speak, he silenced her. "Now please, stop talking to me," he said and looked to see the father smiling at him and the dark haired little child crawling into his lap. Aralé turned away and fell into a tired sleep as the father and Féian fell deep into conversation in their own language.

Aralé awoke to Maveree's voice calling her from sleep. She almost gasped to see her neat and clean. She looked like a little, beautiful, ethereal sprite. Her gown was made of several layers of light incandescent material and flowed about her as she moved.

Her skin glowed and her dark blonde hair hung in waves down to her mid-back. For the first time Aralé could recall, she looked genuinely happy and at peace.

"Come, it is time that we dressed and readied you for the feast." Aralé was then dragged to a spring where a number of other young women were bathing merrily and talking. She readily slid out of her dirty clothes and into the spring beside a girl of a swarthier complexion. She marveled at how wonderful the water felt against her skin.

"Where are the soaps and oils?" She asked and turned to see Maveree smiling.

"They are not used here," Maveree said. "Just come out when you feel that you are clean." Aralé then lay back in the water. She soaked her hair and every inch of her body for nearly a quarter of an hour. Suddenly, she felt perfectly clean and rose to find that her once matted hair was knotless and smooth and every inch of dirt had been washed away.

"I should bottle some of this water and take it back to Laaven," Aralé muttered as Maveree led her behind some trees. A light and flowing gown of soft grey and pink hung from the branches and Maveree helped Aralé put it on.

"It almost feels as if I'm wearing nothing at all!" She exclaimed as she turned slightly. The material billowed behind her slightly as a breeze caught it.

"Yes, they are not particularly fond of clothes here. They find them restricting and only wear them when there are visitors, which there have not been in over a century," Maveree explained but Aralé was not listening as she twirled about joyously in her raiment.

They then walked about ten minutes and came to the center of Merend Zetth. Every witch in the entire village sat in a circle around a large pile of recognizable and also totally bizarre fruits and vegetables. She followed Maveree as she sat beside the Lord and the Lady. They bore no vesture and their naked skin gleamed in the waning light of the sunset. Suddenly, the Lord and Lady stood and all fell silent. Aralé had expected to see fear in the eyes of the witches as they gazed upon the rulers of their city, but instead she found only joy. It seemed that they were happy to show him respect. She had never seen anything like it.

He gave a speech in the language of his people to them and Aralé did not understand. She guessed that he was introducing her, Maveree, and Féian but became slightly worried. Several times throughout his speech, the people laughed. She had lost focus and was daydreaming about sinking her teeth into a leg of pheasant when she felt Maveree's eyes on her.

"Stand up and be recognized," she said and Aralé rose. She saw Féian nearly across from her in the circle seated by the man and woman she had met earlier. The little raven-haired boy she recognized from earlier was clinging to his leg. The witches clapped and then Maveree, Aralé, and Féian sat back down. The feast began.

While Maveree and Féian both spoke to everyone and ate and drank heartily, Aralé sat quietly and picked at the several fruits and vegetables that she recognized. She did not particularly like Merend Zetth. After looking forward to sleeping in a nice warm bed for months, she doubted that the *freaks* (as she called them) had ever even heard of a bed. She sighed unhappily as she bit into an apple.

That night, as they slept on the blankets beneath the stars, Féian suddenly felt an abrupt shift in the atmosphere. He felt a warm breeze caress his cheek and opened his eyes to see the unmistakable figure of the Lady of Merend Zetth beckoning him from afar. He both heard and felt her soft voice. It washed over him and relaxed him. He felt his body tingling almost as if it were aglow.

Come to me child.

Almost of his own accord, Féian rose and walked toward her, his feet leading him through the maze of sleeping witches to the edge of the clearing where the lady stood. She placed a hand on his mid-back, gently guiding him before her and yet leading him at the same time. They walked silently through the city before finally coming to the lush wood that encompassed it. She led him through a forest thick with trees and flowers before coming to one of the ponds where the witches of the city bathed. The lady stepped onto the lake, her golden hair trailing like a train as she walked.

Féian followed and found that he did not sink. He walked beside the Lady, falling into stride with her. He looked down to see small fish swimming about beneath the clear surface of the beautiful lake that reflected the surrounding foliage and the endless night sky. Suddenly, in the very middle of the lake, the Lady stopped. She smiled before jumping into the air and diving cleanly into the center of the lake. Féian followed.

Just as Féian thought he was about to run out of air, the Lady swam through a crevice within the lake's rocky bottom. He suddenly found himself standing in a small circular grotto. It was a fair-sized space encircled in glittering rocks slightly overgrown with viridian moss and flora. At the opposite end stood a large dull black stone sitting on an intricately carved silver table, with two silver chalices engraved with black serpents with yellow eyes of amber on either side.

"What is this place?" He asked as he looked to see the night sky above them. The Lady only smiled at him and nodded before gently leading him to stand before the black stone that rested upon the table. She closed her eyes and suddenly the dull stone turned to reveal a side that was so highly polished that it served as a mirror.

I said that I would grant you the gift of farewell.

He knew that she had not really spoken.

In the night, many find solace, as shall you find yours in the moonlight. Watch your reflection closely.

Féian then turned to the mirror and gazed deeply into his own eyes when suddenly moonlight hit the stone and they began to transform. They became wider and a cold, piercing azure and the skin around them bloodless. He watched as his lighter eyebrows became black as his hair grew past his shoulders and then turned into perfect raven strands. The marks on his face faded to reveal perfect pallid skin and higher cheekbones. He gasped as Nerin's face stared back at him from the mirror.

"Féian?" He watched in awe as the lips parted to speak.

"Nerin…." he whispered, disbelievingly. "Is it really you?"

"Yes," Nerin replied. "But I have to tell you something, something incredibly important and I haven't much time."

"What is it?"

Nerin sighed and looked at him happily. "Their lanterns were unlit. I must return."

"What does that—wait, you are coming back?"

"In a way," Nerin replied enigmatically and Féian let out a frustrated groan.

"What does that mean, Nerin?"

"And they say that their lanterns will not be lit for you either," Nerin continued as if Féian had never spoken.

"What does that—"

"You will return too," Nerin said and Féian decided to stop asking Nerin to explain, as it appeared that he either would not or could not.

"Are you at peace?" Féian asked, hoping more than anything that after the life his friend had lived death would be kinder to him.

Nerin shook his head. "Now, don't give me that look. I was told that I will find peace soon enough, for I have earned it."

Féian nodded. "I only hope for death to be kind to you."

"I must depart soon but before I do I must thank you. While I am sorry that my death caused you grief, you did grieve and that means much to me. If it were not for you, I would not be missed," he said as he looked at the man before him. "I fear I must go now."

"So, this is our farewell then?" Féian asked apprehensively and Nerin smiled.

"You worry too much. All things are as they should be ere long," he replied and closed his eyes. Féian watched as Nerin's face became his again. He turned away from the mirror and looked to the Lady, who sat on a rock, running her fingers through strands of wet hair. Water drops glistened on her body like liquid silver in the moonlight.

"Do you know of what he speaks?"

Yes and no. While I understand him, I cannot fully comprehend him, for he speaks of death and I am the very essence of life.

"Would the Lord know?"

No. I am as the Lord is and he is as I am.

"Oh."

It is time that you returned.

Féian suddenly felt her lips lightly brush his and awoke on a blanket beneath the stars where he had fallen asleep. The little dark haired boy from earlier was curled up against him, sucking his thumb with the snake he was playing with earlier wrapped comfortably about his leg, apparently asleep as well. Across from him slept five little girls curled about each other like kittens and behind them a middle-aged husband and wife laying together, with the husband's arms wrapped possessively about his wife. Féian sighed and fell asleep again.

At the morning meal, Maveree announced that they would be leaving Merend Zetth shortly and resuming their journey. While Aralé was not particularly fond of the witch city and willing to brace the frigid northern weather if it meant finally departing, Féian was not of the same opinion. He had become very close with one of the largest families of Merend Zetth (not to mention that the little dark-haired boy had started to call him Uncle Féian). If it were not for the family that had taken him in, he would have fallen into a deep depression.

The night before their supposed departure, Féian came to Maveree and told her that he would not be leaving with her and Aralé. Maveree was surprisingly apathetic and even though Féian knew that she was not letting him stay out of the goodness of her heart and that she was merely letting him stay because she did not need him anymore, he was incredibly grateful.

On the day of their departure, the Lord and Lady of Merend Zetth gifted Maveree and Aralé two lightweight cloaks that had been enchanted to keep them warm and comfortable, regardless of the weather, and a beautiful flower. Féian stood beside the Lord and Lady of the city with the little boy hanging on his leg, watching as Maveree and Aralé trudged through the snow to a mountain that was barely visible in the distance.

Chapter XXIV
The Final Battle

The entire southern army had been in particularly foul spirits since the departure of the men of the Northern Isles. A week after Captain Larjus' disappearance, they had informed the rest of the army that they were loyal to their captain and had only come because he had convinced them. After arriving, they had only stayed to fight what they knew was a losing battle because Larjus had convinced them. They said very simply that after their captain had deserted, they had absolutely no reason to stay and every reason to leave, such as the wives, children, and friends they had left up north. Only one man of their entire faction stayed, Ilmaren.

While their group had not contributed an overwhelming amount of soldiers, with them gone, the odds of victory went from unlikely to astronomical. It showed plainly on the face of every remaining soldier. The atmosphere that surrounded the camp of the southern army was that of a graveyard. Even though the corpses had been piled and burned, the smell of them was still palpable. Supplies had run low and the hunters had almost no luck hunting.

It took all of the effort of the remaining captains to see to it the soldiers stayed focused and did not succumb to their fear, despair, and tedium and still they were largely unsuccessful. Many had simply given up for it was abundantly clear that they would die. Some had even fallen ill. Fever ran rampant through the southern army and, after the first attack, there were simply not enough healers and not enough medicine. Few who fell ill survived. By the time it had run its course, it had taken nearly a hundred men with it.

It was as they stood burning the corpses of the last of the fallen men and having a makeshift funeral for them that Phallé-Nal attacked for the last time in numbers larger than can be comprehended. The battle did not last long as the majority of those who remained were the untrained men of Amarant. They were quickly disposed of and took very few men of the enemy army with them. Amarant lasted longer than any of them.

The remaining men of Laaven and The Isles of the Sun fought as long as they could with the full understanding that it was just a matter of time. Danen and Ilmaren had been encircled and, side by side, they fought to the death. They had worked out rhythm, each utilizing their strengths and almost fighting as if they were one being with four arms that wielded both a sword and a massive hammer. Ilmaren was the first to fall, his head cut clean from his shoulders. Shortly after, an enemy soldier found a gap in Danen's armor and drove his sword through his thigh. Danen crumbled to the ground and bled to death in the midst of the chaos.

"It wasn't supposed to be this way," he muttered to no one in particular as he looked at Ilmaren's decapitated body, the head of which had been lost in the fray. There was another cadaver not far away, with an arrow jutting from its chest. He felt himself growing weaker and weaker as crimson blood flowed from the gaping wound in his thigh. The last thing he saw was Sern and Amarant standing back to back. In one swift motion, they changed swords to best be able to defeat the enemy soldiers attacking them and then drove the swords through the heads of the northern men.

Grytales and his men, along with a good number of Laaven's warriors, were a good distance away. From where they were, they appeared to be winning, for the men of The Isles of the Sun destroyed everything in their path. Within minutes after their energy started to diminish, the majority of them were slain, leaving only three of the youngest warriors of Laaven. They panicked and were shot down with arrows as they attempted to flee.

The Persian Rug

Within an hour, Sern, Amarant, one soldier of The Isles of the Sun, and two men from Laaven were all that were left of the entire southern battalion. Yet they fought on, knowing that far worse things awaited them in Phallé-Nal. Were they taken as prisoners, then death would await them. Soon, only Amarant and Sern were left. They attempted to fight but not one man from the other side would engage them in battle. An army of mostly blue-eyed men who exuded malevolence only smirked mordantly at the two remaining men.

"They want to take us as prisoners, alive," Amarant said as he stabbed one of the northern soldiers in the neck. The man fell in a bloody heap to the already ensanguined ground and none of the enemy soldiers so much as twitched.

"So our deaths can serve as the after dinner entertainment I presume?" Sern said as he lowered his sword slightly. They still stood back to back, watching the men that encircled them closely.

"Yes," Amarant replied quietly. "Look at how they grin."

"I won't give them the satisfaction," Sern replied and Amarant grabbed his sword hand as he started to raise it.

"Do not," he whispered. "Only a coward dies by their own hand."

The northern men watched as the two men glanced at one another for the longest of whiles. Just as they began to move toward Sern and Amarant, the last southern warriors drove their swords into the other's chest. Both fell to the ground in short-lived agony, blood pouring from their bodies as all grew cold and then light and cognizance faded from their eyes as all grew dark.

By dawn, the northern soldiers had piled all of the dead bodies and burned them in great pyres. Only piles of ash and bone and foul-smelling blood remained as the soldiers ran to the nearby Laaven to steal whatever they could for themselves before returning to their own country. They looted shops, homes, graves of the wealthy, and the Laaven castle, dragging behind them whatever they could carry. They killed mercilessly the few who they found in hiding.

Being that they were in foul spirits for having no prisoners to bring back to torture and not being able to lay waste to the country, the few unlucky men, women, and children who were found in hiding were given the same treatment as Sahena, all though most did not suffer as badly.

After three days of ravaging Laaven as much as they were allowed, the northern men began the return journey to Phallé-Nal.

Chapter XXV
The Empyrean Stairway

"Aralé!" Maveree bellowed as she glowered at the sleeping form of the young woman. Aralé had curled up in the snow and refused to rise. "The mountain is literally four steps away!" Maveree then gestured wildly beside them to the large, snow-covered mountain. Aralé looked up at the mountain and sighed.

"We are going to have to climb that, aren't we?" She asked with a small groan.

"Not exactly," Maveree replied and Aralé only rolled her eyes and let out an annoyed huff. "Why do you think it is called The Empyrean Stairway?"

"Because *The Empyrean Stairway* sounds better than *The Obnoxiously Large Chunk of Ice and Rock Situated Needlessly in the Middle of Nowhere*," Aralé snapped and Maveree sighed. With surprising strength, she pulled the tired young girl to her feet.

"Come, the sooner we make it to the blood fount, the sooner this whole misadventure comes to a close. Don't you want to sleep in a warm bed and stuff yourself with food until you burst again?"

At this, Aralé rose and headed for the mountain. She started to walk up its side only to fall back painfully to the ground. She glared at Maveree.

"Now, for the first time in your life you will be useful,"

Maveree said and she took a sharp silver knife that glinted in the sunlight. Aralé began to panic and slowly retreat. "Cease your cowardice," the seeress snapped. "I need your blood to bring about the actual stairway. Just a drop."

Aralé then cautiously inched forward until she stood before the seeress. Maveree motioned for Aralé to hold out her hand. The young girl did as she was told and closed her eyes as she held out her hand. Aralé whimpered as the sharp edge of the knife cut across the palm of her hand. She nearly fell over as Maveree pulled her so her hand hovered above the base of the mountain. She watched as several drops of blood fell from the open wound in her palm to the white snow. Suddenly, a stairway of ice and snow appeared before them and ascended the side of the mountain. Maveree smiled and stepped onto the first stair. She beckoned for Aralé to follow.

The pair walked until nightfall. They had climbed high enough for it to mean certain death if they fell. They had stopped on a snow-covered rock that jutted out from the mountain. It was then that Maveree took the flower the Lord and Lady of Merend Zetth had given them out of her pocket. She pulled off two petals. One she popped into her mouth and the other she gave to Aralé. She put it in her mouth to find that it not only quenched her hunger and thirst but relaxed her immensely and eased the pain in her sore muscles. Soon after eating, the pair fell into a contented sleep wrapped in their cloaks.

For five days they climbed The Empyrean Stairway in silence. On the fifth morning, after only a quarter of an hour of walking, the stairway ended at the pinnacle of the mountain. Upon reaching it, they found a cave entrance covered in ancient runes. Snow covered the edges of the sacred place but before the entrance to the cave, there was only white stone. The clouds hung so close that Aralé felt as if she could reach out and touch them.

"Aralé," Maveree said as she stood before the archway that marked the cave entrance. "I need your blood to be able to enter." Aralé held out her unscarred hand and Maveree ran the blade of the knife upon it and held Aralé's hand beneath the apex of the archway. Blood dripped from her palm onto the ground. The air grew cold and it began to lightly snow.

"Come along," Maveree said as she led Aralé into the dark of the cave. The cold of the cave bit through their cloaks. Their breath lingered in the air. After nearly an hour of following the old path through the dark of the cave, they came to a large stone chamber. There was a circular hole in the top, allowing light to pour down onto the tiered stone fountain that stood in the very center of the chamber. Crimson blood poured ceaselessly from it and runes covered its base. It looked as if it had been carved from the mountain. A golden chalice rested beside it. Aralé stared at all of this in awe when suddenly she realized that Maveree was nowhere to be found.

"Maveree?" She called as she advanced toward the fountain, which was bathed in rays of light. She started to scream when no answer came from the seeress.

After her fourth cry, she felt a sharp pain in the back of her head and crumbled to the cave floor. Maveree stood behind her. She held a sheathed dagger by the blade. The metal handle jutted out and gleamed in the scant light.

"I am sorry, but it's for the best," Maveree said to Aralé's unconscious body as she quickly walked over to the fountain and grabbed the golden chalice off of the edge. She placed it beside Aralé's outstretched arm and then took Aralé's limp arm and placed her wrist on top of the chalice. She then took the large silver knife from her cloak and dug the tip into Aralé's wrist across the blue veins. Blood began to pour from her wrist into the chalice. Aralé grew whiter and whiter as it quickly filled. Maveree watched and put the knife back in her cloak.

When the chalice was filled to the brim, Maveree peeled Aralé's arm from the top of the chalice and let it drop to the cave floor. She steadily held the cup as she brought it back to the blood fount. She carefully poured Aralé's blood into the fount, praying that it would work. Snow began to fall into the chamber around the fount. Maveree held the chalice under the blood that dripped off of the upper tier of the fountain until it filled to the brim.

She then brought it to her lips, nearly gagging on the contents of the chalice as she fought to drink every last drop. Feeling vertiginous and as if her stomach was about to burst, she clumsily kneeled beside the fountain.

"Return the soul I seek to me in the body of one of the children of Queen Aralevena Caladría II," she said as she gestured toward Aralé's cadaver and collapsed beside the blood fount.

The last thing she registered was darkness and agony, as if her body was being ripped apart.

Chapter XXVI
A Seeress's Advice

Noon was swiftly approaching and the sun high above the Kingdom of Laaven. In the fields, farmers were hard at work and in the streets merchants peddled their wares to passers-by. The rich did their business in lavish offices in grandiose stone dwellings and beggars did whatever they could to get their fill. The Laaven castle, in the very center of the kingdom, was buzzing with excitement for the very next day it would be the turn of the year and the Enembír Festival would take place.

While all of this activity and excitement took place in the kingdom at midday, one old man was just rolling out of bed to face the day. His joints were stiff and the night chill had left him aching. He stiffly rose, stretched, and dressed in blue before shuffling to the front door of his home. He trod across a rich carpet through halls richly decorated with all sorts of artifacts. From his window as he had awoken, he had seen that it was a beautiful day and immediately thought that it would be the perfect day to visit his horses at the stables. He slowly opened the wooden front door of his home to find a myriad of peasants sitting on and around his porch looking rather disappointed.

"Master Eriver," one particularly dirty looking boy called politely from the steps of the large porch. "Would you know if Mistress Eldestchild's about?"

Eriver was about to say that he did not and ask kindly if they would move so he could continue on his way when suddenly a peasant woman who looked too young to have a full head of grey hair stood beside him clutching a piece of parchment. "This was hanging on your door," she said as she held it out to him. Eriver thanked her and took the note. He unfolded it and read it.

Dearest Eriver,

Good morning. I hope that you slept well. I had urgent business at the castle and had to leave at dawn. I should return tonight unless something unexpected occurs (and knowing my life I do not think either of us would be overly surprised if it did).-Eriver chuckled at this- *Since none of the peasants who came to see me today can read, they will have most likely have been standing here for hours by the time you receive this. Tell them that I should return in a fortnight.*

Maveree

By the way: Since you are on your way to the stables can you give Beltaen, Óstara, and Brigantia an apple. Alban is with me.

Meanwhile, Maveree was having an audience with Risúrat in his study. The two had worked their way through half a bottle of wine.

"You could not possibly have come all this way simply to tell me to tell the prince to thank Nerin for helping all of those people during the fever epidemic in his speech," Risúrat said disbelievingly as he poured them both more wine.

"You are right. In actuality, I am here to pay the princess a visit," Maveree said with a sigh, as if she did not particularly want to see Princess Aralevena.

"Really? I was not aware that she called for you."

"She hasn't…yet."

The Persian Rug

"Ah," the man replied. "She is planning her escape no doubt."

"I will not deny it," Maveree said with a small chuckle. "In fact, I should probably go and deal with the wretch now," she said before bidding Risúrat good day and leaving his study. She was inconspicuously making her way through a crowded castle corridor, weaving her way in between legs when suddenly a loud cry of "Your Princess approaches! Look alive!" cleared the hallway so quickly that the frantic people bowled her over on their way to file against the walls. She sat in the center of the hallway, clutching her aching foot. The bulbous servant who had called for the hallway to be cleared took notice of her.

Less than a minute later, a lithe young woman who was fair of face stood at the end of the corridor. Golden hair flowed down her back in rivulets and her amber eyes closed almost entirely as she feigned a yawn to show that her servant had not cleared the hallway as fast as she would have liked. A slender youth who stood only a hair taller than her shifted uneasily beside her. He appeared even paler for his hair was deep black and his raiment was of the same color. His icy blue eyes were fixed on the heavy box he carried in his arms. He looked embarrassed at having a hallway cleared for him.

"The way is cleared," she stated more than asked.

"Yes highness," the short man replied.

"Good, now who will take Nerin's box—" the princess stopped as she looked into the corridor and saw Maveree sitting in the middle of it, obstructing her way. She glared at the small round servant who stood beside her.

"Child, move!" The servant called and Maveree narrowed her eyes.

"I would if the clumsy oaf carrying the house plant had not crushed my ankle beneath his lumbering feet!" She snapped. "Now, I came here to see Princess Aralevena, not be turned to paste under a stampede of incompetent servants!"

"Who *are* you?" The princess spat, growing impatient with

the loquacious little girl who simply would not get out of her way.

"I am Mistress Maveree Eldestchild," she said and the princess paled slightly, realizing that she had just offended the only person who could help her. "And I have come to have an audience with you, Your Highness," Aralé nodded.

"Good day to you, Master Nerin," The princess said quickly and left Nerin standing alone. He looked as if he had been kicked in the stomach as Aralé led a limping Maveree away. She led her through corridor after corridor, which were all cleared for her in a similar fashion, to the very last door in an abandoned corridor.

"This is an old library. I am the only one that comes here," Aralé explained as she opened the door and they walked inside to find walls lined with dusty old bookshelves, several wooden tables covered with a thick layer of dust and a large window with moth-eaten curtains fluttering in the breeze. Dust covered candles in tarnished silver holders sat on all of the tables.

"I was going to send for you this afternoon," the princess said without preamble as she sat on one of the old dust-covered chairs in the library.

"I know. I was nearby and thought that I would save you the trouble for I will not do what you ask."

Aralé looked shocked at being told no before becoming angry. "What do you mean *you will not do what I ask*? I am the princess! You will do whatever I ask!" She half-whined, her arms folded. Maveree rolled her eyes.

"Having knowledge of past, present, and future, I may just be privy to some knowledge that you are not and therefore be capable of making more prudent decisions," Maveree said and the princess only stared at her blankly. "I see past, present and future. I know things that you do not. Listen to me."

The princess considered this for several minutes before looking back to Maveree. "I am listening," she finally said grudgingly.

"Something is coming, Your Highness, and it is not the war you fear. The time to run is not now. If you do as I say, there may never even be a war and you can live happily here for the rest of your days."

"No war? What must I do?" Aralé asked somberly as she stopped drawing patterns in the dust atop the table.

"You must seduce and marry Captain Sern," Maveree said somberly and Aralé rolled her eyes.

"That is already as good as done. He has been madly in love with me for months now. Is that really all that I have to do to forestall war and be able to stay safely within Laaven?"

"Yes, that's all."

Aralé suddenly looked pensive. "He is slightly older than I like my men, honestly," she mused. "But I suppose he is handsome enough. Perhaps he would be more suitable after a sound scrubbing...or four. On the other hand, his eyes are quite gorgeous..."

Maveree excused herself from the princess' company as the young girl continued to think aloud. The seeress painfully limped to the healing wing. Upon entering, all of the young apprentices' faces lit up.

"Mistress Eldestchild!" They greeted her happily as they looked up from their tasks. Some were tending to patients with incredibly minor wounds while the few others in the room organized or cleaned. Their smiles faded as they realized that she was limping.

"What happened?" The group of young boys asked collectively. They looked to be no older than twelve.

"I got trampled in the hall by an imbecile carrying a plant," she muttered as two of the boys who had been organizing small bottles on shelves came toward her. They were dark-haired, cherubic, and obviously related. They quietly helped her to one of the divans in the large open room and sat her down.

"When you fell, the bone popped out," one explained confidently as the other sat before her on the floor with her dainty foot in his hand, examining it. "We are going to have to pop the bone back in. It hurts really bad," he finished and Maveree nodded. She let out a mostly stifled cry of pain as the apprentice manipulated her ankle and the bone popped right back in.

"It will be sore for a while," the other said. "There is a salve for pain we can give you," Maveree nodded wildly, unable to speak. One of the young boys left and returned with a small phial filled with an off-white liquid. He poured some into his hands and began to lightly rub it onto her sore ankle with deft fingers.

"Mistress Eldestchild," Maveree looked up to see the robed form of the Castle Healer, Master Dorin standing before her.

"Master Dorin," she replied. "I've been looking for you. There is something important that I must speak with you about," she said quietly and Dorin nodded.

"That is enough," he said to the apprentice who had been massaging Maveree's ankle for nearly ten minutes when only really three or four were necessary. The boy smiled sheepishly and backed away as Dorin helped Maveree into his study. Once there, he locked the door behind them and helped Maveree into one of the chairs before his desk.

"I have come to tell you something of dire importance. I will only say this once and then I must leave. Do not question me," she said without preamble and Dorin only nodded. "Risúrat knows where you keep your poisons and he is going to break in and steal a phial for the purpose of murder. You must destroy every last poison you possess." Maveree then rose from her chair and limped out of his office and through the healing wing. Upon reaching the busy corridor, she grabbed the first servant she saw.

"See to it that a carriage is prepared for Maveree Eldestchild in a quarter of an hour in front of the castle gates," she commanded and the servant only nodded before continuing on. In exactly a quarter of an hour, she was sitting in a carriage sleeping peacefully as she was driven back to The City of the Wood.

Princess Aralé was still sitting in the forgotten library at the same dust-covered old table when the bell signaling the midday meal rang. She mentally kicked herself upon realizing that she had been sitting alone talking to herself for nearly an hour. She

The Persian Rug

rose, brushed the dust from the furniture off of her dress, and left the old library. Her stomach was grumbling insistently by the time she reached the dining hall. It was rather crowded as she took her seat at the royal table next to her brother, who was staring disgustedly at a piece of pork on his plate.

"Hello brother," she said absently as she shoved forkfuls of whatever was in grabbing distance onto her plate. She was not satisfied until she had a veritable mountain of meat, pheasant, potatoes, pudding, and bread heaped onto her plate. She looked up to see him staring at her large plate of food as if it made him sick. She rolled her eyes and started to voraciously gorge herself.

"Father's too ill to join us I take it," she said through a mouthful of potato and Amíen grimaced and nodded.

"Risúrat tells me that he can barely stand," the prince said as he idly poked at his now cold piece of pork with a fork. Aralé looked up to see Risúrat, a tall, thin middle-aged man with grey hair and a grey beard standing by the entrance to the great hall, looking entirely too pleased with himself.

"When you are king you will get rid of Risúrat, yes?" She whispered, taking the untouched pork off of her brother's plate and starting to eat it after quickly finishing hers. "There is something most unwholesome about him."

The prince mock sighed. "Women are such suspicious creatures. He is harmless. Since father is ill and cannot give the speech at the festival tomorrow he personally helped me write one." Aralé snorted before returning to her ham. After finishing, she gazed about the crowded room as if looking for someone and turned back to her brother who was idly pushing peas around on his plate. He still had not eaten even a bite of food.

"And what of Captain Sern, is he sick as well?" Aralé spat as she poured a double helping of pudding on her plate.

"No, he is in his tree. The man seemed troubled when I spoke with him this morning to find out where you were. Oh and speaking of which, where were you this morning? I wanted to make sure that our festival outfits are not too similar and it was as if you had disappeared!"

"I was…" She trailed off, an idea suddenly striking her and her lips curving into a devious smile. "I will see you later Amíen," Aralé said before taking another bite from her brother's plate.

"What are you planning now?" Amíen replied with an exasperated sigh, but did not get an answer for his sister had already disappeared.

The princess had left the castle and wondered into the warm sunshine pervading the grounds. She walked through the gardens to the back of the castle grounds where the only thing that separated them from the wood beyond was tall, thorny hedgerow. She stepped through the underbrush and stopped before one of the tallest trees. The black clad leg dangling from one of the lower branches denoted the older man's presence.

"Sern?" She called from the ground and watched as his form emerged from the leaves. He deftly swung from branch to branch until he came to one low enough that he could drop to the ground safely. He landed on the ground and bowed in one fluid motion.

"Hello Your Highness," he said and Aralé took his face gently in her hands, forcing him to look her in the eyes.

"If you must be so formal in public you must, but never when we are alone," she said as she truly studied his face and came to the conclusion that he was indeed handsome enough for her to tolerate.

"Very well, Aralé," he said as he rose from his knees. "What brings you out here?" He asked as he sat against the trunk of a tree in the dirt.

"I…" She stuttered as she struggled to think of an excuse that would sound valid. "I have done something terrible," she said and Sern only looked at her, not quite sure of what to expect. He looked at her questioningly but also sympathetically. "The worst thing you can possibly do to a person."

"I doubt that," Sern said with a small smile, knowing that Aralé could be overdramatic. "Come," he said gently, patting the ground beside him. Aralé did not particularly want to sit in the dirt and soil her dress, but at the moment there were more important things than her gown. She sat beside him in the dirt.

"I do not love Nerin," she said and Sern had to hold back a gasp. "He is in love with me and I do not feel the same way. I have known that he's in love with me for months and instead of being honest with him, I have been stalling telling him how I truly feel."

"Why?" Sern asked as he looked at the distraught young woman before him. Aralé sat for several minutes, feigning tears as she thought of a convincing reason and a way to make the conversation suit her purposes.

"Sometimes he makes me forget that I cannot have the one person I want," she replied quietly.

"That is not fair to Nerin," Sern replied quickly, wondering who she felt so deeply for.

"I know," she said sadly. "Have you not ever wanted someone you could not have?"

You do not know the half of it, he thought miserably. "Yes," he finally said and Aralé smirked inwardly.

"Who?" The princess asked and watched as the older man's eyes darted from tree to tree and back, as if somewhere in the woods he would find an answer. He was clearly panicking. She then reached out and gently touched his face as she quickly kissed his lips.

"I…I…" She stuttered. Her face flushed. Sern looked as if he had just died of shock only to find that, in death, a man is given everything he could ever want.

"So it would seem," he said after several long minutes. "That you and I love one another, Nerin loves you, and tomorrow night at the Enembír Festival you will meet your betrothed. This will make for quite an interesting party," he said as he tentatively reached out and took her hand in his.

Chelsea Isadora Teich

Chapter XXVII
Evil Hour

Nerin had returned to the House of Anív, where he did his healing work. He dutifully worked straight through the evening meal and until the head healer Anív forced him to retire. Near midnight, Nerin unwillingly returned to his bedroom that, due to his position as second in command, was private. He could not believe what Aralé had just done. His heart ached for her all week and she had dismissed him happily in a second. While he was hurt, he was not angry for he felt he had gotten what he had deserved regardless of the fact that he had done nothing to merit being swept aside so callously.

He had spent the majority of the night before pacing around his room reminding himself that he was worthless and Aralé had probably found someone better and stronger. He collapsed in a heap in his bed at dawn. However his rest was not peaceful, as he could be heard screaming. He slept until late in the afternoon.

"Nerin, my healer," The young man's icy eyes slowly opened as a soft, lilting voice interrupted his dreams and a gentle hand nudged his shoulder. "You are back among the living I see," Anív said with a small chuckle after he saw the younger man had fully regained consciousness. Nerin looked up at the older man who sat before him, dark eyes regarding him kindly and the lines etched in his face accentuated in the light.

"You looked most troubled in your sleep," Anív finally said after a prolonged silence. His weathered hands were wrapped around one of the many crystals he wore about his neck. Silver rings embedded with stones of all colors covered his slender fingers and he wore gemstone bracelets. He held a small opaque yellow stone of in his hands.

"Only dreams," Nerin replied stiffly. He was clearly done talking.

"Dreams or memories, child?" The elder healer replied, ever patient with Nerin whom, in all of the years he had been there, refused to speak of his past or anything even remotely personal. Men he had known for years could not have even truthfully told where he hailed from.

"Dreams," Nerin replied, trying to stand but being halted by Anív.

"I hold in my hand a stone called citrine. It will soothe your troubled rest. Would you like to tell me of your dreams? You were screaming in your sleep last night."

"As I have done before and will do again. In any case, my foolish nightmares are nothing to burden you with. Keep your stones, they will not avail me," Nerin said and Anív sighed.

"I suppose you do not wish to tell me why you returned from the palace so distraught yesterday."

"I know not what you mean."

"Of course not," Anív replied sadly. "Several times over the past year you returned from your weekly errand at the palace in a similar state, once even near tears, and yet every time you deny it with vehemence. I care deeply for any healer who works beneath me and you are no exception. You cannot truly wish to keep all of your secrets," Anív said as he looked to Nerin's forearm that had been unintentionally exposed in his sleep. White flesh marred with gruesome scars seemed to glow in the setting sun against his black clothes and bedspread. After noticing the elder healer's eyes on it, he swiftly buttoned the sleeve of his shirt and pulled a black glove over his slender hand.

"I have no secrets."

"Very well," the elder healer rose. "Are you going to the turning of the year festivities?"

The Persian Rug

Nerin thought on it. Perhaps if he went there would be the smallest chance that he could corner the princess and talk to her.

"Yes. After all, how often does one get to watch the year one-thousand nine hundred seventy-seven dawn?" Nerin said almost lightheartedly and Anív watched him with slight suspicion.

"Only once an age," the older healer replied. "And before you know the second age will pass and the third will begin."

"I doubt that thirty-some-odd years will fly so quickly," Nerin said. "Now, I hate to be rude but I very well cannot dress with you here."

The older healer nodded and left, leaving Nerin alone to dress and ready himself. Nerin quickly went to the small dresser that occupied a corner of his bedchamber. He pulled out a rich velvet outfit of dark blue and laid it on his bed. He quickly began to dress.

As the festival was about to begin, Prince Amíen the Third sat by his father who lay wrapped up in his bed as he shivered. As a man of only thirty-nine years, he appeared to be at least seventy. His sickly and cadaverous body quaked beneath the thick coverlet, thin dark hair was plastered to his wan face, and his sunken eyes stared blankly into the distance at things unseen. The prince watched in pity and fear as his father muttered something unintelligible.

"I wish that you could be at the festival father," Amíen said sadly, wondering if his father could even hear him. "Sister will be meeting the King of Nallel, as you arranged...and Risúrat helped me write a speech to give tonight at the..." He trailed off, hearing his father croak loudly. Amen was immediately struck with fear. He had seen servants die in similar states. "Father!" He exclaimed, reaching for one of the king's skeletal hands and becoming confused when his father callously shoved it away.

"Get...Risúrat," his father said through his wheezing and convulsing. Amíen looked hurt for only a second before skillfully masking it.

"As you command," Amíen bowed and quickly exited the room. He found Risúrat waiting just down the hall, talking to a servant. He strode over to him and told him that the king had called for him. Risúrat bowed respectfully before heading nonchalantly toward the king's bedchamber. The prince made his way to the festivities.

Risúrat sighed as he turned the doorknob and gently slid the door open, admitting himself without his majesty's permission. He then slammed the door behind him and watched the writhing shape on the bed blench and grimace before starting to convulse. It was only for a brief moment. However, it left the king hoarsely moaning in agony and dripping with cold sweat.

"Risúrat!" The king called as loudly as his hoarse voice and bleeding throat would allow.

"Yes, milord," the man said, bending by the king's bed. The king reached out with one almost transparent hand and gripped the older man's collar with a strength he did not look to possess. Sallow eyes bulged out of his head as he let out a moan of agony for his bones and muscles ached but hurt tenfold whenever he moved.

"Four days!" The king cried before letting go as it hurt too much. He started to shiver again. "So cold."

"Milord—" Risúrat began but was interrupted.

"So cold!" The king bellowed, tears running down his cheeks. "Cannot take…" He trailed of his face suddenly blanching and contorting as he leaned over and retched all over the floor.

"What are you asking of me, milord?" Risúrat asked, though he already knew and he did not bother to hide it.

"Knife," the king said as he rolled himself back up in the blankets, cringing as he did so for even the smallest movement caused him great agony. "There is a knife in the top drawer!" And he started to sweat, no longer feeling cold he threw the coverlets that had been piled atop him away and the king cried as his muscles and bones protested.

"You want me to end it sire?" Risúrat asked mockingly.

"Yess," the king hissed. "Four days! No more!"

The Persian Rug

Risúrat took his time going through the drawer even though there was nothing but a long silver knife, a few letters, pens, and scattered papers stacked neatly within. Then he slowly drew the knife and looked at it, watching the room reflect in its lustrous surface.

"Risúrat!" The king whined and the older man smiled maliciously. "If you try my patience I will have you wait another day," he threatened even though he had no intention of doing so.

The king croaked unhappily. "Sorry! Sorry! S-so..." he trailed off his body started to shake violently. When the convulsions ceased and the king lay limp on the bed, Risúrat took out a small red satin pouch. He stuck the very tip of the knife gently into the pouch, cutting its contents into smaller pieces. He then propped the king up on several pillows and placed the pouch in his hand. The king cradled it and pressed it to his nose, there he inhaled its contents. His eyes rolled back into his head and his body quaked as he inhaled with all of the strength that remained in him. Tears streamed down his face as the sharper shards of the crystalline substance cut his nose and throat. The worse it burned and the more he bled, the more he wanted and the harder it was to stop.

He knew that one day he would simply take so much that it would kill him. Or perhaps one day Risúrat would decide to torture him and simply stop supplying him and wait for the seizures that came with withdrawal to finish him. However, at that moment, all of those macabre thoughts were far from whatever of his mind was left after a decade of torturing his body in such a way. He laughed as blood dripped from a nose he could no longer smell through. He laughed through a face contorted with pain as the jagged shards tore at him. He laughed until he had finally drawn in more than he could take and fell limp against his pillows, eyes open and blankly rolling about in his head.

Risúrat removed the pouch from the king's hand and tucked it back into a hidden pocket in his robes. He looked down in disdain at the king before taking his wrist and putting it to his ear, listening for a pulse. He scowled upon finding one.

"Perhaps next time then?" He said with a sigh. Then he wiped the blood and excess powder from the king's face and pushed his eyelids over his eyes before exiting the room and making his way to the festivities.

The prince and princess sat on their thrones before the fourth of the seven long tables that spanned the garden. Each was piled high with food and wine. The princess was feasting greedily on these while her brother only eyed the food nervously and sipped at a cup of wine. She was a vision in a light purple and silver gown with sleeves so long that they almost trailed the ground. Her long golden hair was wound in intricate designs with silver clasps. Amíen, who sat at the head of the table, was dressed in a glorious outfit of crimson velvet. Small rubies hung from his ears and his hair was pulled out of his face in a crimson clasp adorned with gems.

"Come now brother, eat. One could count the bones in your hands," Aralé said as she took a bite out of a leg of pheasant and got food on her cheek

"And risk bollixing this outfit! Hardly! Do you know how long I had to stand there as they made alterations?" He asked, wincing as his sister smiled, showing the food stuck in her teeth.

"Five–and-a-half days," she said in between gluttonous bites. Amíen found the sight repulsive. "And it would have taken less than three hours if his royal highness was not so fussy," she said taking a bite and her brother huffed.

"It is not my fault that they do not understand that you cannot mix different shades of red and that large buttons are not the fashion anymore," he said and took a sip of wine.

"You should hear yourself. You are such a woman," the princess said through a bite of food and the prince winced visibly at the sight.

"And you are such a slob," he said and grimaced as his sister stuck out her tongue, revealing a repulsive stew of half-chewed food and vegetables. Amíen's eyes suddenly grew wide. "The King of Nallel is here! Oh my! Oh my!" He said as he looked at the group of people entering the gardens clad in grey. He immediately took Aralé's plate of food away from her and silenced her as she began to protest. "Clean off your face and get the food out of your teeth!" He said frantically and did it for her. "Now, King Seraavran will ask you to call him Seraav if he likes you. If he does, just do it and tell him to call you Aralé, but have him call you by your full name and call him by his until he asks you to call him Seraav. His left thigh is wounded from battle and never healed properly so do not brush up against it by accident when you dance or ever. Do not touch it ever. He has a weakness for blondes so if he tries to touch your hair, do not stop him. Oh, and when he makes jokes, which he will for he is a pretty wit and loves a person who can keep up, laugh and touch his arm lightly—"

"You know a lot about King Seraavran, Amíen. Maybe you should become his queen in my stead," Aralé said with a laugh.

"Hardly," Amíen rolled his eyes. "I am just trying to be helpful. You forget that I have known him since he was Prince Seraavran. He has told me all that he looks for in a wife."

"I personally think it a wonderful idea. You already have more jewelry than any queen I have ever heard of," Aralé said and her brother sighed before a genuine smile overtook his handsome face.

"King Seraavran!" He exclaimed and was enveloped into a warm hug by a man nearly a head taller than him. King Seraavran was a well-built man of twenty-two years with a thick head of tawny hair and deep brown eyes. He was dressed far more modestly than Prince Amíen in a simple yet elegant outfit of twilight grey. A silver circlet engraved with serpents and diamonds sat on his head. In Aralé's opinion, Sern was far more attractive.

"Why so formal Amí?" He asked and let go of the young prince. Aralé laughed inwardly at the pet name. "You have grown so tall! I suppose you are beating women off with a stick!" He exclaimed and Amíen blushed slightly. "But you are so very thin! Is your father not feeding you?" He asked only half jokingly and Amíen was about to respond when he remembered the real reason Seraavran had come.

"Seraav, I would like to introduce you to my sister, Princess Aralevena Caladría II," Amíen said as he took his suddenly shy sister by the wrist and pulled her forward so she stood before him. Seraavran had obviously anticipated her to act in such a way and had prepared to charm her.

"Hello, princess," he bowed and took her hand, lightly kissing it.

"Hello King Seraavran," she replied quietly and stepped forward, curtseying stiffly. Amíen watched as his sister and his friend went off to dance. He could not believe how Aralé was acting. His sister did not have a demure bone in her body and yet, with Seraavran, she played the blushing maiden to perfection.

His suspicious thoughts were interrupted by a small group of giggling young noblewomen who encircled him.

Sern stood at the other end of the garden by the musicians, casually glancing at everything but Princess Aralevena and King Seraavran. He was dressed in black and looked almost elegant even though his hair was not pulled back and his face was not clean-shaven. He wore no rings on his fingers or gems in his ears. A silver chain showed above his open collar. However, whatever hung at the bottom of the chain was hidden beneath his tunic.

"Captain." He looked beside him to see a small girl dressed in black and silver sipping from a large goblet of wine. Her long blonde hair fell freely about her face. He thought about how out of place they must have looked, loitering around in black like mourners at a joyous festival.

"Maveree," he said in greeting. He could see Queen Eríé, from The Isles of the Sun, trying to act as if she were not watching him from across the floor.

"Do you really love her?" Maveree asked as she nodded toward Aralé who was still uneasily dancing with the King of Nallel.

"Yes," he replied quietly.

"Do you want her to belong to you and you alone?"

"Yes," Sern replied emphatically after a short pause.

"You two are fated, you know," Maveree said with a

mischievous grin. "And I could help fate along slightly for a price."

"Maveree—" Sern began as he shook his head.

"Do you trust me?" She interrupted.

Sern sighed exasperatedly. "I am not entirely sure."

"Well decide quickly, for I do not often feel so generous," Maveree replied and watched the conflict writ in Sern's face and eyes as he mulled over her proposal.

"What do you want in return?" He asked after a long while.

"I want a seat at the King's Council," she said and Sern sprayed the wine he had been drinking all over the ground.

"Are you insane!? Even as a prince, I would not be able to give you a seat at the King's Council!"

"But you could use your powers of persuasion. Amíen is very easily persuaded," Maveree said matter-of-factly. Sern nodded.

"If you can see to it that Aralé is mine, I will see to it that a seat at the King's Council is yours."

"Very well," Maveree replied and disappeared into the crowd. Sern once again found himself standing alone.

Nerin and Anív had just arrived at the festival to find the party already in full swing. Nerin had every intention of finding Aralé and trying to find a way to discreetly get her somewhere where they could talk. After nearly a quarter of an hour of pushing his way through the crowd, he finally came across Aralé and Seraavran. Neither looked too happy.

"I am sorry." He heard Aralé say as they swayed to the music stiffly.

"It is all right. I understand," he replied dispassionately. "My belated wife was the love of my life. I know that happiness and I would not deny you it. I will just tell your father that I am sorry, but I am simply not ready to marry again, it being less than a year since my wife passed."

"Thank you," Aralé replied with a feigned smile. After overhearing this, Nerin felt almost giddy with glee. It would seem that she loved him after all. He happily walked back to one of the tables and sat down. It seemed that all would be well. He sat at his chair, happily pondering until the time came for the annual speech given by the king.

He watched with almost nonexistent interest as the music stopped and the dancers and loiterers moved to tables. He watched as Amíen walked across the stage to the dais. The second he started to speak, Nerin tuned out and began to study the blades of grass beneath him. Several times, he became semi-aware of short lived bouts of laughter from the people around him but he had absolutely no idea as to what was being said nor did he particularly care.

Suddenly, he felt eyes on him and looked up to see nearly everyone at the festival watching him.

"Come now, my speech is not *that* dull is it?" The prince asked facetiously from behind the dais, causing the audience to laugh and Nerin to blink inanely. The prince sighed. "I just called you to the stage so you could be properly thanked for all of your work with victims of fever during the epidemic five months ago." He then gestured for Nerin to come forward with one of his long fingers.

Nerin blushed as he made his way through the maze of tables to the stage where the prince stood. By the time he stood beside Amíen at the dais, he was crimson. He was lucky that Amíen was both too unconstrained and too inebriated to take his lack of attention personally. Amíen had nearly wedged the poor healer between himself and the dais and had his arm draped about his shoulder as he went on a semi-drunken rant about what a skilled healer Nerin was. Luckily, the majority of the people present at the Enembír Festival were too inebriated to care much.

Nerin had almost grown used to the eyes on him when suddenly Maveree stood up in the midst of the crowd. "Look! There is a man on the roof!" She cried, pointing wildly at the roof. The crowd looked.

The assassin knew that he had been discovered. He also knew that left him with almost no time to complete his task. He quickly readied and fired three arrows before fleeing.

The Persian Rug

One of these arrows struck a woman in the audience in the shoulder, the second hit the stage, and the third pierced Nerin's chest. Screams erupted from the crowd as blood poured, staining the fletching of the arrow red. He had no time to react or to suffer as the arrow had completely pierced his heart, killing him instantly.

The momentum of the arrow sent him falling backward atop the petrified prince. As he fell, the arrow pierced Amíen and the poison entered his blood. By the time the princess had gotten to the stage, the poison had ravaged her brother. He lay dead, bathed in both Nerin's and his own blood. This was the scene Aralé beheld. She let out an ear piercing cry before fainting beside them. The crowd began and there would have been mass pandemonium had Sern not rose from his seat at the warrior's table and stepped behind the dais.

"SILENCE!" He bellowed.

Chelsea Isadora Teich

Chapter XXVIII
The Beginning

Aralé found herself falling into bed after the most trying week she could ever remember having the misfortune to experience. After the death of her brother, there had been a rushed funeral the next day, which almost no one aside from the castle staff attended as nearly everyone in the kingdom had attended Nerin's funeral that was being held in the countryside. Any relatives from other countries could not attend as it would take anywhere from days to weeks for them to arrive. While there was indeed a crowd at his funeral, the majority of them were obviously only there because it gave them a few hours break from their duties.

The single funeral quickly became an unceremonious double funeral after an untimely interruption. When Risúrat had gone to fetch the king, Aralé sent several servants to follow him, as she did not trust him. They had found him helping the king overdose on some foul substance and had dragged him back down to Aralé with the powder still on his fingers. The bag of it in his cloak only helped to cement his fate. He kicked and screamed as two soldiers grabbed him and dragged him away. He would spend the rest of his miserable life imprisoned.

The next thing Aralé knew, her father was announced dead and two healers were carrying him through a crowd of apathetic servants and nobles who were only there to gain her favor. Her father was a useless madman who was apparently addicted to foul street powders and her brother was an overly feminine and equally useless moronic coward. It only seemed natural that no one would truly mourn for them. Nevertheless, an entire afternoon was filled with empty speeches and nobles using every opportunity to flatter the young girl who would one day be their queen.

Scandalized by her wretched father, who she did not at all lament being rid of, and deeply grieving for her brother, she collapsed into bed and spent the night inconsolably sobbing. The fact that everyone else was unaffected by the death of the only person in the world she truly cared for only served to torment her more. After a night of almost no sleep, she stumbled down to dining hall for breakfast where the advisors immediately started to convince her that the first thing that she should do is marry and procure an heir. Not even a day after the only family she had left in the world had passed, the councilmen had a list of potential husbands prepared for her and seemed intent on getting her to choose one of them immediately.

At this, she fled to the old neglected library she often took sanctuary in. she lay on the floor in the dust and sobbed until that night when Sern finally came and found her. She had cried herself unconscious and her head and hands were bleeding and bruised as was the floor beneath them. She had violently bashed her head and fists against the stone floor in a fit of anguish and misguided rage. It looked as if she had done this until she had given herself a concussion. Sern gathered the frail young woman in his arms and took her to the healing wing where she spent three days suffering from a concussion so severe that every time she attempted to move she would either collapse with painful vertigo or retch miserably. Her right wrist was broken and swollen painfully and nearly all of her fingers were broken.

The very second the princess was released the councilmen approached her about choosing a husband. Delirious with pain and also with all of the calming and pain elixirs coursing through her she very groggily laughed and told them kindly that she would have them hanged from the tallest tree in the kingdom the next time they mentioned anything of the like to her. She then collapsed on the ground in fits of laughter and continued to cackle as she was dragged back to the healing wing. It had seemed that one of the healers had unwittingly combined two pain elixirs. While together they did not assuage her pain, they made her too giddy to care that she was in agony.

When the elixirs wore off, she was miserable again but deemed healthy enough for them to start making her immune to poisons. The process would take two weeks. During these two weeks, she would be given enough of certain poisons every day to make her violently ill, but not enough to kill her. She was told that she would build immunity to all of the poisons and then they would stop making her sick. A week had passed and she still spent all of her days in agony and horrendously ill. The healers had told her that for some reason it was taking her longer to build immunity and it might even take an extra week. She was at her wits' end and her only solace was Sern, who held her hair as she retched, held her as she shivered and moaned, and allowed her to use him as a pillow when she slept as she had done when she was a little girl.

She had spent her week grief-stricken and violently ill with very little sleep. It was dark as she awakened in the hospital wing, clutching her stomach as she pondered the worst week she had ever experienced. She had expected to awake to find Sern wrapped around her, holding her protectively as they slept, as he had taken to ever since she asked him to. Part of her was cognizant of how inappropriate that was as she rolled out of the hospital bed and onto the floor where she could retch without soiling the bed. Her body was wracked with spasms as she vomited bile and wondered why Sern was not there. Tears streamed down her cheeks. She felt like a child.

Sern sighed as he rode through the early morning to the deserted City of the Wood. He had to see Maveree and he prayed that she was expecting him and he would find her sitting on her porch, smoking a pipe and inadvertently glaring into the night as if she had a score to settle with it. He sighed, his horse running freely at full speed without any real direction from his rider as he galloped on. Sern relished the freedom he felt as they sped through the nearly silent early morning.

An hour before dawn, he came to the house of Mistress Maveree Eldestchild. She sat cloaked on her front porch with a flask resting in her lap and a pipe pressed between her lips. Smoke billowed ominously about her dark cloaked form.

"Some things never change," she thought aloud without preamble as Sern dismounted. While Sern could not see her thoughtful smile, he heard it in her voice. It was somehow completely apparent that he did not need to answer as she was not exactly speaking to him. He stood in the dark beside his horse, waiting for her to invite him to sit down as he doubted that she would invite him inside as propriety dictated. "You still only visit me when you need something," she finished reflectively and gestured for him to sit on the porch beside her.

"Personally, I do not understand why you would wish to nullify our accord," she said after a short silence.

"How could you possibly—" Sern began to ask but Maveree interrupted.

"Seeress," she deadpanned and let out an impatient sigh before continuing. "Your types always have to make things more complicated than need be."

"What do you mean?" Sern asked as he watched the little seeress inhale some more smoke happily and grumbled exasperatedly.

"We both know that Aralé, now being the last of the noble house of Vénatheln, will become queen when she marries. Marrying her will make you king. Now, you and your endless nobility and ceaseless self-effacement could not just accept that even if you know that is precisely what will happen. You can waste your time partaking in some good old-fashioned doubtfulness and self-deprecation and have all of your dearest friends tell you what a marvelous king you would make before you ask Aralé for her hand, or you can skip all of that and simply walk up to her tomorrow during breakfast and ask her if she would consider you worthy. We both know that she does," Maveree said in a huff.

"Well, firstly that is not exceedingly romantic," Sern replied and Maveree let out a disgusted snort.

"Romance? *Please!*"

"And secondly, I have no royal title, no royal blood, and not a coin to my name. Aralé would have me just as I am, but society is not so kind."

"Do not underestimate the weight your name carries. Men fear you. Remind them that you are the greatest warrior who has ever lived, that should make society *plenty* kind." There was a long silence during which Maveree and Sern drank from her flask before Maveree spoke again. "Admit it. As much as you hate it you know that I am right."

"Of course, you're always right," Sern replied matter-of-factly and Maveree nodded.

"This interesting turn of events conveniently makes it even easier for me to have a reserved seat at the King's Council…" She mused. "What a funny world we live in, eh?"

Sern suddenly felt sick to his stomach. "Maveree, you weren't perchance-"

"Involved in the prince's assassination? You might say that, then again you might not, but that is unimportant. The important thing is that you get your pretty wench and I get my position of power. You only need to know that you have my allegiance and there are none who could ever take it from you."

"Oh," Sern replied. "What did I do to earn such a thing? On numerous occasions you have told me that you serve him or her who best serves you."

Maveree chuckled mysteriously. "I think that you should return to the castle in time for breakfast," she said with a grin. "And no, I will not answer your question."

Sern sighed and rose from the porch. He mounted his horse and sped back the way he had come. He arrived at the castle just as breakfast was being served and as Aralé arrived, he asked for her hand before the entire hall, which broke into wild applause when she accepted. The councilmen were decidedly split. Half of them clapped whilst the other stepped forward to accost Sern. He only smirked at them, which was quite out of character for the usually staid man. Any argument they had ceased with one statement.

"Would you even consider attacking a country that is under my rule?" He asked as he smirked and this stopped any argument from the councilmen who suddenly decided that they did not find the idea of a man with absolutely no royal background to speak of becoming king as loathsome. In the room of ecstatic people sat a very somber looking Dorin and a clearly petrified Danen. They sent each other sad looks across the hall.

Their wedding was going to be held as soon as Aralé recovered from the process of being made immune to various poisons. It was obviously going to be a rushed affair since people cared more about having a king on the throne than Sern and Aralé having a beautiful romantic wedding. Not everyone was so happy about the impending marriage. Nearly all of Sern's friends attempted to dissuade him, claiming that Aralé was "pure evil" and that "her claws and fangs would come out shortly after marriage and he would be hopelessly chained to some sort of creature for the rest of his life." He ignored them. The majority of the upper class was averse to the marriage as well. They knew that Sern would be a king of the people, meaning that he would serve the poorer majority.

Regardless, their wedding day finally came on a relatively cold and rainy day in February. In a last effort to talk some sense into Sern, Danen tried to convince him that the rain was an omen. Sern did not listen.

Being that Aralé had only distant family remaining and Sern had only a mother and a sister he had not seen or heard from since he was a child, all customs involving the families of the betrothed were ignored at their wedding. They simply said their vows in archaic and outdated language before the entire kingdom and the many royal guests from other kingdoms who stood in the rain in the southern gardens. Both were clad in ethereal sere raiment.

Sern placed the silver crown of the queen on Aralé's head and Aralé placed the golden crown of the king on Sern's head.

They then shared a brief kiss and the after ceremony festivities began. Aralé and Sern chose to forgo the last half of the night of wild revelry to make merry on their own.

They received the customary five days of rest after the wedding. On the sixth, their duties began. Sern's first order of business was removing all of the useless castle employees with positions they did not deserve and did not live up to. Many people with powerful connections were angered and many wondered if Sern would be assassinated before he could procure an heir.

None were shocked when he offered Mistress Maveree Eldestchild a seat at his council. However, no one could believe it when she had actually accepted. Being a seeress she was offered such positions by various monarchs and wealthy men almost daily. It was common knowledge that she was offered ridiculous amounts of land, money, and power. It seemed that Sern had offered her no bribe and the only thing he had really given her was the option not to start until April twenty-eighth of the same year. No one knew precisely why, but the kingdom was ecstatic to find out that their king would have a seeress serving him, regardless of when she started.

It seemed that Sern was exactly what Laaven needed. Soon after becoming crowned, he had started repairing all of the damage the belated King Amíen and the corrupt monarchy beneath him had done. The army was being rebuilt along with the kingdom. With Sern as king, crime became nearly nonexistent almost instantly as all of the thieves were desperately afraid of him. He swiftly began to rebuild the economy as well.

And just as people became convinced that things could not get any better, after nearly a year of his rule, it was announced that Queen Aralevena Caladría II was with child.

Chelsea Isadora Teich

About the Author

Chelsea Isadora Teich is an American high school student. She currently lives in the northeast with her family, which consists of her parents, several younger siblings, and five pets. She is a polyglot and interested in poetry, music, acting, tarot cards, and horseback riding. She is a nature lover and it was in part nature that inspired *The Persian Rug*. The works of Shakespeare, Dumas, Tolkien, Hugo, Homer, Poe, Dante, Stoker, Sophocles and also the Bhagavad-Gita and New Testament both inspired and influenced this novel. The mythologies, religions, and histories of such peoples as the Vikings, Celts, Romans, Ancient Egyptians, Native Americans, Japanese, Arabs and the general history of Europe's people also influenced this novel. She could not have gotten through the arduous publication process without her Jethro Tull CD's.